A
FAMILY
WOMAN

T.B. Markinson

Published by T. B. Markinson
ISBN: 978-1-98-581556-8

Visit T. B. Markinson's official website at lesbianromancesbytbm.com for the latest news, book details, and other information.

Cover Design by Erin Dameron-Hill / EDHGraphics
Edited by Karin Cox and Jeri Walker
Proofread by Kelly Hashway
Book layout by Guido Henkel

— Chapter One —

I released an audible sigh and rubbed my sweaty palms on my jeans. The news we'd just received from the OB-GYN continued to churn through my mind.

"You okay, Lizzie?" Sarah flicked on the windshield wipers to clear away the beginning flakes of a snowstorm. She peeked out of the corner of her eye, not wanting to take all her attention off the road as we approached a red light on the corner of College Avenue and Drake.

The clock on the SUV's dash ticked one minute past noon.

I nodded, my tongue and vocal cords unable to function.

The light turned green, and we continued along Drake.

"I know it was a shock," she said, placing a hand on my thigh. "Talk to me."

How could I express my thoughts after hearing that news?

"Hey, you aren't the only one who's living through this. Stop being this way." Her voice hardened, but her squeeze of my thigh let me know she wasn't completely annoyed; she understood the enormity of the situation.

She was right, per usual. I had a habit of clamming up when my world was rocked to the core, as it had been earlier today.

More often than not, it was the worst choice to make when it came to discussing "things" with Sarah, who was an open book.

"I'm fine. I promise." Try as I might, I couldn't banish the quiver from my voice.

Sarah exhaled and drummed her fingers on the steering wheel. "You hungry?" Without waiting for an answer, she added, "I'm famished."

It was then that it dawned on me: she was driving toward her favorite Vietnamese place, not toward our home, which was in the opposite direction. At the moment, I thought the mere whiff of food would send me running for a toilet.

My nerves weren't just jangled. Rattled wasn't the right word, either. It was worse than that. Much worse. Whenever this level of fear and shock roiled through my system, it didn't take much for the idiot in me to say the wrong thing, hence why I typically shut my trap. If there was a manual for idiots who struggled with social situations, the first rule would be: when in doubt don't say a word. Maybe I should write the manual, since everyone close to me was constantly pointing out areas where I needed work so I could interact better with human beings.

My mind backtracked to the matter at hand. Sarah wanted lunch. I think that was what she'd said. "Uh, sure."

Sarah parked close to the entrance. Inside, the joint was deserted. A woman behind the hostess podium smiled warmly and waved for us to follow her past the empty tables and booths to the far end of the restaurant, as if there was only one table left. Maybe she expected a large lunch rush at any moment.

Sarah ordered for both of us: noodles with stir-fried lemongrass chicken for her and a simple beef and rice bowl for me. After the woman left, Sarah stroked my hand. "It's going to be okay. You and I are going to be okay." She lowered her head to meet my gaze.

Even her gorgeous chocolate-brown eyes couldn't comfort me. I forced a smile. *Okay? How was everything going to be okay?* I wasn't equipped to handle the situation—from birth, my family had handicapped my ability to deal with…

Sarah interrupted my train of thought. "You know, when I was in college, my favorite meal was the two cheeseburger meal at McDonald's." She cocked her head as if the memory fixed everything. "Know why?"

Puzzled, I cupped my chin with my hand to support my drooping head. Besides verbally shutting down when scared, my mind and body like to shut off completely too.

"Because two is sometimes better than one," Sarah continued.

I laughed, finally. "I see some flaws in that logic."

She slapped my hand. "You would. Come on. Talk to me."

"It's a shock, really. I wasn't expecting… *that*." I raised both hands in the air, finally showing some life.

Sarah straightened in her seat, seeming relieved the emotional zombie was sparking back to normal. "It was a possibility. It's always been a possibility for us. The way we did it—using more than one of your eggs to increase our chances."

I remembered hearing that, but I'd always shoved it out of my mind, thinking surely it wouldn't happen to me. To us. I fiddled with the corner of a paper placemat printed with a map of Vietnam.

Sarah's eyes misted, and she dabbed each one with a napkin. "I still can't believe it. When we heard the first"—she blotted her eyes again—"and then the second…"

I nodded, hearing the thudding sound, like it was muffled or underwater, in my ears again.

"All this time, we didn't know." She shook her head in amazement.

It was amazing, considering. Terrifying but also mind-blowing. Were two better than one?

"For thirteen weeks," Sarah said, smoothing a hand over her belly, "I've been talking to one."

"Not two." I swallowed.

"Not two." A flush of excitement surged in Sarah's cheeks, and her smile lit up the room, connecting to my soul. "Twins, Lizzie. We're having twins."

A waiter set down our bowls, gave us a subservient bow, and left us in peace. I always found it odd that Sarah preferred this modest place over the wildly popular Vietnamese restaurant on College Avenue, which was decorated to the nines and had an hour-long wait, even for lunch. Maybe she preferred the quiet here, without the line snaking out the door. Or quite possibly, she didn't want me, the socially inept, to embarrass her in front of the who's who in Fort Collins.

Neither of us picked up our flimsy wooden chopsticks. Our eyes were locked on each other, communicating a thousand ideas at once.

"We may need a bigger house." Sarah finally broke the trance.

"Trust me, our mini-mansion is large enough for twins."

"Mock the *mini*-mansion all you want. You love our house." Sarah split her chopsticks apart and stirred the noodles and chicken.

I reached across the table and enveloped her hand. "I love you."

She smiled and dug in, ravished. I picked at my meal. After several quiet moments, Sarah set her chopsticks to the side and asked in all seriousness, "So you aren't mad?"

"Why would I be mad?"

"About the extra baby."

"Hey, at least it's not quadruplets." I closed my eyes and sucked in a breath. "I would never be mad about having more than one baby. It's just a lot to process." I tapped the side of my noggin.

"Careful. You might anger the bats in your belfry." She swirled the chopsticks in a circle in front of my face.

I smiled, shaking my head. "Are you going to let me talk?"

Sarah mimed zipping her full lips, but her endearing smile didn't make any promises.

A cleansing breath escaped my mouth. "My mind doesn't make leaps like this very easily. All along, I've been focusing on having a baby—one baby."

"Ha! I bet your therapist has told you that a thousand times, about your mind not making leaps, and you're finally accepting it."

I shook my head playfully. "Be nice."

Sarah's facial expression softened. "I'm sorry. I'm feeling a bit punchy."

"You always go above and beyond." I winked.

"We used your eggs. This isn't all on me."

"Two of me are in there." I pointed to her belly with my chopsticks.

Sarah paled.

"Geez, don't look so scared when I put it that way. You'll give me a complex." I shoveled in rice and spicy beef doused with a healthy spritz of sriracha sauce, which made my nose twitch.

"Two Lizzies. What have I done?" She smothered her eyes with a palm.

I flinched as if she'd thrown ice-cold water in my face.

"Such easy pickings," she mocked, laughing as she scooped in a mouthful of rice.

"You think you're so funny."

"I really hope having a sense of humor isn't genetic."

I jabbed my chopsticks in the air. "Take that back!"

"Or what?" She parried my chopsticks with hers.

"Or…"

The shimmer in her eyes knocked the words out of my head, and the confident arch of her left brow showed she was aware of her power over me.

Sarah put down her chopsticks and folded her hands on top of each other on the table. "What's really troubling you?"

"I don't… I mean, I want to be, but what if I suck at being a good parent? Knowing we'll be responsible for two humans— and let's face it, I didn't have a stellar childhood." I rubbed the top of my head. "I don't want to fuck up our children. I really don't. To this day, I still don't have a great relationship with my father or brother. What kind of example would I be for —?" I pointed to Sarah's stomach.

Sarah reached across the table and patted my hand, quieting my emotions with her touch. "No one knows what they'll be like as a parent. The only thing we can do is love our children and each other. That's all." She trailed a fingertip along the top of my hand. The ticklish sensation muted my discontent, replacing it with desire for her. "You aren't the only one who's scared. It'd be weird if we weren't."

Oddly, that struck the right chord inside my brain.

"The thing that helps me get through each day is knowing how much you love me. You need to give yourself more credit. You can be infuriating at times, with your stubbornness, keeping secrets—"

"Isn't this supposed to be a pep talk?" I nudged her foot under the table.

Sarah laughed. "You're right. It's just hard not mentioning your flaws whenever I can."

"One of *your* many flaws, that's for sure."

"Oh, really." Her voice increased an octave. "Do tell. What are my other flaws?" She playfully crossed her arms over her chest, snaring my attention away from the negative.

"You don't show off your cleavage enough."

She snorted and covered her mouth with a palm.

"They're beautiful and getting better each day. You should share them with the world."

The lines around her eyes crinkled with pleasure. "The world?"

"Maybe not. With me, though. Always with me."

Sarah leaned forward, exposing enough for a sweet glimpse. "Any other flaws of this nature that I should address?"

"Take me home and find out." I waggled my brows.

Sarah rummaged around in her purse, extracted three tens from her wallet, and tossed the bills on the table. Apparently, I wasn't the only one who was hot to trot. "Maybe we should have more heart-to-hearts if this is the outcome."

"Don't ruin the moment."

"Does it ruin the moment if I say I want you inside me?" Her sensual pout was even more convincing than her words.

I whisked her hand to my mouth and kissed her fingertips. "That could never ruin a thing."

We stood and made a mad dash for the car.

Over her shoulder, Sarah batted her eyelashes at me. "Can you hold on until we get home?"

"Why is it when you're in a hurry, roads that are typically empty are suddenly packed?" I groaned as Sarah eased the car a few feet forward before the traffic light turned red. It was the third time we'd had to wait for the same red light. Although we left the restaurant ten minutes ago, we'd barely traveled a block. I peered out the windshield. "The snow is melting before it reaches the road, so that can't be the reason."

"Karma's a bitch."

"How is this karma?" I jerked my head toward the gridlock and then leaned over to nibble on her earlobe.

Sarah moaned. "Anything's possible, knowing you." She kinked her neck, giving me better access to her milky skin.

"Why do you always assume I'm the one being punished? You, my dear, are not innocent. Like the time you jumped the gun and believed William when he said I ruined Meg's life — forced her into prostitution."

Sarah slapped my leg. "Is that how you treat the mother of your children, bringing up things from the past?"

"Because you never do? Besides, you're always preaching that I should be honest. I, for a fact" —I traced my index finger down the front of her shirt—"know you are not pure. Not completely. I distinctly remember you sitting on my face last night." I licked her neck, my tongue landing right behind her ear.

It made her breath hitch. "Lizzie—" she started to speak, but snapped her mouth shut.

"Wise woman."

Again she visibly curbed her words, cinching her beautiful lips tight.

"It'd probably be faster to drive to Estes. What's going on?" I peered through the windshield again, trying to spot the source of the holdup.

"I'm not sure I want to know. Traffic like this usually means one thing: a terrible accident."

I nodded in agreement. "Turn around."

"What?"

"I don't want to see it, and I know you don't either. So let's not. No reason to kill the mood." I slid my hand down her thigh and cupped her pussy, relishing the warmth through her jeans. "Turn here."

Sarah put the blinker on and eased the car into position to turn onto the side street. "Now what?"

"Fancy a night away? Or a weekend? Otherwise, I may never get into your pants."

An opening formed in the traffic, and Sarah claimed the space, merging into the lane. One step closer to freedom. "Really? The whole weekend?"

I laughed. "We just found out we're having twins. In a few months, our chances to drop everything will be nil for the next eighteen years."

"Eighteen years," Sarah echoed, a tremble in her voice.

"Come on, sweetheart. Let's live on the edge." I grabbed my cell from the coin holder under the radio. Rule two for my guide for the socially inept: if you manage to convince a beautiful, sexy woman to marry you, make sure you continue to up your game to keep her interest. Spontaneous weekends away certainly qualified.

"What about Hank?"

"I'm already texting Maddie, best friend extraordinaire, to look in on the fiendish feline, although there's enough food in his automatic dispenser for the week."

"He's not a fiend."

"You should have seen him last night when I made him come inside. Hank has no idea what lurks in our neighborhood at night." I attempted to cackle like a witch, but it sounded more like an old woman choking to death on her dentures.

"Acting isn't in your future." She flipped a U-turn on the side street, getting into line to turn onto the main road, heading away from the traffic.

"Sadly, no. Luckily, I have a beautiful wife to support me." I grinned at her.

"Not to mention a substantial trust fund. What about clothes?" Sarah rounded back to the matter at hand.

I swiveled my head. "Puh-lease! You can smell a shopping mall a mile away."

"I'll need maternity clothes soon. Things are starting to get tight." She tugged on the waist of her jeans.

"Not what I had in mind for the weekend, but I'm sure we can squeeze it in."

"Oh, really? What'd you have in mind?" She widened her eyes.

"Clothes-wise, not much—if you want me to stick to this honesty thing you've been cramming down my throat." My cell chimed. "Maddie's in. She's actually going to stay at our place."

"What about Doug?"

I read the text aloud, "*Perfect timing. Doug is driving me crazy. Will stay at your place.* I think she wants time alone."

"Uh-oh."

"I've said it before; Doug is a nice guy. The excitement doesn't last long with the nice ones."

"But I like Doug. After all the shit your brother put her through, she needs someone who'll treat her right." Sarah steered back onto the street we'd been stuck on for over ten minutes, but now heading south out of Fort Collins.

"I know. But you don't have to sleep with him."

"Is that it? You think Doug's a bad lay?"

It was difficult to picture anyone named Doug getting groovy between the sheets. "I wouldn't say that. I'm sure it's not everything. Maddie has seemed antsy lately, like she has no clue what she wants when it comes to career, love life—anything really. Remember how she signed up for all those cooking classes because she got a wild hair about buying a restaurant, and then she didn't bother going back after the first class?"

Sarah nodded, lost in thought. She headed out of the city on a back road through uninhabited fields, and the road was as clear as can be.

"Boulder?" I asked.

"What?"

"Are we going to Boulder?"

"How'd you know?"

"Just a guess, considering the route you're taking. I'll make a reservation for a hotel." I swiped my phone screen and started to look up places.

"Don't forget a dinner reservation," she barked.

"Easy, bossy pants. So much for spontaneity." I poked her with my elbow. "It's a sad day when I'm the laidback loosey-goosey one in our relationship."

"Sorry. All of a sudden I have a hankering for Mexican tonight." She chewed on a hangnail.

"Not a surprise—"

Sarah walloped my leg. "What does that mean?"

I retreated close to the door. "Ouch! What was that for?"

"Calling me fat. Just because I'm preggo doesn't make it okay for you to make weight jokes."

"Are you kidding me? I did no such thing." I rubbed my thigh to temper the burning sensation.

"You were about to." She clenched the steering wheel with both hands.

"No, I wasn't. I was going to say that we left before finishing our lunch—didn't even bother having it packaged to go. Remember?"

Sarah's cheeks reddened, and her shoulders lost their tension. "That's right. We did."

"Geez. When have I ever called you fat or insinuated it?"

"Have you thought it?" She rubbed her belly, which barely offered a hint about her condition.

Of course, I knew what caused her insecurity. Everyone loved to remind me I was clueless, but I'd have to be a complete moron not to realize that in six months Sarah would be as large as a house—for two. "Sarah, you are absolutely beautiful. Now and always."

"Even when I'll inevitably blimp out?"

"I wouldn't call it blimping out."

"What would you call it, then?"

"Being pregnant." I shrugged. "With twins," I added for good measure.

She sighed.

"Besides, you'll be the most beautiful blimp." I cowered against the car door again, protecting my face with raised hands, and closed my eyes.

"Lizzie!"

We both laughed.

"Kidding, of course." Sneaking a glance to make sure the coast was clear, I leaned over and massaged her stomach. "Don't ever doubt how attracted I am to you. Not ever."

"Willing to put your money where your mouth is?" she countered.

"I would rather put your pussy there."

That earned me a chuckle. "That's on the agenda. Don't fret." She licked her lips.

"Let me guess. After shopping and a fancy dinner?"

"You know me so well." She gunned the SUV to pass a car on the two-lane road.

After she'd safely merged back into the right lane, I continued, "I hope so. Can't imagine what it'd be like starting a family with a stranger."

"It still knocks me for a loop every time we mention starting a family. You?" Her voice confirmed her feelings.

"At least I don't faint each time anymore." My mind flittered to my own messed-up family. The fear of becoming like them, even a scintilla, was hard to shake. One saving grace was that I kept reminding myself our marriage was much stronger than my parents'. Surely having a stronger bedrock increased the odds of raising well-adjusted children. And if one turned out to be a sociopath, from the research I'd done, there wouldn't have been much we could have done to prevent it. Wait, was it psychopaths who were born that way and sociopaths were made, or vice versa? Did researching this crap say something demented about me?

"Admit it. You nearly swooned this morning when we heard the second heartbeat." Her hand grazed my thigh.

"I did not!" I flat-out lied.

We drove past a deserted gas station, and an idea materialized. I jerked my head back toward the dilapidated building. "I'll make you a deal," I said.

"Does it involve sex?"

"And shopping. Turn around and park behind that gas station. The backseat reclines. Let's get our groove on, and then I'll buy you everything your little heart desires."

"You make it sound like I expect gifts in exchange for sleeping with you." She was already slowing down, looking for a space to turn around. No cars were in sight.

"Expect…? No! But if it helps me get inside you right now, I'd buy you an entire shopping center."

— Chapter Two —

After an afternoon of shopping, followed by a relaxing meal at a hole-in-the-wall Mexican restaurant Maddie had recommended via text, Sarah and I stepped into the hotel elevator a little after nine. We were the only two occupants. I managed to juggle the shopping bags enough to press the button for the ninth floor.

Sarah crashed against the mirrored interior, yawning.

"Bedtime?" I smiled.

She returned my smile guiltily. "Maybe." Her eyes fell on the lingerie bag in my left hand. "Would that be horrible of me, after everything you've done to throw together this romantic getaway?"

"Yes, it would. We should just go home," I joked, intentionally softening my tone.

Sarah shook her head, keeping her eyes on mine. "Whatever. Besides, you already got a taste."

"True. But that was only a tease." I elbowed her ribs. "Let's get you in pajamas and into bed."

"Which ones?" Sarah motioned to the Victoria's Secret bag.

"The knit ones, if you plan on getting any sleep." I made goo-goo eyes at her, and she smiled again, still looking guilty. "We have the whole weekend, and if you want to rest the entire time, I'm fine with that. I promise. You are growing my babies."

The elevator dinged, and I darted out an arm laden with bags to hold the door open for her. "After you, madam."

"I should get pregnant more often if this is how you treat me."

"Easy now. We have plenty of room for the twins, but if we keep having kids, we will have to move to a bigger place, and you know how much I hate change." I set the bags down outside the door to fish the keycard out of my back jeans pocket. After the third swipe, the door unlocked.

Hotel staff had prepared the room per my instructions when I checked in. The lights were dimmed, and rose petals decorated the bedspread. A bottle of non-alcoholic sparkling wine sat in a silver ice bucket.

Sarah's eyes swept through the room, noting the setup. "Now I really feel guilty." She patted my cheek before letting herself fall back on the bed, her arms spread out. A single petal floated into the air, and she grabbed it and inhaled its heady scent.

I crammed all the bags in the far corner, next to the nightstand, and then lay beside her on the king-size bed. "Don't be. Making babies is a 24/7 job." I skated my hand under her sweater and fondled her tummy.

"That feels nice," she murmured, her eyes closed.

"Would you like a massage?"

"Really?"

The eagerness in her voice made me laugh. "It's the least I can do."

"True. You got me into this."

"Me?" I squeaked. "If I remember correctly, you had the IVF doctor picked out before you even told me you wanted a baby."

Sarah ignored me and rolled onto her side. "Massage, now."

"What, no please? I see how it's going to be. Do you want to take your clothes off?"

"I'm too tired. I never thought being pregnant would be so exhausting—I have to fight to stay awake past eight o'clock these days."

"I remember the days when you took me to bed early for different reasons. And you couldn't keep your clothes on!" I pinched her side. "Now you don't even want to get naked for a proper massage."

"Don't worry. I booked us for real massages tomorrow. This is just a warm-up." She tucked her hands under her chin.

"Us?" I dug my fingers into her shoulders, kneading carefully.

Sarah let out a satisfactory groan. "I'm going to need you to be on your toes, so we both need to get some rest. Come August, we won't stop for almost two decades."

"Two decades! Way to sell this whole parenting thing." I walked my fingers down her spine. Her shirt and sweater didn't allow much room to maneuver. "Silly question. Can you have a real massage?"

"Yep. I checked. The place caters to pregnant women."

"I should have known. You've already researched how many times you should be peeing every day."

"I thought every hour was excessive!" She bumped me with her hip.

"Just wait. Soon it'll be three times every half hour, according to some pregnancy research I've done."

"Lizzie!"

I lay down next to her. "Don't get all huffy. I know you're loving this. You were born to be a mother. Our children are lucky."

She turned to stare into my face, her dark eyes gleaming. "Hold me."

I peeled back the covers, and Sarah snuggled into my arms, falling asleep almost instantly. Leaning back against the headboard, I watched the city lights outside the window sputter against the inky night.

"Lizzie," Sarah whispered.

"Everything okay?" I asked in a groggy voice, doing my best to strong-arm my brain fully awake with a single shake of my head.

"Yeah. Just checking whether you were asleep." Her fingers teased one of my nipples under my cotton T-shirt, demanding my full attention.

"You woke me in the middle of the night to ask me whether I was asleep?" I teased.

Sarah rolled me onto my back and straddled my stomach. Reaching up, she eighty-sixed her sweater and T-shirt, revealing a ruby-red satin and lace bra. "Are you complaining?"

I gripped the sides of her stomach. "Nope. No complaints."

The intensity on her face excited me far more than her sexy lingerie.

I cupped her cheek. "Why are you staring at me like that?"

"I want to fuck."

I smiled. "I figured."

Sarah placed a finger on my lips. "Shhhh. Listen to me. Earlier this afternoon, while you were in the bookstore" —she rolled her eyes because it was impossible for me to pass a bookstore without stepping inside—"I hopped into a store around the corner and bought something for us. Remember when you said you'd buy me anything my heart desired?"

I signaled for her to go on.

"We've never used one together, and I thought it'd be fun."

"Used what?"

She bent down. "You'll see."

Before I could ask another question, Sarah stretched her sleek body on top of mine and slipped her tongue into my mouth, greedily. I knew from past experiences that when Sarah was this frisky it was best to go with the flow. Not to mention I would be a fucking moron to turn down a half-naked woman who was grinding into my pussy in a way that meant, "I'm about to rock your world."

Her hand slid under my shirt, and she raked her nails down my side.

I moaned.

"You like?" she purred, her tongue warm where it licked my earlobe—one of my many weaknesses that she took advantage of. Not that I minded.

I flipped Sarah carefully onto her back.

She laughed. "You do like it."

I ripped my shirt off and cast it onto the plush hunter-green hotel carpet.

"I like it when you don't speak. The strong silent type can be a turn-on." Sarah prodded my crotch with her hip.

My fingers sauntered over her skin, lingering briefly on her bra. She'd known for years that I was a sucker for what I called "fuck-me lingerie," and she wasn't even wearing one of the items we'd purchased earlier. I was particularly eager to see her in the black Chantilly-lace baby doll slip that had caught my eye in Victoria's Secret earlier.

The bra and panties she wore now must have been the ones she'd left the house in. Sarah was a planner, even when we didn't have plans. It was like she had a sixth sense about fuckathons. I'd be lying if I said I wasn't overly curious to find out what she'd bought earlier. My wife was usually the one who instigated our sexual adventures—wonderful, exciting escapades that only we shared.

Sarah sat up, encircling my torso in her embrace and peppering my neck with kisses. I slipped my hands around her body to unclasp her bra. As much as I loved it, I wanted to see her—all of her.

The kiss we shared could only be described as a "slow burn." It wasn't the kind to kick our arousal into full speed; its purpose was to show how much we loved each other. Sensually passionate—the type of kiss I replayed in my mind whenever I was away from the love of my life. These were the nights I wished would never end.

I stroked both of her cheeks and took them in my hands, staring deeply into her eyes.

"I love it when you look at me like I'm the only woman on the planet who can turn you on." She nestled her cheek into my right palm.

"You are. Always."

The depth in her eyes seemed endless, like her love. We remained locked in the gaze for several blissful moments, neither of us able to resist the meaning of such a look.

"I want to show you how beautiful you are," I murmured.

Our lips met again, our desire ramping up rapidly. Our touch becoming hungrier, clawing at clothes. Fisting the hair on the back of her head, I guided her mouth to mine, going deeper, wanting to feel the flames sparking from the depths of our souls.

Sarah fell back onto the bed and elevated her butt to allow me to frantically dispose of her jeans and panties in one swift motion.

"Fucking hell, you're gorgeous." My eyes roved over her nakedness, taking in every curve, freckle, and the slight bulge of her stomach. My fingertips massaged the swell there. Sarah's arms were up above her head, and whenever I touched her bare skin, her body writhed beneath me.

I spent more time than usual kissing and licking her abdomen. "You're amazing." I rubbed my cheek against her belly. "I can't believe you are creating life in here."

Sarah's eyes misted. "God, I'm terrified."

I moved up to cradle her in my arms. "I'll be there every step of the way. That may not be comforting, considering… and if you need to cuss me out at times, I totally understand."

Laughter rumbled inside her. "Shit. Be careful, giving me permission to do that." She rapped my head with her knuckles. "Twins will test your limited patience and your need to schedule everything."

"Oh, please. You act like everything is always my fault."

"Are you saying you're innocent?"

"Completely." I peppered her neck with kisses. Her breath quickened when I took her nipple in my mouth, sucking it gently, feeling its firmness with my teeth. "Is this my fault?"

"What?" she asked breathily.

"That I can't keep my hands or my mouth off you." My tongue continued to tease her nipple.

"No, but this is." Sitting up, she rolled me onto my back on the soft hotel sheet. It must have had a thread count befitting a princess. She mounted me with such fervor that I immediately forgot all about the sheets.

I was about to add my two cents when her lips captured mine, silencing what probably would have been an inane, not to mention counterintuitive, comment anyway.

Remember the first rule, Lizzie. When in doubt, stay quiet.

"Shhh," she murmured into my ear, as if in tune with my thoughts. "Just enjoy us."

She pinned my arms over my head. Clearly, Pilates was paying off. Sarah separated my legs with her hip, gyrating against my pussy, all the while manipulating my right nipple with her tongue. Her hands smoothed up and down the sides of my body, releasing a torrent of goose bumps. Sarah's touch was akin to saying I love you. No one had ever made me feel the way she made me feel. Not ever.

"I'm going to let go of your arms, but leave them where they are. I want to be in control. Complete and total control." The hunger in her eyes initiated a tremor in me and made me nod in agreement.

"Good. Maybe you are trainable." Sarah straddled my mid-section, her fingers trekking over my skin. Judging by the crooked upward twist of her lips, she got off on watching me squirm with anticipation. After several minutes of this treatment, I lurched up to kiss her, but my wife, who was slightly smaller than I was, manhandled me back to the mattress.

"I told you not to move. Enjoy."

"I enjoy touching you," I grumbled playfully.

"And you will. Soon. Not now." She indicated for me to lift my ass so she could do away with my blue-and-white-striped pajama bottoms.

Her tongue took over for her fingers, tasting and exploring my neck, collarbone, breasts, nipples, ticklish sides, and the hypersensitive skin below my belly button.

The intensity of my need accelerated. My eyes closed, my breaths coming in rasps that excited us both.

Sarah shifted her weight—and her tongue—further down my body.

If it was possible to taste desire, I was gulping in delicious mouthfuls.

Part of me hoped she'd bypass the area dripping in anticipation to explore my lower extremities, but the other part didn't think I could hold on much longer.

I needed Sarah to make love to me. The buildup was becoming painful, delightfully so, but still painful. I chanted in my head: *Good things come to those who wait.*

"You look like you're about to erupt." She skimmed a finger over my wetness.

I slowly opened my eyes, wanting to savor this moment. In the pale moonlight, Sarah's dark hair contrasted with her creamy skin. Her heavy breasts heaved with each intake of breath. Her swirling chocolate eyes smoldered.

"I may."

"I want you to. I want you to let go completely."

My hips rubbed against hers. She wanted to be in control, but I couldn't stop this part of my body; it had a mind of its own. Sarah didn't admonish me; instead she rode me.

"Yes, yes, yes." She flung her head back. "This is what I wanted tonight."

"To ride me?" I jacked up both eyebrows.

"Exactly. Are you ready for your gift?" She ran a finger the length of my upper body.

"Does it involve you?"

"Absolutely." She leaned over the side of the bed, rustled in a plastic bag, and pulled out a strap-on—the attachment already, um, attached.

I laughed, slightly fearful. "You've got to be joking."

Sarah slapped my stomach. "Not a joke. Not at all. You and I have never used one."

"Have you with someone else?"

"Does it matter?"

I hesitated. Was it a piece of information I wanted permanently etched into my memory bank?

The commanding pleading in her eyes was more powerful than the pulsing between my legs.

"Not at all." I eyed the device. "You or me?"

"I want you to wear it first."

I shivered. The black-corset harness didn't intimidate me; the enormous cock did. Would it ease into my pregnant wife without slamming into the twins? Granted, the babies were still minuscule at the moment, but this was not the average-sized penis, at least I didn't think so. My experience in that department was nil.

Sarah bent over the side of the bed again, keeping me in suspense with a mischievous glance out of the corner of her eye. She soon vaulted back up with a tube of lubricant. "Go on. Slip it on."

I sat up, dangling the device by a strap between my thumb and forefinger, giving it a once-over.

"Surely even you can figure it out," Sarah teased.

"Hmmm… I wouldn't give me too much credit. Did you assemble it before waking me?"

Sarah plucked it out of my hands. "Trust me. I don't give you that much credit, and to answer your question, it came assembled." She gestured for me to lie down and to scoot my ass up so she could hoist the harness over my lower body. Its softness took me by surprise.

"Tell me the truth. Have you had something so—large and uh… purple inside you?"

"Would you have preferred a rainbow one?"

I shook my head.

She laughed at my stern head shaking. "Didn't think so." Her eyes softened. "I want us to keep experiencing new things, even now."

"What do you mean? Even now?" I gawked at the thick cock poking upward from my crotch.

"Now that we're on the cusp of becoming parents. You and I still matter." She placed one hand on her chest and the other on mine. "I always want a place in our lives that includes only us, where we do things that only we know about. It's important to me. Vital for our relationship."

It wasn't the first time she had expressed this wish. As soon as we'd found out Sarah was pregnant, she'd kicked our relationship into the center of everything. Her parents never divorced, but her father had died when Sarah was a child. Growing up with only one parent made Sarah determined that our family would always have two parents at the heads of the table—parents who never divorced and whose love deepened each year. Distance, even physical, was not an option.

Understanding how much it meant to her, coupled with my own desire to stay in touch on all levels, ignited the switch in my head. If she wanted us to stay close, by all means, I'd never fight her on it. If that meant fucking her with a strap-on, well, I was game, even if I wasn't all that confident about my thrusting skills with the appendage.

"How do you want to do this?" I tentatively gripped the dildo with my right hand.

She tittered. "You've seen movies right? Or do I need to start buying straight porn?"

"Have you been buying lesbian porn and not sharing?" I slanted my head.

"That's an idea." She clapped her hands. "Porn!"

"Can't wait to see all the adverts when I log onto the computer after your first porn purchase."

"People don't buy porn anymore. It's all over the Internet." Sarah squeezed some lube into her hand and smeared it over the purple penis. Was the color significant? At least it wasn't banana yellow. That would ruin the mood for sure.

I jabbed my hand out for her to add lube and helped lather the entire eight inches. Surprisingly, it was kinda hot. "Top or bottom?"

"I want to be on top. Like I said, I want to ride you."

"Giddyup." My upward hip thrust motioned that I was ready.

Sarah's pussy hovered over the dildo, her eyes wide. I remained still, waiting for her to make the final decision. It was all fun and games until someone got stabbed with an eight-inch cock. Again, I had to wonder how realistic the size was. What would pop up in my browser if I googled "average penis size"?

"What are you thinking?" she asked.

"N-nothing at all. Just waiting for you to make your move."

Sarah flashed her *here goes nothing* grin. The tip entered her, and her eyes widened further.

"Changing your mind?" I winked at her, slightly moving my hips.

"Not a chance. Taking it slow. Enjoying the experience."

"I've got all night." I eyeballed the dildo as it was slowly swallowed by Sarah's pussy. "And we don't need any Viagra."

"Only you would turn this into a competition." She adjusted and began the ride. "Come on, cowgirl. Show me what you got."

I drove my hips upward.

Sarah welcomed the thrust with an excited, "Oi!"

Her response was the impetus I needed. I wanted to make Sarah come on top of me. Typically, my view while eating her pussy was obscured when she climaxed, but with her on top, riding me, I had the best seat in the house. I picked up the pace, and Sarah flopped about like a rider on a bucking bronco. Hopefully, that didn't imply I was inept with a strap-on.

Her back arched, and her head lolled back, thrusting her tits, which were getting fuller every day, toward the ceiling. Her hand traveled up and down her body, clearly in ecstasy. I was fairly certain my eyes were boggling over the image playing in real time. Every movement inside her was reciprocated with an excited quake in her breath and body. She bounced up and down on me, while I concentrated, blotting out the fancy hotel room, the ornate wallpaper, the crystal chandelier, and the countryside paintings that conjured up images of the queen having tea in Buckingham Palace. The sophisticated suite was probably used by straight couples assuming the missionary position—if they fucked at all—not a lesbian getting her jollies with a purple plastic accessory.

My goal was to get her to climax, but the pressure from the harness rubbed my clit in such a way that I was on the precipice of an orgasm myself. Maybe she sensed that, because we both dug deep to pick up the pace. We'd moved from making love, smack dab into full-on fuck mode.

Sarah's body gyrated frantically as she murmured through ragged breathing, "Jesus fucking Christ, don't stop."

There was no way in hell I would stop until I'd drained every last ounce of energy. My eyes were gummed shut now, preparing for an earth-shattering climax, but I needed to hold on. My orgasm would hit me hard, I knew, but I couldn't succumb until Sarah got there first.

"Oooooo." She urged me on.

My muscles were fatigued with exertion and anticipation. Sweat glistened on both of our bodies. The slapping sounds of our bodies colliding into each other intensified and alerted me to the fact that it was now or never. If I was exhausted, Sarah was nearing the point of no return, considering she was doing most of the work. Her hips slowed, and I opened my eyes, not wanting to miss out. Her face had squished up into her pre-orgasm state. She needed my help to get there.

I thrust my hips up as far as I could, emitting a primal rumble from deep inside—a sound that had never slipped out before during lovemaking or ever.

"Oh God, yes!" Sarah's legs began quivering. I only had to hang on for a few more seconds before I could give in to my own sexual bliss. Her eyes snapped open, staring into mine. She'd never looked sexier, bringing both of us there... and beyond.

Moments later, Sarah curled up in my arms, resting her head on my chest. "Sometimes you surprise the shit out of me."

I laughed, not taken aback by her honesty. "What do you mean?"

"Don't be mad, but when I purchased my new favorite sex toy, I was pretty sure you'd scoff at the idea. I thought it would take some serious begging to get you to even consider it."

I snapped my fingers. "Damn. If I'd only known."

"What? Didn't you like it?" Her head popped up, and she gave me the evil eye.

"I think it's safe to say I loved it. But if I'd known the level of begging you were willing to stoop to, I would have forestalled the fuck fest." I caressed her delicate cheekbone. "You do have a certain way when pleading in bed."

Sarah thumped my shoulder, not pissed at all.

"Can we go back? Start over?"

"What? My historian wants to rewrite history?" Her eyes agreed with the idea.

"Absolutely. I'm a strong proponent of getting things right, no matter how many times we have to try. That's the teacher in me."

Sarah yawned. "I'm in but not tonight."

"Tease." I wrestled her back into my arms. "Are you comfortable, sweetheart? I can't have the mother of my children suffer in any way."

"I like that."

"What?" I nuzzled my cheek against the top of her head.

"That you can see me as a mother and as a woman. Once they become moms, women are sometimes put solely in the 'mother' box. I don't want that, especially from you."

"Ah, you still want nights like this? I don't think that will be a problem, my little sex pot."

She burrowed closer, murmuring into my ear just before she drifted off to la-la land, "Just you wait for tomorrow's adventure."

— Chapter Three —

"That's the best building on campus." I pointed toward a brick building with a recent addition made of glass. "I've spent many happy hours there, still do whenever I get the chance."

Ethan and Janice, friends and colleagues during my grad school days, burst into laughter.

"That explains so much." Ethan's wiry upper body shuddered with hilarity, and he put a hand on Janice's shoulder for support. Their merriment morphed into an odd, conspiratorial joy.

"What building is it?" Bailey, Janice's bespectacled younger cousin, asked, eyes wide.

"The library." Janice continued to laugh.

Bailey's eyes narrowed behind her rectangular tortoiseshell glasses. "Really?" She studied my face. "Are you yanking my leg?"

"Not a chance. She's being completely real with you." Ethan attempted to rein in his laughing fit.

Sarah looped her hand through my arm and gave my bicep a supportive squeeze, her smile proving she was laughing at my expense on the inside. She whispered in my ear, "Not many high school students give a rat's ass about libraries."

Dottie, who was Bailey and Janice's grandmother, smiled. "If Bailey comes here, I'm putting Lizzie in charge of monitoring her study habits."

What type of spreadsheet I'd set up flashed through my mind, and I couldn't curtail a smile.

It was a Saturday morning during spring break, so not many undergrads were on campus, if any, although a decent amount of grad students and a handful of professors buzzed to and fro. Even though it was the second week in March, thick clouds clung to the foothills, threatening snow. Stark tree branches against a gunmetal sky conjured an eerie feeling, more fitting for autumn than spring.

Janice was visiting her alma mater with her grandmother and cousin, who was making a whirlwind tour of five colleges in three states in under nine days. She'd invited Ethan and me to tag along this morning to show Bailey the highlights. Sarah, a CU alum, joined us after I'd made her promise not to undermine our objective: wooing Bailey to become a CSU Ram, not a CU buff—at least not while on CSU's campus.

"How in the world did you ever find a woman?" Janice teased.

"She didn't. I found Lizzie in the history department chair's office." Sarah spoke to Janice's back as we brought up the rear of the group.

Janice gaped over her shoulder and said, "Wow! It must have been a dream come true—true love in the history department."

"She found me in the library." Ethan tapped his chest with one finger; his other hand gripped his daughter's. "Lizzie and I worked there together for a couple of years."

Janice rubbernecked over her shoulder again and winked. "Life has worked out for the biggest nerd I know."

I scowled, which didn't intimidate the plucky San Franciscan, of course. "Somehow, I've managed to muddle through life one nerdy day at a time."

Dottie rubbed her hands together. "I hate the cold."

"Then why do we live in San Francisco instead of LA?" Bailey sniped, rolling her eyes.

"Because culture matters, not nightclubs." A formidable woman in stature and tone, Dottie's lined forehead made one thing clear: she didn't like having her authority challenged. Only the softness in her eyes lessened the fear factor. After Bailey's mom died in a mountain-climbing accident, Dottie swooped in to raise her three-year-old granddaughter. Bailey's father had never been in the picture.

"I know a good place for coffee," I said.

"As long as it's not the library." Bailey rounded on me, her withering look smashing my hopes of her completing a daily spreadsheet.

If she moved here, it was clear I'd have to come up with an ingenious plan that would enable me to track her studies without her knowing. I loved a good challenge.

Dottie had agreed to visit colleges in California, Colorado, and Oregon, but she had her heart set on Bailey attending Stanford, much closer to home. Oregon was next on her list. Bailey, however, had narrowed it down to three schools that were at least a day's drive away: UCLA, CU, and CSU. Janice had confided to me that the odds of her getting into UCLA or Stanford were slim at best. It'd be safe to say the library probably wouldn't be Bailey's favorite place on campus. She'd likely never set foot inside, a shameful thought.

Later today, our group was heading to CU—sans Ethan, who had to take his daughter, Casey, to hip-hop dance lessons. I had a hard time envisioning a group of kindergarteners dancing, let alone to hip-hop. Then again, the last time I danced was on my wedding day, and that didn't go well.

Sarah loved to email the clip of me tripping over my gown as she attempted to twirl me around without telegraphing the move first. If Ethan hadn't been standing next to the three-tiered cake, I'd have crashed right into it, ruining Sarah's chance of smearing my face, even after she swore up and down she wouldn't.

Inside the student center, Janice and I shepherded the group to some tables near a glass wall.

"All right, what can I get everyone?" I clapped my hands together in a waitress-like way.

"What's available?" Bailey stared at me as if my answer determined whether she'd accept CSU. She had a smidge of California snobbery about her.

I stripped my jacket off. "Uh, it's Saturday during spring break, so not much. However, if you want a coffee and something sweet, I think that can be arranged."

"Coffee. Black." Dottie tightened her scarf. How was the woman still freezing, even inside?

I fumbled in my bag in search of a small notebook and fished a pen out of my shirt pocket.

"I see she hasn't changed much since I moved home years ago." Janice grinned. "Vanilla latte and a cinnamon roll for me."

"Ditto for me." Sarah took a seat next to Casey and Ethan.

"Espresso." Bailey strained to see over my shoulder, out the window. "And a cinnamon roll," she muttered casually as if she really didn't want it—or the calories. She had the type of build that packed on weight easily; she'd probably never be thin.

"Can you watch Casey for me?" Ethan asked Sarah as he stood. "Even with the notepad, Lizzie will find a way to bollix everything if left to her own devices."

"Says the man wearing one navy New Balance and one black Nike shoe." I aimed my pen at his mismatched shoes.

Ethan smiled sheepishly. "Casey helped me get ready this morning."

"You're putting the blame on your daughter? That's low. I'm used to you giving me sh—" I sized up Casey, to see whether she'd caught that I almost said shit, but she was too busy doodling on a napkin with pens Janice had magically produced from her purse. "—trouble, but tossing your child under the bus to save face…" I tsked.

Ethan put a hand on my shoulder, leading me away. "Come August, you'll understand. I only have *one* child. You have twins on the way. I won't be surprised if you leave the house without a shirt on. I've always wondered about your lingerie choice: sexy or grandma to match your penchant for sweater vests?"

I rolled my eyes. "Please. I have action plans in place for when the twins arrive." I held my left wrist aloft. "This watch has ten alarms, and I already use seven of them. You aren't scaring me. Organization is my thing."

"Good Lord, why in the hell would anyone need seven alarms?"

"I can show you." I tapped my watch.

Ethan smothered my hand. "You know, for the sake of our friendship, I'd rather not know your BM schedule."

"I don't poop on command."

"If you say so. But here's a tip: people might think someone who's so uptight they need seven alarms shits on a schedule." Ethan approached the registers, snatched the notepad from my hand, and placed the orders in a strong baritone voice. He added at the last moment, "Oh, can you add a couple of blueberry muffins? I haven't had one since I finished my master's." His giddiness was matched by the change in his tone, nearly squealing like a child.

By the time we returned with the drinks and snacks, Casey was teaching Sarah, Bailey, and Janice a few hip-hop moves. Bailey's cell phone provided the music. Dottie looked on with a blend of condemnation and grandmotherly pride.

"No, Bailey, like this." Casey stepped side to side, snapping her fingers clumsily with both hands. Then she surged forward, stomping her feet and tossing her arms about.

Bailey mimicked her. "I think I got it."

Janice and Sarah followed suit.

Sarah grinned at what I assumed was the shocked look on my face. "You're a natural teacher, Casey."

The child giggled.

"If I somehow get signed up for hip-hop classes, I'm going to kick your ass," I whispered to Ethan.

"I think Sarah gave up on your dance skills on your wedding day."

Casey eyed the gigantic muffin Ethan held, and all gyration came to an abrupt end. She reached up for it. "Please, sir, may I have some more?" Casey wasn't just a good teacher, but a great listener. I had taught her the *Oliver Twist* line weeks ago. I wasn't an expert, but Ethan's child was in the top one percent when it came to intelligence.

Ethan settled next to her and broke the muffin in half. "You can have the rest for dessert tonight."

"So, Lizzie, you went to school and taught here?" Bailey tore a tiny piece off her cinnamon roll.

"Correct." I sipped my chai. "Ask me anything. I'm a CSU expert."

Janice perked up. "What does clam jam mean?"

"I said I'm a CSU expert, not an expert of idiotic phrases."

"It's serious. All people like you should know." Janice overlapped her arms, and she and Ethan shared another conspiratorial smirk. It was hard to believe we were all finished with school and married with kids or babies on the way. As soon as Janice and Ethan saw each other, their antics had regressed to high school level.

"What about people like me?" Even though she was mocking me, it was nice that we had fallen back into the groove of grad school. I hadn't seen Janice since her wedding day, before I finished my PhD. Since then, she and her husband, Collin, had welcomed two children. She'd left the kids behind with him in San Francisco for this trip.

"If you knew the term, you'd know what I'd meant." Janice's smile contained the perfect splash of arrogance, just to goad me.

Sarah laughed. "Even *I* know what it means."

"Me too," Ethan piped in.

I regarded Bailey and Dottie. From the grin on Bailey's face, she knew, but Dottie was in the clueless boat with me. "Okay, I give. What's clam jam?"

Janice covered Casey's ears. "The lesbian version of cock-blocking."

"You may have to define"—Sarah covered Casey's ears as well—"cock-blocking."

Ethan inched closer. "It means preventing someone from scoring. You know what scoring is, right?"

"Something you and your wife never do."

"*Touché*." He smiled proudly. Ethan's aversion to bodily fluids complicated sexual relations, hence why they'd adopted Casey.

Dottie tutted. Apparently discussing clam-jamming, cock-blocking, and scoring weren't Dottie-approved topics of conversations while shopping for a college for her youngest granddaughter, or ever. I full-heartedly agreed, but Janice's Californian openness was known to test my boundaries.

"I have one." Bailey slapped the tabletop. "What's a gold star?" She turned to me and boosted a brow.

"Ah, like in school for good behavior," I mumbled.

They all started laughing, even Dottie. I hadn't pegged her as the traitorous type, but clearly I was wrong.

Sarah whispered behind her hand to the adults at the table, "She is one and doesn't even know it."

"One of what?" I demanded.

"You've never been with a man?" Dottie hefted an eyebrow.

How in the world had I gotten myself into this position? Even after all of these years, Janice still knew how to play me like a fiddle.

"Seriously, who in their right mind has the time to learn phrases like 'gold star' or 'clam jam'? I can list a hundred useful things that everyone should know but doesn't." I stabbed the air with a finger.

"She wanders the library, updating the list daily." Janice tittered.

I scowled.

"You didn't answer my question, dear. Have you ever" — Dottie looked sideways at Casey, who was happily doodling on a piece of paper — "canoodled with a man?"

Janice's grandmother fixed her steely eyes on me.

"Have you ever canoodled with a woman?" I countered.

"Yes. Two, in fact." She turned to Janice and Sarah. "It was nice, but something was missing."

Everyone but Casey snickered.

I swiped a palm across my brow. "You know, labels are for keeping everything and everyone in a box." I couldn't stop myself from blinking excessively. "All of you should be ashamed of yourselves."

Janice responded, "We should be ashamed of ourselves? You don't appreciate your LGBTQ heritage and culture." She laughed and turned to Sarah. "She's probably a pillow princess to boot."

Confounded, I queried Sarah for an explanation. For the first time during this exchange, Sarah colored. She whispered behind her hand, "It means you don't reciprocate in bed."

I huffed and turned on Janice. "That's a lie. I love eating my wife's pussy," I exclaimed much too loudly, neglecting to cover Casey's ears.

"Why would you eat Hank?" Casey asked, referring to my cat. Thankfully, the brainiac hadn't learned the other definition of pussy yet.

"Because she's a mean lady," Ethan said. "Only mean ladies eat cats and brag about it in front of children."

Casey squinted one eye, sizing me up. "She's not mean."

Ethan relaxed in his chair. "What is she then?"

"My friend."

"At least I have *one* at this table," I grumbled.

Janice stood and looped her arms about my neck. "Don't be mad. I've missed teasing you; that's all." She squeezed. "It's not my fault you make such an easy target."

"You can't help yourself, can you?"

"Nope. As a mom-to-be you need to remember one thing: don't lose your sense of humor. Some days, it's the only thing that will keep you from losing your mind. And surround yourself with those who love you. You'll need all the support you can get."

"You're going to be a mom?" Casey's eyes widened.

"Yes. Lizzie and I are going to have a baby." Sarah rubbed her baby bump. "Two. Twins, actually."

Casey whipped her head back to me. "How can you have a baby if you don't know *The Little Mermaid*?"

Even Casey had serious reservations about my parenting skills.

She stared at me, a serious frown on her young face. "Oh boy, you have a lot to learn."

In bed that night, Sarah asked, "Do you miss being on campus?"

My first thought was: *Does she know Dr. Marcel offered me a teaching position this fall?* The semester would start days after the babies' due date. My second impulse was: *Quick! Wave a shiny object to get her off the scent.*

I rolled over and nuzzled my face into the crook of her neck.

Sarah shoved me off. "That means yes."

"My trying to seduce you means I miss teaching?"

She sat up and fluffed some pillows behind her back. "Ah, I didn't mention teaching."

Again, my instinct was to distract. "You got me. What's my punishment?" I traced my fingertips along her jawline as sensually as possible.

She laughed and swatted my hand away. "The secret you're keeping must be good."

"Why do I even bother?"

"Keeping a secret?" She shrugged. "Who knows? You aren't good at it."

"Not that. Trying to seduce you."

"Please, if you really wanted to have sex, you'd have succeeded by now." Sarah laid a hand on my chest. "Something's troubling you. You may not know the full truth yourself, but I know there's angst inside. Why don't you talk to me about it?"

"If I don't know the full truth, how can I talk about it?" I groaned.

Sarah let out an exasperated sigh, the one she'd perfected years ago. I liked to call it the *I love you, Lizzie, but it ain't easy* sigh. "Talking things over may help you realize what's bothering you." Her eyes pleaded with me.

I stared at the blue and taupe paisley pattern on our new comforter. "Talking things over isn't one of my strong suits."

"Really? I hadn't noticed."

"Okay, wise guy. I get it. I'm imperfect and the source of all our relationship issues, and you are the goddess of positive chi."

Sarah cuffed the back of my head. "Don't be an ass. I want to help you. Let me in, please."

I propped one pillow beneath my lower back and squashed a mint-green decorative pillow against my chest. "I haven't been able to write a word in weeks now. For some reason, I can't stop researching to focus on the real task at hand: getting words written."

"Why do you think that is?" Sarah sat up, flashing her supportive face.

I faced her. "Really? You're going to act like my therapist? Lob questions back at me to get a gut reaction?"

"Does it work in therapy?" She smiled knowingly.

"Ye—hey, you did it again."

Sarah tugged my tank top up and stroked my stomach with soft fingertips. "Keep going."

"Shouldn't I be saying that to you?" I pinched my eyes shut, focusing only on her touch.

"Later. Right now, let it out. Don't think; just speak."

Keeping my eyes shut, I said, "I like researching. Learning new things, even about things that have been studied and analyzed from fifty different angles by even more historians.

Shutting down the curious aspect of my brain to write is much harder these days."

Sarah's hand worked its way toward my right breast. She focused on the areola, not making contact with my hardening nipple. "You've always liked researching, but you've been able to synthesize the research in a presentable way. What's stopping you now?"

"That's the thing. I don't know. I've set deadlines. I've tried insisting that if I don't write a certain amount of words in a day I can't go for a bike ride, or some other form of punishment. But it's not working. I'm losing my focus, and it's scaring me." My eyes opened and fixated on her worried face. "I don't want to slide into oblivion."

"Oblivion—that seems a bit dramatic. No wonder you're scaring yourself." She straddled my stomach and cupped my chin with her hand. "I'm not an expert, but I know you. You have a fabulous way of making a mountain out of a molehill. And the way you accomplish that best is by putting too much pressure and expectations on yourself. Nothing major will happen if you don't write your next book—"

"Thanks for that," I cut her off.

She smiled her *you're about to get laid* smile, which quieted me instantly. "Let me finish. What I mean is no one will die if you don't write it. No catastrophic tragedy will wipe out the human population—"

"I am writing about the Nazis, so part of your theory is wrong. That whole *if you don't know your history, you're doomed to repeat it* shtick." I winked.

"Because no one else has written about Nazis and the Holocaust?" The sarcasm in her voice matched her quirked brow. "Are you going to let me finish?" She lowered her mouth to an inch from mine.

I nodded.

"Blot out the fear, the fear of writing a crappy first draft. Swipe away the possibility of being wrong—that's what your editor and specialized beta readers help with. Not everyone has Dr. Marcel, the preeminent historian in your time period, as a first reader. Just sit down and write the words. Try setting a timer for twenty minutes and just type. See what happens. I know for a fact that your watch has a timer."

What she said made sense. Sarah pressed her lips to mine, and I responded eagerly for thirty seconds before breaking away and wiggling out from under her.

"Where are you going?" She rolled onto her back.

"To write for twenty minutes. Can you hold that thought?" I waved to the lit candles and her sexy lingerie.

"You want to start now?" Her face wasn't annoyed, albeit slightly perplexed.

"Is there a better time?" I slipped one arm into a navy cardigan.

Sarah laughed. "Serves me right for being so good at guessing what's going on inside that brain of yours."

I crouched down and kissed the top of her head. "That's right. This is all your fault. I'll be back in twenty."

"You better be, or I'll take care of myself." She slid her hand under her pink silk panties.

My resolve started to waver.

Sarah flicked her hand. "Go. And then come back and get busy. Sexy busy."

———————— ⌒⌒ ————————

Approximately twenty-three minutes later, I tiptoed into the bedroom and eased under the covers. Sarah's back faced me. Unsure whether she was asleep, I nuzzled against her backside, peppering the back of her neck with kisses.

She reacted a little.

My hand reached around and slithered up her nightie, heading straight for her burgeoning breasts.

My caress elicited a moan from the now half-awake Sarah. "Gentle." Her breasts were becoming increasingly tender as the pregnancy progressed.

Regretfully, I abandoned the tempting titties, although I had to suppress a disappointed sigh. Instead, I rolled her onto her back and staked my claim on her mouth. Sarah met my passion, upping the stakes by bolting upright and yanking her nightie off.

"Damn, they're gorgeous." I attempted a wolf whistle.

Sarah ignored my feeble attempt and followed my gaze to her breasts. "It doesn't seem fair. I've always loved having you fondle my girls, but now that they're in peak form, I can't stand to have you touch them."

"It's a travesty, and I study travesties for a living, so I know." I tapped a confident thumb on my chest.

"Did you just compare my boobs to the Holocaust?" She tilted her head to the side, which made her smile appear even more sarcastic and seductive. A sliver of moonlight reflected in her stunning eyes.

"Uh… of course not. Who would do such a thing?"

"Only an idiot." She laughed—a laugh that implied I was indeed an idiot but that it was one of the things she loved about me. I'd never understand how that attracted her to me—neither of us did. Her eyes roamed over my body. Tugging on my cardigan she said, "I think you're a mite overdressed, Professor."

"Now that's a problem that can be resolved as quick as"—I freed my arms from the sweater and shed my tank top—"that."

Sarah pushed me onto my back and positioned herself over my body. "Now these are not off limits." Slowly, she descended, not stopping until she sucked my right nipple into her mouth, teasing and biting.

My head sank down into the plush pillow. "Thank God for that." My hands cupped her ass cheeks, easing her into my hot zone. I could feel her desire wetting the lining of her panties. I massaged her ass with greedy hands. "These are mine, all mine."

"You like?" She craned her head over her shoulder, eyeing my hands as I grabbed her ass.

"I love your body. I'm still unsure how I was able to get you to fall in love with me."

She swung her head around to stare down at me. "I'm still unclear about that as well."

I beckoned her with a finger. "Shut up and kiss me."

"Is that all you want?"

"It's the starting point."

"For what?"

"Fucking."

"I love when you talk that way."

I gripped the back of her head and forced her mouth to mine. The need for talking was over. Action was what I craved, and from the silent need in her eyes, Sarah wholeheartedly agreed.

I flipped her onto her back, startling her but ratcheting her yearning up a few notches. My tongue delved into her mouth, savoring the taste of craving. Her fingers bunched the hair on the back of my head, luring me further into her.

I let my tongue work down the side of her body, bypassing her breasts, although I studied them longingly as her chest moved up and down with each rapid breath. I focused on the area right below her belly button, licking and nipping her expanding belly. Tenderly, I smoothed a palm over the apex of the growth, not uttering my feelings aloud. By the way Sarah draped her hand over mine, I was certain she understood what I was communicating. Together we were creating a family: one we would cherish through thick and thin.

My teeth raked her pubic hair, causing her breath to hitch. Slight variations in her breathing always affected me, driving my need to please her, to prove how much I loved her, how much I craved her pussy. Tasting her. Smelling her. Being inside her.

She raised her hips off the light-gray sheets, alerting me she was ready.

I tugged off her panties and flicked her clit with my tongue, using enough force to cause her to moan but not enough to overplay my hand. Separating her lips with my own, my tongue glided all the way down through her warm tunnel and back up to stake my claim on the spot she so desperately wanted me to invade. I meandered to her inner thigh, concentrating on the softness of her skin, the top of my head nuzzling her love zone, keeping her stimulated, promising more.

And I so desperately wanted to give her more. Sometimes, it was difficult to determine who it was harder on: Sarah or me. Foreplay had significant advantages, but it wasn't a game for the weak-willed. Holding off, even for a few moments, intensified the experience, transforming it into an act of love and not mere fucking.

With this in mind, I continued my migration to the tip of her toes, sucking each one into my mouth. Sarah writhed underneath me, each twitch connected directly with my heart and soul. Both of us were in blissful agony, keen for the release while savoring the buildup to a mind-blowing explosion.

"Please," she begged.

That was the trigger I'd been waiting for. Repositioning my body so my head was between her legs, I peered into her eyes before embarking on the final act of stage two. Her expectant smile and nod commanded me to continue.

I eased my tongue inside her, making way for two fingers to increase my efforts. Sarah gasped, arching her back. My mouth found her bud, throbbing and waiting to be plucked. I circled it with my tongue, sucked it into my mouth. Fuck, she tasted good. The wait was well worth it.

Her gyrating hips compelled me to go deeper. More force. Another finger. I doubled my efforts on her clit. Her eager gasps and moans helped me kick it up even further. Soon, our bodies melded into one. Every touch burned for both of us. Every flick of the tongue elicited an electrical current, and I was willing to bet each beat of our hearts was perfectly in tune.

Sarah's fingers clawed the back of my head. She shuddered, her back arched so far I was amazed she hadn't snapped in two.

"Jesus, don't stop," she commanded.

No way in hell I would. My only wish was to make Sarah happy, to give her the orgasm to outdo all orgasms. My fingers hammered inside her, thrusting with as much force as I could muster. My tongue went into overtime, lapping as if it would never tire or cease.

I wanted Sarah to explode like she'd never done before.

"Oh my God, how are you doing this?"

I didn't care about the how; I focused on achieving my goal.

Her scream was the first proof that I'd succeeded. The second clue was the juice flooding my mouth and chin. The climax was upon us.

"Holy fucking shit," she hollered, her body convulsing.

I held my fingers and tongue in place as the waves continued, rocking every muscle in her body. I didn't move until every ounce of sexual frenzy had worked its way through, leaving her motionless on the bed, gasping for breath.

Then, I cradled her in my arms, nuzzling my face into the warmth of her neck. She leaned into me, unable to speak. I loved that we no longer had to say *I love you*—or as Sarah liked to say in the beginning of our relationship, *I heart you*— to be heard loud and clear. In the stillness of the moonlit room, I'd never felt more alive, more secure. I'd never been so happy in my personal life.

— CHAPTER FOUR —

"WHY DID WE INVITE PETER AND TIFFANY TO DINNER?" I SPRAYED LEMON PLEDGE onto a rag and wiped down the deep-cherry coffee table that sat between matching leather sofas in the library, the de facto room for drinks before and after dinner.

"We? I don't remember you being involved."

"I know! So why did *you* invite Peter and Tiffany to dinner?" I shook the yellow can at her. "Not to be horrible, but after Mom passed, I thought my interactions with my family would subside or stop altogether."

"Subside? You have no relationship with them. How can that subside? You didn't even see them at all the first year we were together." She perched on the arm of a wingback chair and caressed her five-month baby bump. "Is it cold in here? Shall I light the fire?" Without waiting for an answer, she flipped the switch to ignite the fireplace on the far wall. "I seem to remember you mentioning that not having a relationship with your family would be a bad example for our children."

She was right about that, but actually forming a relationship with them seemed more daunting than the German army successfully invading Russia.

"This conversation is moot. This is all Tiffany's doing. She pretty much wrangled the invite out of me. She wasn't kidding before her wedding when she said she wanted to fix your relationship with Peter. Besides, I think she likes stirring the pot, and one surefire way to accomplish that is getting more than one Petrie in the room."

I groaned. "Don't answer the phone when she calls. I don't."

"Lizzie! She's your sister-in-law. How can I ignore her?" Sarah's face flushed a lovely shade of rose. Sometimes it was worth getting her riled up. She grinned as if in tune with my thoughts.

"Simple. Follow my example." I yanked my cell out of my pocket and chucked it into a drawer of my desk near the bay windows that overlooked our quiet street.

Sarah staggered back onto her feet and continued straightening the room, ignoring my histrionics. Fluffing pillows. Organizing the crystal decanters on the bar. "I can't remember. Is Peter a bourbon or a scotch man?"

"Bourbon, I think." I'd moved on to polishing the small crimson end tables.

"What's the difference between bourbon and scotch anyway?" Sarah didn't bother waiting for me to answer, knowing I didn't have an inkling. She brandished her cell. "See, this is why I can't lock mine in a drawer. Most normal humans can't live without the convenience of a phone."

"For centuries, great minds in history managed." I gestured to a row of novels by Dickens. "Charles didn't need a cell phone, and look what he accomplished." I tsked. "Heaven forbid my brother doesn't get the drink of his choice. This is our house, not a bar—even though you've been stocking up lately. Odd, since neither of us is drinking these days."

Sarah pantomimed for me to zip it. "My mother raised me to be a good host. Your mom—"

"Raised animals. I know, I know." I held my hands up, one still grappling with the canister, the other a wet dust rag. "But I have a pretty good argument that my mom didn't rear me at all. Luckily, I had a nanny."

Sarah's tight-lipped smile wasn't comforting. "Not sure you want to go around telling people that, my dear. Okay…" She waved her cell to and fro to get me back on track. "According to the Internet, scotch comes from Scotland—that should have been obvious—and it's made from malted barley. Bourbon is distilled from corn in the US.'"

"I feel a hundred times smarter now." I feigned a curtsy.

She snatched up a bottle. "Scotch whiskey—not bourbon." Sarah scrunched her face and looked to the ceiling before settling her gorgeous eyes on mine. "Would you mind?"

I nearly discarded the cleaning supplies onto the sofa, but Sarah's pinched face said *Don't you dare*. Carefully placing them in the cleaning bucket, I asked, "Do we need anything else?"

"For such a neat freak, it amazes me how much you hate cleaning." Her narrowed eyes were more condemning than her words.

"That's why we have Miranda—to do the cleaning. Maybe we need to find someone who's on call 24/7 for when you make the mistake of answering the phone. Or maybe we should hire live-in help, instead of Miranda coming in twice a week."

Her eye roll put me in my place, but she couldn't restrict her impulse to pound the final nail in. "You're unbelievable. You know that?"

"Kidding, of course." I wasn't, and we both knew it. "Do we need anything else?" I repeated, retrieving my phone from the drawer.

She shook her head.

On my way out of the library, I stopped to kiss her cheek and place a hand on her belly. "Bye, little twinkies."

"Wait!"

I veered about in the doorway. "Tiffany has a sweet tooth. Get some chocolates. Nice ones, Lizzie, and don't skimp on Peter's bourbon, either. He's your only sibling." Her stare bored into the center of my forehead.

I leaned against the doorjamb. "You might want to start pronouncing her name the way she likes: Tie-Fannie."

"I only pronounce it that way when she's around. Like you do, I might add."

It was true. I found Tiffany's insistence of being called Tie-Fannie completely absurd.

Before I had a chance to make my exit, Sarah added, "Don't forget the chocolate or bourbon." She stabbed two fingers in the air, making a determined victory symbol.

"How could I forget two items?" I counted them on my own splayed fingers. "I don't even need a list."

Sarah's withering look said she'd feel better if I jotted them down. "That's another thing that amazes me about you. How much you hate shopping and how you can mess up buying a gallon of milk." She smiled sweetly to take the sting out of her honesty.

During her pregnancy, I'd been going to the store regularly and botching each trip almost every time. If she wanted creamy peanut butter, I for some reason purchased extra crunchy. Strawberry jam morphed into orange marmalade in my mind. Last week, she'd had a hankering for beans and franks, but I'd purchased Vienna sausages instead of hot dogs. Sarah chalked it up to sabotage since shopping resided in my *only if I absolutely have to* category, but I didn't like to contemplate I was subconsciously selecting the wrong items. I preferred to think I simply sucked at shopping, not to mention

I usually wouldn't take the time to ask someone to direct me to the proper aisle or item.

Sarah waved for me to go, dismissing me like I was one of her minions. And I was the rude one for wanting a cleaner available seven days a week!

Less than ten minutes later, I wandered through the aisle of the fancy liquor store on the outskirts of Old Town. Aisle upon aisle promised one thing: I'd flub the operation. I excelled when there weren't so many options. Maybe I should have lived in East Germany during the cold war; one option for everything, if there was an option at all. I could practically hear Sarah saying, "Oh, you'd find a way to screw up no matter what, just to make a point."

I rooted in my jeans pocket for my cell and hit speed dial for Maddie.

"Ha! Sarah texted that I'd probably hear from you." Maddie laughed.

"Did she tell you my mission?"

"Nope. She said it was a surprise."

"What type of bourbon does Peter like?" I asked as I carefully maneuvered past a craft beer display that resembled a house of cards—one wrong move and it'd all come tumbling down.

"Why in the hell are you asking me about that no-good asshole?" Her tone didn't contain an ounce of wrath.

I sighed. "I'm sorry. But you're the only person I know who knows him."

"He's your brother, not mine." She laughed again.

"I think I remember that. I have vague recollections of him growing up under the same roof. But you almost married him. That makes you the Peter expert in this situation."

A clerk, who was straightening a disheveled shelf, hiked up an eyebrow at me.

I covered the phone and whispered, "I'm okay." She gave me the once-over that most sales clerks give, making it clear she knew I couldn't shop my way out of a wet paper bag.

"Peter's a Blanton's man."

"Blanton's," I parroted, nodding. I squinted at the items in front of me, realizing I was in the vodka section. Rising myself on tippy-toes, I tried to see whether the next aisle over had brown or clear liquids. "Is it expensive?"

"What do you think?" I could picture the derision on Maddie's face.

"Right." I moved to the end of the vodka and gin aisle and found the correct one. "Okay, I see Maker's Mark, Rowan's Creek, Knob Creek, Fighting Cock." I turned my face upward and continued to scan the top rows. "Rebel Yell, Very Old Barton, Wild Turkey, Basil Hayden's, Booker's, Elijah Craig, Ancient Age—hey, that's kinda historical and not in a Confederate way."

"Don't you dare. I told you. Blanton's."

"I don't see Blanton's."

The woman who had been straightening up seconds ago appeared, snatched a bottle from right in front of me, and placed it in my hands. It was a round bottle featuring a man riding a horse on the top. I read the label aloud, "Blanton's Original Single Barrel."

"That's it. Anything else?" Maddie chirped, clearly enjoying rescuing me, Lizzie the Bungling Idiot Shopper.

I pawed the phone's speaker, whispered thank you to the lady, and then muttered into the phone, "Chocolates. Sarah said Tiffany has a sweet tooth." I marched to the register to pay for Peter's bourbon. Not minding my manners, I kept Maddie on the phone as a rail-thin man with a wispy goatee rang up the purchase. My eyes boggled at the ninety-dollar total. Gritting my teeth, I handed over my Amex. After signing the screen, I thanked the clerk and stepped outside, clutching a bottle that Peter would probably only have one drink from—two tops. This was the first time Peter had been invited to my home, and I prayed it'd be the last. At least booze didn't ever go bad.

"Can you talk yet?" Maddie asked. "Some of us have things to do today."

"Like what?"

"Laundry." She tried to make it sound exciting, but no one can make laundry sound exciting.

"Trade you. I'd rather clean my knickers than have Peter sit down at my table."

She laughed. "Be glad you aren't cleaning Peter's knickers. Two words: skid marks."

I nearly dropped the ninety-dollar Blanton's onto the pavement. "Jesus, Maddie. That's one fact about my brother I never needed to know. Skid marks in his tighty-whities." I cringed and shook my arms and head to cleanse my soul.

"Ask him about it at dinner."

"I can just picture it. 'Peter, can you pass the salt? By the way, Maddie says you have skid marks in your underpants. Is that true?'"

"Underpants!" Maddie chortled. "I love it."

"Focus, Maddie." I stood on the sidewalk of the shopping center. "Chocolates. I need chocolates."

"Yep, that's the color of Peter's—"

I wrenched the phone away from my ear and counted to five before placing it back.

"Peter's skid marks," she continued.

How did the woman do it?

As if in tune with my thoughts, Maddie responded. "You're so predictable."

"Quick question, if Peter was so disgusting, why'd you almost marry him?"

"I fell for him. It's amazing what you can live with when you're in love." She said it with a sincerity that shocked the hell out of me. How anyone could love my brother was unfathomable.

Unsure how to manage this can of worms, I stayed quiet.

She cleared her throat. "Now, you need chocolates. Where are you?"

"On a sidewalk outside the liquor store, trying to erase the image of Peter and his..." I left the rest unsaid so I wouldn't puke all over my new Keens Sarah bought me last week.

"Which shopping center?"

I looked around and saw a King Soopers across the way. A gas station. Wells Fargo. Domino's. "I don't know. The one that's ten minutes from my house."

"Huh." I could practically see her scratch her head, lost in thought. "Not much there. Head to Old Town and go to Filene's."

"Old Town?" I consulted my Timex. "They'll be at the house in thirty minutes. Can't I just buy her a Snicker's or something? Doesn't every woman love Hershey's kisses? I do, and King Soopers will have them."

"No, you cannot!" she screeched like a howler monkey being separated from its mom. "Sarah will skin you alive. She's all about family these days, including yours for some insane reason. You really need—"

Once again I extracted the phone from my ear until the tirade ended. By the time I reached my SUV, I figured Maddie's rant was over. "Okay, okay. I'm getting in the car now. Settle down."

"Good girl. Maybe you are trainable after all. God knows Sarah's been trying her best with you."

"I'm not a puppy or something."

"True. I hear they're fast learners. Even Hank has learned to play fetch with a balled-up piece of paper, and he's a cat."

"There aren't many cats like my boy." I smiled. "He takes after me."

"Did you teach him how to lick his ass in front of the television?"

I groaned. "You need serious help."

"Says the woman who's so competitive she thinks her cat is the smartest cat in human history."

I sucked in too much air through my nostrils. "Always a pleasure. I'll call if I need more help," I said.

"Which you will. Talk in a few."

The phone went dead. I hated that she was 99.97 percent right.

"Welcome." Sarah waved Peter and Tiffany into our home.

Right behind them stood a man I didn't recognize. Had Peter hired a driver like Dad?

"Hope you don't mind, but we brought my baby brother. His fiancée has a business obligation, and he's completely lost." Tiffany looped her arm through her brother's. I'd never met him—not even at Peter and Tiffany's wedding. Of course, that day was one big nerve-wracking blur since Tiffany had insisted I give a speech. I could have met the Pope that day, and I still wouldn't remember.

"The more the merrier," Sarah chirped.

I gulped. Tiffany and her brother were in my home, meaning they knew where I lived. I loved our house, but at the moment I wanted to pack up all of our shit and move far far away—maybe to Alaska or Canada. Tiffany wasn't the easiest person for me to relate to, and now I was faced with two of them.

Of course, there weren't many people I got along with. Theories as to why I was so socially inept ranged from being a book nerd (Sarah's go-to theory) to being an alien child trapped in a human body (Maddie's theory). My reasoning was that most people sucked, so why bother? Whenever I spouted this reason, Sarah claimed that unless I got to really know people, I wouldn't be able to get past that stumbling block. She followed that up by suggesting I was highly judgmental, which was code for *too much like my mother and Peter*. Most intelligent people were, but I kept that thought to myself. Did Einstein have tons of friends? I mentally added that question to my *need to google* list.

Sarah extended a hand to Tiffany's brother. "I'm Sarah, and this is my wife, Lizzie." Sarah rarely introduced me as her wife, but in Peter's presence, she loved to needle my uptight, homophobic brother a smidgen. It meant the world to me that she did. Hopefully, our twins wouldn't despise each other.

"Where are my manners?" Peter puffed out his chest. "This is Christopher." He waved to me. "And this is my sister, Elizabeth."

I reached for Christopher's proffered hand. "Nice to meet you, Christopher."

"Kit, please. All my friends call me Kit." His smile was genuine, not calculating like Tiffany's, and there was a hint of mischief in his eyes. Plus, he didn't try to pulverize my hand, a pleasant surprise. Tiffany had the grip of a python. Right when you thought she was done torturing you, she squeezed harder.

"By all means, call me Lizzie." I glared at Peter for the umpteenth time after making this announcement, hoping it would finally sink in that I hated my formal name: Elizabeth. His eyes wandered over the entryway of our home, sizing up the staircase to the immediate right, the red and gold oriental rug on the original hardwood floor, an antique table with a Tiffany lamp dating back to the early 1900s, a pair of Chippendale chairs, and the arch with crown molding that led to the rooms on the main floor.

Typically, I didn't notice people's reactions to our home, but I took great pride watching Peter soak it all in. His expression showed neither approval nor disapproval, and I took that as a positive sign. If he found any fault, no matter how insignificant, he'd rub my nose in it. One of the first criticisms I remember from childhood was him saying, "You can't do anything right. You even have two dimples in your right cheek and one in your left."

After I took their coats, Sarah clapped her hands together. "Let's have a drink in the library." She led the way, while I hung their jackets in the hall closet, treating Peter's Burberry jacket rougher than necessary. There was sibling rivalry, and then there was Peter and I. All-out sibling war. Maybe I could encourage Hank to spray my brother's jacket. He'd never had an accident in the house, but there was always hope. Maybe I could google *How to encourage your cat to ruin your cocky brother's jacket*. Sarah might be proud of me, searching on my phone like a normal, twenty-first-century person. The thought brought a smile to my face, and I did a quick Internet search. Dang. All the articles on the first page were about getting your cat to stop spraying. I didn't have time to concoct the perfect search terms. I let out a sigh and joined the party in the library.

"Wow! Lizzie, have you read all of these books?" Tiffany waved to the leather bound tomes that filled the floor-to-ceiling shelves.

"Not yet, but a good portion."

"What's with all the Swastikas?" Kit directed the question to Sarah, for some reason, pointing toward the shelves mostly hidden from view near my desk or under the bay windows, where Sarah insisted I store my research books. It was dusk — my favorite time of day — so the drapes hadn't been completely drawn, letting a violet light wash the room.

Sarah tittered. "When we started dating, the first time I strolled into Lizzie's apartment I almost made a run for it." She stood behind me and placed a hand on each of my shoulders. "Lizzie is an historian, and her specialty is the Nazis — of all things." She tightened her grip, letting me know she wasn't judging. At least I think that was what she meant by the caress. Quite possibly, she meant, *Don't launch into a history lecture.*

"Would anyone like a drink?" I clasped my hands together and bowed slightly like a waiter. "Peter, we have Blanton's."

He actually smiled and nodded as he took a seat on the couch on the far side of the room. Gesturing to the Oriental rug under the couches and coffee table and then the one under my desk, he said, "Do you have a problem with moths?"

Sarah sloped her head to the left. "Excuse me?"

"Moths — eating your sweaters. A buddy of mine says that all the moths infiltrating the US come from the Middle Easterners who bring their rugs into the country to sell them. I noticed you had another rug in the foyer." He tugged the sleeve of his cashmere cardigan as if warding off evil Middle Eastern insects.

I was in mid-pour of his drink, and the mental lapse made me spill the ninety-dollar liquid all over the top of the bar. I mopped up the mess with a cloth, contemplating whether I could wring the towel out into Peter's glass without anyone noticing; that would be much easier to accomplish than training Hank to spray his jacket.

"An interesting theory." Sarah's voice was flat — it was the tone she often used when I said something foolish but she lacked the energy or desire to start an argument.

Kit raked his overly manicured goatee and sought out his sister, who was still wandering the room, taking in everything. Noticing that Tiffany was either ignoring Peter or hadn't heard him, Kit flashed me a guilty smile. Did he feel like he had to apologize for Peter? If he started that now, he'd never stop.

"What can I get you, Kit?" I waved to the bottles on the bar.

He moseyed over and put a hand on his hip, accentuating his thin waist as he studied the selection. "Oooh, I love grappa."

"Grappa it is." I retrieved an hourglass flute of the Italian brandy from the cabinet below the bar top. "Tie-Fannie, what about you?"

She was admiring the view of our tree-lined street out the window and didn't bother turning around. "Wine, please."

"Red or white?"

"Bartender's choice." She smiled coquettishly over her shoulder.

Sarah and I exchanged glances. Mine tried to convey: *This is why I don't like having family over.*

Peter was an arrogant ass, and apparently a racist one, and his wife was an airhead. I placed all the drinks on a silver tray, including ice water with a slice of lemon for Sarah, and carried it to the coffee table. Once sitting opposite Peter, I reached for my Coke on ice.

"Still can't stomach a real drink, Elizabeth?" Peter glommed onto his cut-crystal tumbler and swirled the honey-colored drink.

"It doesn't seem fair to have a drink when my pregnant wife can't."

Sarah parked on the armrest of the couch and draped her hand over my shoulder. "Ever since Lizzie found out we're pregnant, she's been more responsible than I thought imaginable. She's mapped out all the routes to the hospital and has actually done several dry runs at different times of day."

"Aw, that's sweet." Kit sat in the wingback chair off to the side, crossing his legs. He had the skinniest ankles I'd ever seen. He was shorter than Peter by at least five inches, and I bet he weighed well under one hundred and fifty pounds. "I hear you're having twins."

"That's right. A boy and girl."

"Will you have more?" Tiffany took a seat next to Peter, sweeping her wineglass up to her lips like a parched sailor.

"Not sure, really. Time will tell how difficult twins are." Sarah smiled and massaged her belly. "So far so good, but soon we'll be up to our eyeballs in diapers, bottles, and long nights."

"At least Elizabeth doesn't work." Peter leaned forward and placed a slice of chorizo on a wheat cracker.

"Then you'll be a stay-at-home mom?" Kit speared an olive with a toothpick from the array of snacks Sarah had set out while I was on the bourbon and chocolate run.

"Not quite. I'm working on my third book... Well, I'm in the early stages." I motioned to the stack of books on my desk, many with dog-eared pages and countless slips of paper sticking out. I had banned Sarah from stashing this particular pile, since it consisted of the sources I was knee-deep in at the moment. I had a process, and I didn't want to disrupt it for anyone, least of all Peter and a ditzy blonde who insisted on being called Tie-Fannie.

"How hard can reading and writing be?" Peter's haughty smile didn't go unnoticed. "A couple of hours a day for what... a month?" My brother's vacant expression made it clear he thought that was all it took to research and write historical nonfiction. Was he that clueless, or did he think only people in the finance business understood hard work and dedication?

"Then you two have more in common than I thought." Tiffany grinned, the points of her pearly whites seeming to sharpen before my eyes. "With all your golfing and *whatnot*, you can't tell me you've put in a full day at the office since your cushy promotion."

I zeroed in on her annunciation of "whatnot." I'd learned from Maddie, years ago, that my older brother was a philanderer. I'd assumed Tiffany knew that about Peter before they married, but for some reason she either accepted it or thought she could change him. Now, I was guessing he hadn't altered his ways and that Tiffany wasn't going to let him get away with it, not entirely. Did she get some perverse joy of making jibes about his cheating to let him know she was on to him? Or was it to embarrass him in front of others?

Peter cast a withering glare at his wife, who smiled innocently before fixing another cracker with port-wine cheese.

"What about you, Kit? When's the big day?" Sarah turned her back on the crackling tension between the couple opposite us.

"What?" Kit mumbled around a mouthful of chorizo.

"Your wedding, of course."

"Oh, *that*. We haven't set a date yet."

Kit and Tiffany had a habit of stressing insignificant words, which modified the entire tone of the conversation. Did the whole family speak in code? And if that was their code, even I, the usually socially tone deaf one in a group, had already cracked it.

"Our family wants a June wedding, but Kit, here, is being difficult." Tiffany swished her wineglass, almost dumping the burgundy liquid onto her pale amethyst dress.

"I'm not being difficult. Mom and Dad were married in June. I don't think we should share their month; that's all." He shrugged as if it was no big deal.

I wasn't an expert in people, not living ones anyway, but his reasoning stank of a man trying to stall getting hitched. Interesting. Tiffany had been dead-set on getting her claws into Peter, but Kit came across as a man who didn't want to relinquish his independence. I was starting to like him, even if there were a few curly chest hairs poking out of his mint-green gingham poplin shirt. His sleeves were rolled up, and from the thickness of his arm hair and evidence of chest hair, I gathered he was quite hirsute.

"There are thirty days in June. Surely you can pick a date that doesn't step on anyone's toes." Peter relaxed into the couch cushions, both arms spread along the back of the sofa. "You don't want to let a woman like Courtney slip away, Christopher. Beautiful, successful, and well-bred."

"Kit," Kit and I simultaneously corrected him.

Peter smiled, like he used to do when we were kids and he thought I was being a pussy. But there were grown-ups present, which prevented him from calling me names. Peter had always hated any sign of weakness. Years ago, I thought it was because he didn't have any weaknesses. Now, I suspected my brother was one of the most fearful men I'd ever encountered. That stoked conflicting and vacillating emotions in me, ranging from satisfaction to pity.

Tiffany's brother acknowledged my support with a slight dip of his head. The room grew silent, and four out of five of us looked to the drinks in our hands as if we were praying a safe conversation would magically start.

"Who's this?" Tiffany swiped a frame off a side table.

"Hank," I replied. "Our cat."

"You have a pet?" Tiffany's face exhibited confusion. "That's odd."

Sarah crumpled her forehead. "How so?"

Tiffany's eyes briefly landed on her husband. "Peter would never entertain getting a pet."

"Waste of money if you ask me. How much are the vet bills? And for what? A nuisance that becomes an obligation."

"Does that mean you don't really *want* children?" Kit shifted in his seat, crossing his other leg and draping his hands primly in his lap. "That obligation lasts a lifetime, and I imagine the cost is at least quadruple that of pet bills."

"Of course I want children." Peter scoffed. "Every man should want a family. Even these two are starting a family." He waved to Sarah and me.

"Even these two," Kit reiterated. "What do you mean? Lesbians?"

Peter's face flushed. My mother loved to pronounce the word as *les-bi-an* to get a rise out of me, but Peter usually tried to be subtler. Not that a deriding *even these two* was all that better. He sipped his Blanton's, refusing to explain himself. How odd that Peter had married a woman who spoke in condescending code and never outright verbalized what was on her mind.

From the angry crinkles around Kit's eyes, Peter didn't have to explain.

Sarah placed a hand on my thigh, turning to me with a tight smile. I returned my own version.

"I don't want kids." Kit pinned his eyes on Peter, expectantly.

"I'm not surprised." He glared at Kit.

I had to admit the only manly thing about Kit was his hairiness; not that Peter exuded masculinity either.

Tiffany levered herself off the couch, drifted into my line of sight like a ghost, and interjected, "I want to see the nursery." She faked excitement by clasping her hands together, childlike.

The tension between the three of them sizzled. Maybe I wasn't the only one with an effed-up family.

Peter didn't roll his eyes, but I sensed that if Sarah, Tiffany, and I hadn't been watching his reaction like a hawk, he would have. The only disapproval he allowed himself to show was the thinning of his bloodless lips to the point where they almost disappeared into his mouth.

I noticed Kit's eyes glistened with curiosity as the five of us tromped upstairs to the nursery.

When inside, Sarah waved her hand. "Welcome to the zoo."

Everything depicted zoo animals in bright colors; however, none of them were associated with the female or male sex. The decals and pictures on the walls. Stuffed animals. Quilts. Mobiles over each crib. There was even a six-foot stuffed giraffe in the corner, next to a wooden rocking chair.

Sarah rubbed my back as the group took everything in. My fascination with zoos had started late in life. Months ago, after learning that my mother was dying from colon cancer, Maddie had taken me to the zoo to snap me out of my funk. It was the first time I'd ever been. Not the first time since I was a kid; the first time *ever.*

The visit proved two things. One: my family was bizarre. While most families did family things on occasion, ours never even went to the zoo, which was less than thirty minutes from my childhood home. Two: zoo animals, whether a decal, stuffed animal, or the real thing, made me smile.

Tiffany twirled around. "Oh my God." Another handclap. "This is adorable, in all caps." She snapped her fingers and continued to wheel about on four-inch heels, causing my heart to flutter as I envisioned her crashing into one of the cribs and having to put together another one. Assembling baby furniture was the true test of any relationship. Sarah was dead set against paying someone to do it—not even Maddie, our interior designer. "Isn't this adorable?" She turned to Kit and Peter, waiting with her fake smile.

Kit's smile comforted me.

Peter grabbed a stuffed otter from the dresser. "It's something, all right."

"We can't take all the credit. Our designer pulled it all together for us." Sarah pinned Peter with a friendly but not too friendly stare.

He didn't take the Maddie bait, lowering his eyes to the plush carpet.

"Hello!" someone hollered from downstairs.

Sarah kinked an inquisitive eyebrow at me. I gave a quick shake of the head to let her know I certainly hadn't invited Maddie over, not today, of all days.

Maddie's heels clicked on the polished floors in the hallway leading toward the kitchen. "Anyone home? Lizzie? Sarah?"

"Be right down, Maddie," Sarah shouted.

Peter's face went up in flames, and he twisted the otter with both hands almost de-stuffing the poor thing.

Tiffany's face contorted with malicious delight. "Is that *the* Maddie? Your ex-fiancée?" Her smile was many things, but certainly not supportive or kind.

Peter squared his shoulders and plunked the otter back in place, not saying a word.

"Maddie's a close friend of ours," Sarah explained to Kit, not mentioning Maddie had ditched Peter at the altar.

My brother's face continued to change colors. Right now, he was working on a deep shade of eggplant—heart-attack color.

Sarah joined her hands together like a tour host. "Shall we go back downstairs? Have another drink before dinner?" Her smile suggested she'd rather gouge out her own eyes. I wanted to remind her this was what happened when she answered Tiffany's phone calls: uncomfortable family situations.

Tiffany sprinted out of the nursery like a child hurtling toward a Christmas tree to open presents. Did she see this as a golden opportunity to make Peter suffer? Tiffany was the kind of woman who loved to make others suffer—just like my mother.

Peter nodded bravely, to no one in particular, and I wondered whether he was psyching himself up to see his ex— the one who'd humiliated him in front of all his friends and business associates.

Kit's crinkled forehead was the only natural emotion on display in the room. He tweaked my arm. "Ah, Lizzie. What's this?" He pointed to a plastic white container standing next to the changing table.

Torn about helping Sarah handle the Maddie situation or outright ignoring our unexpected guest, I opted to stay behind. "It's a Diaper Genie."

Kit stepped back half a step. "Oh. That's the downside to kids and dogs—cleaning up their shit."

"Never had a dog," I said, not mentioning I wasn't too keen on changing diapers either, even though Sarah had made it perfectly clear I'd be doing my fair share.

Kit rolled back onto his heels, threading his arms over his chest. "I'm more of a cat man, myself."

I nodded. "Maybe Hank will make an appearance." I looked at the nursery door expectantly.

Kit followed my eyes and laughed. "A ghost cat or an imaginary one?"

I smiled. "Both. Since moving in here, we allow him to go outside. He makes rare appearances, but a portion of his kibble is gone each morning."

Voices from the first floor drifted into the nursery. So far, no shouting or door slamming.

Kit studied my face and then leaned in. "Does Peter treat everyone with such disdain or just…?" He paused, and scouted over his shoulder with the skill of a Nazi spy, hardly showing his true intention. "Or just people like *us*?" He stressed the word us.

"Uh, Peter can be a bit much at times. I wouldn't take it personally." I placed a hand on his shoulder. Why wasn't Sarah here? She'd know how to handle this conversation. I was better at analyzing the downsides of the Versailles Treaty and how it led to the rise of Hitler and World War II than I was at explaining why my only sibling was a complete asshole.

Kit plucked up the plush sea otter Peter had mangled earlier and fluffed it back into recognizable form. "So cute." He tickled the toy's belly. "My *friends* call me Otter. You know what I mean?" He exaggerated a wink.

I smiled, remembering the otters at the Denver Zoo and how I could watch them for hours, at peace and happy. "I do. Deep down, we're all otters." I motioned to him, the stuffed animal, and then tapped my chest.

Kit's face screwed up into a question mark, but then his facial muscles relaxed. "Yeah, right." He nodded. "We are, aren't we?"

Peels of laugher from downstairs caught my attention, and even though I was one floor up, I distinctly made out Sarah's SOS laughter.

"We should head downstairs." I motioned to the door.

"Rescue Sarah." Kit grinned.

"Exactly. We're definitely on the same page."

———————

"Who's this?" Maddie's attention locked on to my new buddy Kit, or should I say Otter?

"Maddie, I'd like you to meet Tie-Fannie's brother Kit." Like a salesperson on a showroom floor, Sarah waved across the library as if Kit was the most expensive and special item in the joint.

"Hi, Kit." Maddie sashayed toward him and grasped his hand delicately, not her usual crushing clutch to test someone's moxie. Was that one of Peter's dating criteria? Blondes with the grip of death?

Kit placed one palm over their conjoined hands. "It's lovely to meet such a bewitching creature." He stared into Maddie's Mediterranean blue eyes.

Maddie blushed. Another first.

"You're the one Peter let get away?" Kit squared his shoulders.

Peter, for a brief moment, lost his usual swagger, but then raging emotion flared in his eyes.

Tiffany jumped into the fray, sidestepping the Peter storm. "Now, Kit, don't be naughty. It all worked out for the best." She affixed her arm on her husband's. Peter didn't physically shake her off, but his stiffened spine and condescending sniff indicated not all had worked out according to his plan.

Maddie's genuine smile conveyed much. "Tiffany's right." She turned to Peter, and her cat-that-ate-the-canary smile quickly became saccharine. "It worked out for everyone."

"Tie-Fannie," Tiffany corrected.

Maddie eyeballed the airhead. "I'm sorry?"

"My name. It's pronounced Tie-Fannie." She bounced on the balls of her feet like a child waiting in line for a carnival ride.

"Oh." Maddie's blue eyes queried Sarah's face to see whether Tiffany was fucking with her. Sarah's gaze pleaded *Play nice*.

"Is it all right if I call you Tie?"

"Of course. That's what my girlfriends call me." Tiffany dropped Peter's arm in a flash and hooked her arm through

Maddie's, drawing her out of the library, destination unknown.

Maddie surveyed over her shoulder, shell-shocked. I waved and mouthed, "Toodles." It was nice to see someone else as perplexed by the woman as I was. Right then and there, I decided to refer to her as Tie, a much more palatable choice than her hideous pronunciation.

Peter marched to the bar to refill his bourbon.

Kit followed him with his eyes, no doubt relishing seeing the usually commanding Peter off-kilter. "So, Peter, do you always have a backup girl wherever you go?"

Peter raised his glass and swallowed half, quickly pouring more Blanton's into the tumbler and alleviating my fear that the booze would be wasted. I should thank Maddie later. I was intrigued to know why she'd shown up tonight, knowing Peter and Tie were here.

"Maddie's a good friend of ours, always popping by when least expected." Sarah threw me an accusatory look, but I gave a slight shrug of *Don't blame me.* I only called her to find out what kind of bourbon to buy Peter. Not once did I say, "You know, it'd be wonderful for you to stop by and say hi to the man you jilted an hour before the two of you were supposed to tie the knot for life."

"She's the most beautiful woman." Kit's attempt to needle Peter worked like a charm.

"Hands off!" he shouted. Realizing his error, he squared his shoulders and added, "You're engaged, remember?"

Kit waved him off. "We haven't set a date." He flicked a piece of lint off his shoulder. "No reason not to test the waters, ensure I'm making the right choic—"

"The right choice about what?" Tie and Maddie returned, and his sister released her hold on Maddie's arm to swoop up her nearly empty wineglass from the coffee table. She promptly handed the glass off to Peter, the new waiter for the night, to refill.

"About Courtney." Kit knocked back the dregs of his grappa.

Tie stopped in her tracks. "Are you thinking of breaking off the engagement?"

Kit motioned for Peter to refill his grappa, too, not bothering to affirm the answer, which seemed so obvious to everyone except Tie and Peter. I wasn't the famed code breaker Alan Turing, but it didn't take brilliance to decipher that Kit was hiding something.

Maddie thrust her hip out, pushing Peter to the side of the bar so she could pour herself a glass of merlot. Apparently, she'd decided to dig in for the night. What game was she playing? After taking a sip, she said, "In my experience, if you're doubting the relationship, you should end it. Now." Without a glance at her ex, she added, "I waited too long, and I suffered for it."

"*You* suffered?" Peter growled. "I was the one standing in front of everyone—"

"Wait?" Kit sprang up. "Did you stand him up at the altar?"

Tie whipped her head around at spine-cracking speed to give her husband a withering look. I wondered if this was for show. Was it possible Peter had been able to keep this tidbit under wraps?

"I regret that." Maddie placed a hand on Peter's arm, but he brushed it off and hoisted the tumbler to his lips. "It was cruel."

She turned to Kit. "I don't recommend doing that. As soon as you know it's not right, break it off. That's what I did tonight."

"Wh*at*?" Sarah turned the word into two syllables.

"Doug asked me to marry him. I said no." Maddie whirled the wine in the glass, looking as unsteady as the liquid sloshing inside.

"You were dating a man named Doug?" Peter's lips curled up. "D-ou-G or Dougie?"

"Because Petey is much manlier." Maddie held her glass to her mouth, eyebrows raised, inhaling the wine fumes.

"No one calls me Petey."

"I did. If I remember correctly, you used to love it when I did. Or the moments when I did."

I tried to shake off the slimy feeling of listening to this conversation between my rigid brother and my best friend—in front of Tie.

"I'm going to start calling you Petey." Kit moved closer to Maddie, staking his claim.

"No you won't. No one will. Ever." Peter distanced himself, literally, storming to the other side of the library and selecting a book off the shelves. He instantly pretended to peruse the pages.

"Do you know what I'd call you if we dated?" Maddie purred in Kit's ear, loud enough for all to hear.

"Otter," I said.

Kit choked on his grappa, while Sarah and Maddie reeled around to glare at me as if I'd said the absolute worst thing possible.

"What? Otters are cute and playful. Not to mention highly intelligent. They're one of the few animals that make tools," I rambled, trying to cover whatever blunder I'd committed.

"I like that name," Tie cooed to her brother. "I'm going to start calling you *that*."

I studied her face and detected a glimpse of malice.

Maddie and Sarah appeared ready to throttle me.

"And, you're hairy and skinny, like an otter. You have been since birth." Tie appraised her sibling with cold eyes, not entirely clueless to the blood rage coursing through the atmosphere.

How was I suddenly in more trouble than Peter? Not that he bothered to notice. He was still busily thumbing through the pages of the book.

Maddie regained her composure and fastened her arm on Kit's. "I would call you Kitty."

"Ha! That's wimpier than Petey," Peter said, proving he was listening and absorbing every word.

Maddie turned her back on him. "Kitty's love other pussies, don't they?" she purred.

I met Sarah's eye, trying to grasp the unreal scene playing out in our library. Was I dreaming? My wife seemed just as perplexed.

Kit whispered something in Maddie's ear, something saucy, from the way her face flushed. The two of them continued their private conversation.

Tie looked on with interest. Peter devoted his attention to the book in his hands, leafing through the pages like a mad librarian trying to locate a passage that would save the world.

Sarah cleared her throat. "Maddie, are you staying for dinner?"

For the first time, Maddie's brazen attitude wavered. "Uh —"

"What? Do you have another man's life you need to ruin?" Peter spoke without looking up from the pages.

I'd never considered the possibility that my brother had been in love with Maddie. I'd always thought she was just a piece of his master plan. Yet, the man in my library was acting every bit like someone who'd had his heart crushed by his one and only. I knew what it felt like to lose the one and only.

When Sarah left me for weeks after I made a horrible mistake, I didn't think I'd ever get her back. Those were the worst days of my life.

Tie looked to Peter and then to Maddie. A new energy coursed beneath the surface of those icy blue irises. I shuddered.

"Thanks for the invite, Sarah, but I should be going. I wouldn't want to intrude on your family dinner." Maddie downed the rest of her wine.

"Don't be silly. You're family." Sarah's words, I assumed, were meant for Peter, letting him know not to say anything snide.

He didn't.

Maddie wavered. "No, really. I'm meeting up with some friends at a club."

Kit whispered something in Maddie's ear again.

"Oh, my! You're fun!" Maddie thwacked his arm. "You're more than welcome to join me. What do you say?"

"By all means." He signed for Maddie to lead the way.

"What about dinner?" Tie asked.

"*Que sera sera.*" Kit sang a few more lines of the song.

"You can't leave." Peter chucked the book onto the couch, and for a moment I was unclear as to whom he was bossing around: Kit or Maddie. "I forbid it."

Maddie smiled. "Forbid what, Petey?"

"Forbid you to leave with… with… that thing." He stretched a finger at Kit.

"And you think you have the power to stop us?" Maddie stood closer to Kit, placing a hand on his chest. I cringed, remembering my glimpse of his chest hair.

Peter stared her down but didn't physically try to block the exit. After the two disappeared from the room, and we heard the front door close, Peter grabbed another book from the shelf and hurled it across the room, nearly hitting Sarah.

"Whoa, whoa, whoa. Watch out for my pregnant wife." Surprisingly, it was easier to rein in my older brother than I remembered.

He waved an apology to Sarah before straightening his sweater and his expertly creased trousers. "I think it's time we left."

"Why?" Tie asked. "Kit's never been one for finishing things, you know that." She met his glare with steely eyes. "Besides, we shouldn't be rude to your sister and Sarah, who were kind enough to invite us into their home."

I stifled a laugh with the palm of my hand. Tie had gone to great lengths to force an invite from Sarah. Was her reason just to piss off her husband?

Peter's defeated, though still defiant, grimace indicated he had backed down.

"Shall we have dinner?" Sarah valiantly asked, barely any emotion in her voice.

I was in Peter's camp. It was time for him to leave, but the set look on Sarah's face made it clear I shouldn't tell him that. My mind was racing with everything that had transpired over the past thirty minutes. It'd take me weeks to process everything.

"Why in the world did you out Kit in front of Tiffany and Peter, of all people?" Sarah shook her head at me as she carried a stack of dishes to the kitchen sink.

"*Out* him? What are you talking about?" I tailed her, my hands full with water and wineglasses.

"*Otter.* Ring a bell?"

"He told me his friends called him Otter. Why can't I call him that?"

"His friends? Did he mention these friends?" Sarah melted against the kitchen counter, one hand protectively placed on her belly.

"Come on." I pulled her arm. "You're exhausted. Let's sit, and then you can lecture me properly."

She didn't put up a fight, but as soon as her butt made contact with the chair in the TV room, she picked up where she'd left off. "Don't you know what an otter is?"

"A mammal. Thirteen different species. Only the sea otter spends the majority of its time in the water. Many think they're related to the beaver, but they aren't. They're actually distant cousins of the skunk." I grinned at my superior knowledge. Ever since my first visit to the zoo, I'd been watching documentaries about these fascinating creatures.

Sarah's mouth formed an O. "You really have no idea, do you?"

I collapsed on the couch, slipped my Keens off, and propped my tired feet up on the coffee table. "About what?"

"Gay men who look like Kit are called otters?"

"Ooo-kay. I didn't know that." My mind went into warp speed, trying to ferret out the problem. "But why does that matter?"

Her brown eyes scorched my clueless blue ones.

I pitched my hands up.

"Seriously, sometimes I wonder how you've been able to survive for so long. Kit's friends call him Otter because he's gay!" Sarah slapped the armrests of her chair.

"What are you talking about? The man is engaged, although that didn't stop him from hitting on Maddie."

Sarah rested her elbow against the armrest and rubbed her forehead wearily. "It took Maddie less than two seconds to figure out Kit's situation, and she went into absolute hyper-drive to throw Peter and Tiffany off his scent. Plus, I think she enjoyed getting a few zingers in. Didn't you wonder why she was putting on such a show with Kit in front of Peter?" Sarah sighed audibly. "Maybe I should offer classes for the clueless on how to act around normal humans. You can't be the only one on this planet who is utterly stupid."

"Geez, Sarah. Don't hold back." Although, the lessons would help me write my guidebook for the clueless, at least.

She took a deep breath and then another. "Kit may be engaged, but I'm telling you right now: he's gay. He's as gay as they come."

"If he's engaged, doesn't that make him bisexual?"

"No. No, it doesn't. It means he's in the closet. He's hiding his sexuality, although I suspect not from everyone."

"From whom, then?"

Sarah leaned her head back and closed her eyes. "My guess is from his family and from Peter."

"That's absurd. Why would anyone in the twenty-first century hide their sexuality. It's legal to marry now."

"That doesn't mean everyone is on board. Peter doesn't exactly accept you."

"No, but I don't care." I shrugged.

"Listen, we don't know Kit well enough to understand his motive, but I do know one thing: he's gayer than Liberace."

"Prove it. Kit's mint-green shirt wasn't even close to one of Liberace's outfits."

"So only men in outlandish outfits are gay?"

"Of course not. But when you say he's gayer than Liberace, it paints a picture—and that picture doesn't match Kit."

Sarah, too tired to argue over Kit's sexuality, whipped out her phone and motioned for me to come over to the chair. I perched on the arm while she showed me the most recent text from Maddie, containing a photo of Maddie and Kit in a gay bar. Kit wore a tiara and was dancing with a burly man—the way you dance with someone you want to fuck.

"So I can't call him Otter, but Maddie can post a photo of him dancing with a dude?"

The faint lines around Sarah's eyes crinkled like they usually did when she thought I was being melodramatic. "She didn't post it online—she sent it to me to show you. Maddie probably knew I'd have to sit down and explain a few things to you."

"Bu-but… Peter's just as dumb as I am. He won't know what otter means, will he?" I sounded too hopeful.

"He probably doesn't. But Tiffany isn't as dumb as she pretends to be. You need to watch yourself around her, Lizzie."

"Only gay people know, right? It's like a secret code?"

"You're gay, and you didn't know, which goes to show you can't count on people knowing things because of their so-called labels or lack of them."

I waved her off, which she took in her stride since I had never been in tune with anything gay. I'd only known Liberace was gay because we recently watched a documentary on him.

"No, it's not code. Anyone who watches shows like *Modern Family* will know the term. Not all gays are in hiding. Most people, even grandmothers, know more about popular culture than you."

I rubbed my eyebrows, rustling the coarse hairs back and forth. "So I may have outed Kit to his homophobic sister?"

"You may have. However, I suspect she knows. She just hasn't informed Peter or anyone else."

— Chapter Five —

MADDIE SNAPPED HER PHONE SHUT. SHE WAS SITTING ON A BARSTOOL AT THE island in our kitchen, a full day after her surprise visit.

"New phone?" I asked.

"Got it yesterday." She waved it in the air.

"When I had a phone like that, everyone teased me, called it ancient." I folded my arms, leaning against the doorjamb in the kitchen.

"Adele's video made flip phones cool again." She rotated on the stool and smiled condescendingly. "Besides, I like the ability to slam it shut." She demonstrated.

"Adele, huh?" I jabbed a thumb at my chest. "She's cooler than I am."

Maddie quirked a combative eyebrow. "Do you even know who she is?"

The name pricked a distant memory I couldn't bring to mind. It didn't stop me from saying, "Of course. Who doesn't know Adele?"

I continued to rack my brain. Was she that YouTube sensation Maddie had been following when she decided she wanted her own YouTube channel to make a fortune? That whim had lasted only marginally longer than her cooking classes.

Maddie locked eyes with Sarah, who stood on the opposite side of the kitchen island. Sarah gave her a sheepish grin and shook her beautiful head, as if to say, *Why do you set yourself up like this*?

"Who is she, then?" Maddie asked.

"Oh, please. I'm not in the mood for foolish tests." I squished my index finger and thumb together as if squashing a bug.

My action didn't fool her.

"Just admit you don't know who she is. Not knowing or remembering is one thing; being a fake is completely different." Maddie's left leg bounced up and down on the barstool footrest. She was fidgeting more than usual.

Sarah turned to me, winked, and then murmured, "Hello." Her smile was genuine in a baffling way. She regularly ganged up on me when that shit-starter Maddie was around.

"Hi," I responded, throwing her a half-hearted wave.

Sarah's smile plummeted from her face, and Maddie burst into laughter.

"Even after your wife gives you the biggest clue possible, you don't know." Maddie's shoulders heaved up and down with her dramatic sigh.

"Hello" was a clue? How?

"Be nice, Maddie. Lizzie's special."

"Doesn't excuse lying." Maddie squared her shoulders.

"I didn't lie," I said.

"You didn't tell the truth," she countered.

I rolled my eyes. "Whatever, Maddie."

"Someday, you'll need to learn. You're bringing a baby into the world."

"Babies," I corrected.

"Yes, babies. An even better reason for you to smarten up. Don't be like Peter."

"How does this equate to being like Peter?"

"Equate?" She looked to the heavens. "That's a start. You and Peter are stiff in casual conversation."

I started to defend myself, but Sarah silenced me with a shake of the head.

"Okay, Maddie. You've had your fun at Lizzie's expense and made your point. Now, why are your panties in a bunch?" Sarah swooped in and saved me before I foolishly took Maddie to task, knowing full well I was more like Peter than I cared to admit.

"I'll spill if Lizzie can define 'panties in a bunch.'"

"To become overwrought about something trivial." I stuck my tongue out at her.

"Wow, I've never heard it defined that way, but bravo, that pretty much sums it up."

Sarah took a seat on the barstool next to Maddie, placing one hand on her arm. "Tell us. You're clearly on the warpath, and you're taking it out on Lizzie."

I moved to stand on the opposite side of the counter, close enough to feel included in the conversation but far enough away from Maddie's sights. Sarah was dead-on about her mood.

Maddie rested her elbows on the counter and propped her chin on her hands. "I'm confused."

"Me too. Why in the hell did you show up knowing Peter was over?" I blurted.

Sarah's eyes bulged; however, she'd be lying if she denied wanting to know the answer.

"I forgot he was coming over." She chewed on her thumbnail, a pretty clear sign she was lying. "I was so distraught and needed someone to talk to."

I bought she was upset, considering the Doug part. "How could you forget after helping me pick out Peter's bourbon a couple of hours before?"

Maddie smothered her face with her arms once more, causing Sarah to give me the *not now* glare. I rolled my eyes, which didn't go unnoticed by Sarah. Was Maddie so curious to meet the woman Peter married she decided to barge in without an invite? Or was there something else I couldn't put my finger on?

"Do you want to talk about Doug?" Sarah asked in a tone that implied I should back off for now.

"Yes… No. Yes!" Maddie spoke into her arms.

Sarah and I exchanged an *uh-oh* glance.

Sarah leaned over and rubbed her back. "Go on."

Maddie popped up and sniffled. "I met someone."

"Really? When?" Sarah's expression brightened.

"Two nights ago."

Sarah's eyes widened. "Not Kit. Please tell me you don't mean Kit."

"What?" Maddie giggled mirthlessly before wiping her nose on her sleeve. "No! I haven't fallen for a gay man. Come on. Give me some credit."

"But you were at a gay bar," I said and then held my breath, knowing I should have kept silent. Remember the first rule.

They both eyed me, but the spark vanished from Maddie's face. "Yes. A bar for gay men and lesbians."

"You met a woman?" Sarah put two and two together way before I did.

For as long as I'd known Maddie, who was bisexual, she'd never dated a woman.

"What's her name?" Sarah asked.

"Courtney."

"Ha! What a coincidence? Kit's fiancée is named Courtney. I don't think I've known a Courtney, and in a little over twenty-four hours I've heard of two." I thrummed my fingers on the granite countertop.

Maddie's shoulders drooped, and Sarah's furrowed brow got me thinking. "No! No way. This can't be happening." I placed both palms on my head. "Peter will take this out on me. Not you. Not Kit. Me!" I slammed an open palm into my chest.

"I know, but—"

"How'd you even meet Courtney?" Sarah made it clear I should allow her to steer the conversation.

"She joined us after Kit and I left here."

"She knows, then, about Kit?" Sarah's soft tone was completely free of judgment.

Maddie nodded. "Turns out Lizzie isn't the only one with a complicated family. Both Kit and Courtney..." She left the rest unsaid.

Were Peter and I the only ones in the dark?

"What's she like?" Sarah continued.

Maddie smiled. "A minx—the female version of Kit, really. Funny, gorgeous, and man, can she dance. The three of us closed the bar down. I haven't felt so free in months—years, really. I was with her all day yesterday."

The mere mention of Kit's name reminded me of the real issue. "I'm putting my foot down. You cannot pursue Courtney."

Maddie blinked, and Sarah glared at me, aghast.

"Who do you think you are?" Maddie asked without her usual verve.

"How many people are on this planet? More than seven billion and growing each day. And you fall for Kit's fiancée?"

Maddie's face contorted with perverse excitement. "Are you suggesting I fall for a baby born today?"

I jammed my fist down on the counter. "Don't get off topic. Do you have any idea what it was like growing up in the Petrie family? I'll be clear. It was hell."

Maddie's face softened. "Kit thinks it's great if Courtney and I hook up—keeping it in the family, so to speak. Less chance the news will spread."

I drew my eyebrows together. "Peter already thinks I ruined your relationship with him—Lizzie the Lesbian, destroyer of all. Now he'll blame me for Kit and Courtney, too."

"You didn't ruin our relationship. Peter did—by cheating." Maddie lifted her gaze to meet mine. "I can have a sit-down with him and make it crystal clear that this has nothing to do with him anymore. And nothing to do with you."

"He'll never see that. He probably thinks I'm the one who outed his mistress in the first place."

Maddie chewed her bottom lip. "Yeah, right. You never suspected Peter and your father had mistresses. I had to tell you."

"He won't see it that way. The one thing I know about my brother is he has a chip on his shoulder the size of Uranus."

Maddie broke out into fits of laughter. "Why'd you choose Uranus? Out of all the planets?"

"Conditions have to be ideal to be seen without optical aid." I shrugged. Didn't everyone know that?

"That's one of the things I love about you. You're hilarious, but you have no idea why." Maddie smiled to take the sting out of her backhanded compliment. Her reassurance might have worked better if her smile didn't coil up in a way that suggested I really was an effing moron.

Sarah shifted on her barstool. "How do you feel about Courtney being in a committed *relationship* with Kit?" She made quote marks in the air. "You were just busting Lizzie's balls for being fake, yet this seems like ultimate fakeness to me, even with the complicated family stuff—or whatever." Sarah made her feelings known with the last word. She wasn't buying Kit and Courtney's excuse lock, stock, and barrel.

Maddie's lips clamped shut, and she turned her head to the ceiling, offering only a limp shrug.

"I'm not sure that would fly with me," Sarah continued. "God knows Lizzie is one of the most clueless people in the world, but she's always been out of the closet."

I wasn't sure how I felt about that statement. At what point would I become less clueless? I'd been looking up a word on the Urban Dictionary every day for months, trying to up my cool factor. Today's word—*napahoe*—referred to a hot chick slumbering in your bed. Seriously, when would I ever need that word? Despite its uselessness, it was locked in my brain forever now.

When Sarah wasn't home, I binged on popular TV shows. I'd even enlisted Ethan's assistance, years ago, to round out my music selection. Not that I'd confess that to Sarah or Maddie, and I'd sworn Ethan to secrecy. So far, he hadn't stabbed me in the back. Knowing him, he was waiting for the opportune moment. I was wary of trusting him completely, but I needed someone on my side. Even Batman had a sidekick. Ethan was my Robin.

My fear was being *that* parent: the one my children and their friends made fun of. I remembered all too well how cruel children could be. Children could sniff out fear, and they had no issues shredding the weakest link. And shit, with the information superhighway, bullying had taken on a whole new level.

Lesson one, Lizzie, don't ever say "information superhighway" aloud! Two-year-olds with iPhones will mock you.

According to the Urban Dictionary, that term had died with the nineties. World Wide Web was also a no-no. I made a mental note to research the newer, cooler term for the Internet.

Sarah snapped her fingers. "Lizzie!"

I shook my head. "Sorry. What?"

"Would you make me a cup of tea?" Sarah's face had visibly paled.

"Of course, sweetheart." I flipped around and filled the kettle. "Are you feeling unwell? Do you need to take a nap?"

"I'm fine. I just need something soothing." She cradled her belly.

I nodded. My other fear and the most pressing—besides being the nerdiest parent in human history—was something happening to Sarah or one of the babies. Threatening terms like subchorionic hemorrhage, preeclampsia, placental abruption, and choriocarcinoma rattled around in my head. I tried to force the fear back into the recesses of my mind. "Maddie, tea?"

"Please."

I opened the cabinet to the left of the stove and singled out the golden Tea-for-Two pouch. "What kind?" I asked over my shoulder. "Considering our conversation earlier, I'm assuming you don't need pregnancy tea."

"Oh, so funny. Mock my situation." She smiled, appreciating the dig. "Darjeeling."

"Not Lady Grey?" I cracked.

"Wow, two jokes in less than five minutes. Careful your head doesn't explode from kicking into overdrive." Maddie's eyes blazed with merriment. That was one thing I loved about her—the more shit someone dished out, the more she enjoyed being around that person.

"Did you wake up with a napahoe in your bed?" I had my back to both of them, so I allowed myself the tiniest of grins at my own joke.

"A what?" Sarah asked, shell-shocked.

I continued preparing the tea, ignoring them. Let them figure it out on their own, if they really wanted to know.

"Ah-ha!" Maddie exclaimed.

I about-faced.

Maddie slapped the countertop with one hand, holding Sarah's iPhone in her other hand. "I do believe Lizzie is boning up on slang. Napahoe is one of the terms on the front page of the Urban Dictionary." Maddie hunched over to show Sarah so my confused wife could confirm it.

Sarah's grin hinted she'd already suspected, but she winked at me anyway. It used to unnerve me: how well Sarah knew me. I'd learned over the years that having someone perfectly in tune with you was one of the greatest gifts.

That emboldened me. "Come on, Maddie. All the cool cats know it and don't need the Urban Dictionary."

"Yeah, right. Lizzie, you aren't clueless; you're a jive turkey."

Jive turkey?

I swatted the thought away, making a mental note to look that up when the coast was clear. "Whatever. If I'm so clueless, why is my life perfect and you just dumped Doug and have the hots for a lesbian who's engaged to a gay man who happens to be my sister-in-law's brother and the brother-in-law of your ex-fiancé?" I whistled, amazed I got all that out. From the open-mouthed looks I was receiving from both Sarah and Maddie, I still needed to work on my delivery. "Um, that came out wrong, didn't it? Too heartless?"

Maddie held her thumb and index finger half an inch apart. "Just a scootch."

Sarah drummed her fingers on the countertop. "Try researching the word *finesse*. Maybe watch more Cary Grant films—God knows you love him."

My eyes roved the kitchen, searching for a solution. They fixated on the box of chocolates I'd failed to send home with Tie. "Chocolate?"

Both of them laughed.

"Nice save, Einstein." Sarah hoisted her body off the barstool. "Would you mind bringing the tea to the library? I need a cozier chair."

"Anything for you."

Muffled voices drifted from the library. I clutched the tray that held three teas and a box of chocolates. Outside the door, I called, "Can I come in?"

"No!" Maddie responded.

It was good to hear the playfulness return to her voice. "I remembered the chocolates." I positioned the tray in the open door so Maddie could see the collection of truffles.

She craned her neck. "What kind?"

I inched into the room. "A selection of raspberry, amaretto, cognac, cherry…" I checked the box again. "Passion fruit, salted caramel—"

"Bring them." She ushered me in with a flick of her wrist.

Sarah eyed me with a look I couldn't decipher. Was she warning me to go easy on Maddie about the Courtney thing? Lately, all of Maddie's projects, or whatnot, had been short-lived. Or was my wife simply tired? Now, everything made her tired; sometimes, just brushing her teeth wiped her out.

I placed the tray down on the coffee table, and Maddie flipped the lid on the box and scanned all the goodies. She popped a truffle into her mouth and sank into the couch. After chomping down a few times, she swallowed and then added, "As much as it pains me to admit it, you spoke the truth earlier." But her smile was false and the sadness in her eyes troubled me. If I picked up on it correctly, Sarah was now on high alert, which worried me. She was busy growing two human beings in her belly. Maddie drama would only drain her more.

I lowered myself onto the couch next to Sarah, placing my hand on her knee. Maddie sat opposite, her legs tucked underneath her body.

"Tell me about Courtney." I mimed waving a white flag, signaling I'd do my best not to judge.

"I don't want another lecture," she grumbled, clearly not buying my act. She popped another truffle into her mouth.

"Truce, okay. I'm just curious about her. Not many people turn your head. She must be special. Besides being a good dancer, how so?"

Sarah squeezed my hand.

Maddie sank onto the couch, clasping a pillow to her chest. "I'll do better than that. How about the four of us do dinner this week?"

Inside I was screaming, "Nooooo!" If Peter or Tie got wind, I'd never hear the end of it. However, at the moment I was teetering on my pregnant wife's shit list. "Sounds great. What night?"

Maddie tugged her phone out of her back jeans pocket. "I'll text her now."

Fantastic. They were already texting buddies, soon to be fuck buddies, if they weren't already. Since they'd spent the weekend together, I assumed they'd done the deed. Was there a term for lesbian fuck buddy?

I turned to Sarah and smiled my *This is what happens when my family comes over for dinner* smile.

CHAPTER SIX

THE FOLLOWING DAY, I MET ETHAN IN THE CAFÉ AT BARNES AND NOBLE. HIS wife, Lisa, was with Casey in the children's section for story time with Dr. Seuss, meaning a book, not the author whom I thought was dead. Shouldn't a parent-to-be know if he was alive or dead?

"Why the long face?" He plopped his gangly body down into a metal chair, looking like a wrung-out Raggedy Andy doll. Several hairs sprouted like weeds from his typically trimmed moustache, and his *Catcher in the Rye* T-shirt defined the word rumpled.

"Nothing." I took my seat at the table and sipped my chai, puckering my lips.

"I know. You only like the chai at a legit Starbucks, not one crammed into a bookstore. I guarantee you it tastes the same."

"It's not that. It was hotter than normal; that's all."

His mocking smile didn't offer a hint of apology. "Soon, you'll understand why I'm killing two birds with one stone."

"How do you mean?"

His eyes twinkled behind his thick lenses. "Juggling work, kids, and coffee breaks." He stirred his coffee. "How's Sarah?"

"Good. Tired but she's a trooper. I don't know how she manages, really." I rested my face on my hand propped on my bent elbow.

"Women are amazing. I complain about never having enough time, but Lisa is the super-parent in our home." He stared vacantly out the window at the vast parking lot. Slowly, he settled his gaze on me. "Will Sarah take time off after the babies are born?"

"She's thinking of taking a year, but I have a feeling it'll stretch into several. She loves teaching, but my money is on the twins." I smiled.

"Kids have a way of winning over even the hardest of hearts." Ethan hadn't been so gung-ho about fatherhood when he and his wife adopted Casey. Ethan had agreed to the arrangement as a way to appease his wife for putting up with his fluids aversion. However, it had only taken days for the baby to change his tune. Now he was a devoted dad, except when it came to diaper duties, and there was talk of expanding their family.

"I have to ask; what's up with your shirt?" He gestured with a coffee-stained stir stick.

I assessed my navy blue T-shirt. "What's wrong with it?"

"Since when did you start liking beer?"

He jabbed the stir stick again at the Ben Franklin quote: *Beer is proof that God loves us and wants us to be happy.*

I shrugged.

"Out with it. You hate beer."

"I don't hate beer. I just prefer other things."

Ethan laughed. "It's hard to believe he actually said it. A nice thought, but come on—it has to be a gimmick to sell T-shirts."

I grinned. "History isn't perfect. Besides, Sarah bought the shirt for me, said it made her think of me."

"Ah, now I see. Anyone ever tell ya you're pussy whipped?"

"Worse things could happen to me."

"Ha! You are evolving. I remember when the mere thought of a relationship sent you running for the hills." He stretched his arms over his head. "So what's new with you? I'm sensing some tension." He stroked his moustache.

I sighed. "I've been offered a teaching job."

"I see." He took in my sagging posture. "Doesn't look like you're thrilled."

I straightened, nodding while I tried to figure out how to answer. "I don't know, really. Dr. Marcel wants me to teach a couple of classes a semester to lighten his workload. He's getting old. And…" And what?

Ethan raised a thin eyebrow above his frames.

"It'd be nice. I've been out of the classroom for several years now, and maybe the stimulation would help. I've been floundering a bit. Might need more structure in my life." I tapped the side of my forehead.

"Sounds like the perfect opportunity, then."

"Yeah." My voice cracked. "But not the timing."

He crossed his arms and groaned. "Let me guess; you haven't told Sarah?"

A guilty grin forced its way out. "Bingo."

His delicate fingers drummed against the side of his cup. "Scratch what I said earlier about you evolving. You really don't learn, do you?"

I put a hand on my chest. "Hey, I think it's a great sign that I'm feeling guilty. That has to be some kind of progress for me."

The dip of his head acknowledged the point, but his face told the full story. "True, but take the extra step. Be honest with Sarah from the start. This is a decision you two should make together. Both of you have enough going on. You don't need unnecessary drama. Look where that's gotten you in the past. You nearly lost her. Do you want to risk that again?"

I pinched the bridge of my nose. "I know, I know. But I'm scared to tell her."

"Why?" He scrunched his face.

"We're having twins. How will Sarah feel if I say, 'Hey, it's great about the babies, but I also have some exciting news that involves me working outside the home?' The timing couldn't be worse."

"Seriously? You're worried Sarah will be mad that you got a job offer? News flash. Most parents work. These days, both parents work."

I sliced the air with my hand to interject.

He swatted my objection away. "Yes, we all know you have enough money and you don't need to work. But if you tell Sarah how you're feeling... What'd you say? Floundering? I'm sure she'll understand. And it's not like you'll be shorthanded. Her mom and Maddie will be around. Teaching a class or two will take up some of your time, of course, but it's not full-time. I'm guessing you've already started prepping, even though you haven't formally accepted."

I shifted in my seat.

"I knew it. Hire Maddie as your nanny. She doesn't seem happy in her design job anymore."

"I think she loves her design job, except that it doesn't pay all of her bills."

"Politicians keep saying the economy is improving, but I haven't noticed it." Ethan's pursed lips spoke volumes.

I crossed my left leg over my right. "Speaking of Maddie, she has her heart set on riling up unnecessary drama in my life. She's decided to pursue Tie's brother's fiancée."

Ethan shook his head as if trying to shake the words into understandable order. "Come again?"

"Tie, who is married to my brother Peter, has a brother named Kit. Following?"

"Amazingly, I'm still with you." He smirked.

"Kit is engaged to a woman named Courtney."

"And how does Maddie fit in?"

"This is where it gets a bit kinky. Kit is gay."

"Does Courtney know?"

"She's also gay."

Ethan licked his lips. "So the marriage is a way to stay hidden, perhaps?"

"I guess so. I haven't asked him outright. I've only just met him. The rumor is he and Courtney have *complicated* family situations."

Ethan's eyes grew big. "This is juicy stuff—the kind of thing I overhear in the hallways at the high school. Too bad you don't write novels. Your life is full of drama." His facial expression changed from surprise to knowing. "It's only a matter of time until you put your foot in it."

I clenched my shirt over my heart, feigning being mortally wounded, and then smiled. "Tell me about it. We're having dinner with Maddie and Courtney this week."

"No Kit?"

I groaned. "I hope not, but who the hell knows with these people? You say I'm not evolved or committed to my relationship. Shit, I'm heads above these jokers."

Ethan chortled. "Given the situation, I'm not sure you should be bragging about it. You know, for someone who has always distanced herself from the Jerry Springer family lifestyle, you can't stay out of their tangled webs."

His words were true, making me wonder if I could ever have a healthy interaction with family members, even for the sake of our twins. "I'd have to move far away. Not sure there are malls suitable for Sarah in Alaska," I joked in an attempt to move away from the Maddie, Kit, and Courtney snafu.

"Probably not." Ethan rubbed his chin as if he was actually contemplating the issue. "But think globally. Paris? London? Istanbul?"

"Istanbul not Constantinople," I sang.

"Ah, I see the music lessons are working. That's a fun one. But how are you getting along with songs from this century?" He narrowed his eyes.

"Been listening to Adele on the YouTube. Have you heard of her?"

"*The* YouTube?" Ethan's sneer overtook his features. "Your unborn twins have heard of her, and it's called YouTube," he felt the need to add.

"How am I ever going to catch up so my kids aren't embarrassed of me?"

"You're having twins. You're never going to catch up with anything. Never again." He crept closer. "But it's a great sign that you're trying. You really want to be the best parent you can be, don't ya?"

I nodded.

"Don't look so scared. Like this bullshit with Maddie—it'll blow over soon enough. Things have a way of working out. What really matters are the ones you love." He watched as Lisa and Casey made their way to us. "Once the twins pop out, you'll know exactly what I'm talking about. Let the rest roll off like water off a duck's back." He waved to his family.

"Daddy!" Casey squealed.

Ethan opened his arms in the nick of time as Casey crashed into him. "How was story time, munchkin?"

Casey, distracted by the sweets in the glass case behind Ethan, pointed. "Can I have a cookie?"

I hiked one brow up to Lisa, who nodded her assent. "Come on." I put my hand out, and we took our place in line.

Casey squeezed my hand and swung our arms. "What are you doing two years from now?"

Geez, did the kid know about my secret job offer? Wait, that didn't make sense since she was asking about two years from now. *Guilty, Lizzie.* "I don't know. What are *you* doing?"

"Going to Disneyworld for my birthday. Want to come?" Casey dropped my hand and smooshed her face against the case, adding another smudge. The employees must've hated how all the sugar-starved tykes swarmed the café after story time. Four other kids were standing in line behind us. "That one." She tapped the glass, indicating a cookie topped with M&Ms.

The woman behind the counter placed the cookie into a paper sleeve and handed it to me. I ordered another round of coffees for the adults, while Casey zipped over to her mom, holding the bag aloft as if showing off treasure.

When I retook my seat, passing out the fresh coffee for Ethan and Lisa, I said, "Disneyworld?"

Ethan ruffled the top of Casey's head. "It's all she can talk about—going to Disneyworld for her seventh birthday."

I studied Ethan's face for any trace of unease. All I saw, though, was gaiety. Lisa and Ethan weren't exactly rolling in dough. Most of their vacations since bringing Casey home had involved traveling to see grandparents.

"Sign us up." I sipped my chai.

Ethan swiveled his neck. "You? At a family resort?"

"Hey now, in less than four months, my family will be larger than yours." I tipped my drink in his direction.

His eyes widened as if reality hit him hard, but the shock soon morphed into a grin. "Maybe you won't be so bad after all."

"What does that mean?" I had a pretty good idea.

"As a mom. You actually seem excited."

"Ethan!" Lisa scolded.

Undeterred by his wife's condemnation, he finished the conversation by adding, "Just don't mess up your marriage by keeping your secret."

That piqued Lisa's interest. "Secret?"

Casey sat in her lap, gnawing on the cookie, oblivious to the conflict. *God, to be a kid again.* I wished a cookie had the ability to take me away from all the Petrie family drama.

"I was offered a teaching position at the university, part-time," I confessed into my chai.

She nodded. "Right. And you haven't told Sarah."

She stated it, rather than questioning, which made it clear my reputation for not being the most honest partner was bordering on asshole level.

"I haven't figured out how to break the news," I defended myself. "My start date is so close to the twin's birth."

"Not sure you need a game plan. Sounds pretty straightforward." Ethan crossed his arms.

Casey giggled and asked out of the blue, "Do you know Elsa?"

"Is she a twin?"

That made her laugh harder. "No! She's queen of Arendelle."

"From the movie *Frozen*." Ethan filled me in.

Casey slid off her mom's lap and approached me with a terrifying smile. "You need to learn the movies." She climbed into my lap.

I wrapped my arms around her. "Do you think you can help me?"

"Yes!" She grinned.

"Shall we go buy the DVD?"

Casey's eyes narrowed. "Don't you have the Internet?"

"Of course."

She laughed. "They just appear now."

"Like magic?" I tickled her side.

"Internet magic." She giggled.

"She means Netflix, not pirating films." Ethan sipped his coffee.

"Netflix is the coolest." Casey nibbled on her cookie.

"Casey," Ethan said with just enough authority to get her attention. "Do you think it's nice to keep a secret?"

Casey shook her head.

"Well, Lizzie, it took you three decades, but you finally met someone who can guide you through life." Ethan laughed.

— Chapter Seven —

"Any chance you can hurry? We're meeting Maddie and Courtney soon." Sarah leaned against the bathroom counter.

I wrenched my toothbrush out of my mouth and spat into the sink.

Sarah perused the screen on her cell. "We're supposed to be there in thirty minutes, and the drive takes at least twenty."

"Okay, okay. I'm ready." I was all about proper oral hygiene, but Sarah's pinched face made me set down the mouthwash, skipping a step that would have only taken thirty seconds tops. I motioned for her to walk ahead. "After you, my dear."

Sarah patted my cheek as if she understood my fear of the lecture.

We settled into the car with me behind the wheel.

"I know going to dinner tonight is one of the last things you want to do, but I don't want to be late." She pressed my right thigh with enough force for my foot to push the gas pedal. "Get the lead out."

"Where are we going?"

Sarah huffed. "How do you never know the details?" Leaning forward, she typed the restaurant's name into the GPS.

"Because you two never include me in the texts."

Her head spun around. "And do you want to know why?"

"Because I'd tell you it's insane to plan a dinner with Maddie and Kit's fiancée, and that if Peter catches wind of this, he'll make my life a living hell. And *you're* the one who keeps saying Tie is smarter than we think. How will she handle this?"

Sarah chortled. "For someone who's always going on about not caring what her family thinks, you sure act like you care."

"This is the moment you decide to discuss this? Minutes away from the dinner from hell?"

"So touchy!" Sarah cradled her hands on her pregnant belly. "I hope you two take after me," she murmured.

"Hey now! That's hitting below the belt." I shook my head, smiling.

"What's really bugging you?" Sarah slipped her shoes off her swollen feet, wincing. She rotated one foot.

"I don't know. It's just weird, going behind Kit's back. I like him."

"But you know he's gay, right? Courtney isn't going behind his back. I'm assuming this is the arrangement they've agreed to. I'm pretty sure he has dates with men."

"How do people come to this kind of arrangement? Acceptable cheating?"

Sarah started exercising her other foot. "It's not really cheating, though, if they've agreed to it. Is that what's bugging you? This is hitting too close to home?"

I briefly took my eyes off the road. "What do you mean?"

"Your father cheated on your mom for years. Peter cheats."

"Maybe. I wasn't my mom's biggest fan, but still—how does one ever justify adultery?"

Sarah remained quiet.

Once again, I peeked out of the corner of my eye, trying to root out the cause of her silence. Cheating was a sensitive subject in our relationship after I'd made a terrible mistake and made a pass at Maddie. At the time, Sarah was pushing me to settle down, propelling my commitment-phobe streak into full-fledged self-destruction. Thank God Maddie had slapped me and brought me to my senses before I had the chance to ruin the best thing that had ever happened to me. Sarah left me when I confessed, of course, but I was able to win her back.

Letting out an anguished sigh, she leaned her head back against the headrest. "Not everything in life is black and white. I don't know Kit and Courtney's reasons for their sham of an engagement, but if you ask me, it's sad that they think they have to live like that. I can't imagine living that lie, day in and day out. And you thought you had it bad."

"Wait, how did I just get thrown under the bus?"

She laughed. "Les-bi-an."

"Ah, yes. My mom had loved to stress every syllable of *that* word."

"I still remember the first time I heard her say it. I had no idea what to do—rush to your defense or tuck and run."

"I think you chose deer in headlights." I squeezed her thigh.

"What would you have done in my place?"

"The same. No question."

"Tonight, remember how your mom used to make you feel and try to be kind. Don't judge. Just let things be." Sarah's tone was soft and supportive, tinged with enough firmness to let me know I should take her words to heart or face the Sarah firing squad later.

"I'll do my best."

"That's what I'm afraid of." She patted my leg, flashing her winning smile.

"You think you're so funny!" I tickled her side.

"Stop or I'll pee!"

I heeded her advice, not wanting to replace the SUV's leather seat.

"Actually, can you pull over? I really do need to pee."

I checked out the digital clock on the dash. "Twenty-one minutes since you last went. A new record."

"Now who thinks they're so funny? Why don't you try being pregnant?"

"Not a chance in hell. Have you taken a good look at your swollen feet lately?"

Sarah turned to me and gave me a death stare. I smiled sweetly back at her.

"Sarah, you look lovely." Maddie stood and helped my wife to her seat, nodding hello to me.

It was strange seeing Maddie so well behaved.

She turned to the woman sitting to Sarah's left. "This is Courtney."

The woman tipped her head as if she was the Queen of England. I had to admit, though, she was a fucking knockout. The line from Christopher Marlowe's *Doctor Faustus* came to mind. "Was this the face that launch'd a thousand ships?" Honey-colored locks were piled on top of her head in a haphazard way, perfectly so. Her complexion was flawless; her eyes the textbook definition of sea green on a stormy day. Courtney's low-cut blouse allowed more than a glimpse of her goodies. No wonder Kit had wanted her as a trophy wife—no one would ever question why he was marrying such a divine creature. Was she all looks and no substance? A quick examination of her cunning eyes answered that question.

Did she know she was the whole package? The hand she put out in greeting screamed, "Hell yes, I know it!"

"Court, I'd like you to meet Sarah and Lizzie."

We both smiled, but I knew Sarah's welcoming look held much more warmth. Courtney's eyes flickered to mine and then landed on Sarah's, staying put. "It's lovely to meet you."

Sarah blushed under Courtney's intense stare. "Likewise, I'm sure."

Was this woman serious? Ogling my pregnant wife while I sat at the table?

Wide-eyed, Maddie soaked in her presence like she was sitting before a statue created by Michelangelo. I wanted to say, "Fasten your seat belts, ladies. It's going to be a bumpy ride."

Maybe, for once, I wouldn't be the one making a complete ass out of myself. Perhaps I would take a shine to Courtney for that reason alone. Then again, Maddie was one of my dearest friends. She teased me mercilessly, though, and paybacks could be a bitch. The only downside was that if Courtney was a player, like I'd already assumed, she wouldn't be in the picture long enough to give me much of a reprieve.

I unfolded an oversized red-and-white checkered linen napkin in my lap. "I've never been here. What's good?"

Courtney turned her head like she was on a runway. "The question is: what isn't good here?" Her words and posture dripped with confidence.

"Wow," I stated, responding to her demeanor rather than her claims about the restaurant.

She smiled at my answer, obviously thinking I was impressed with the joint. Let her think that.

Sarah's swift kick under the table informed me I hadn't gotten away with it completely. Maddie, though, rested her chin on her palm, gazing at Helen of Troy—er, Courtney.

"May I be so bold as to order for the table?" the she-devil asked.

"By all means," replied Sarah.

Maddie nodded, speechless.

I swallowed. It wasn't a secret I wasn't the most daring diner. However, the fact that we were in a BBQ joint buoyed my nerves. Even the "Don't Mess with Texas" sign over Maddie's head didn't rattle me; however, I wasn't particularly fond of the "Don't Tread on Me" with a coiled rattler mural on a vibrant yellow wall.

The waiter arrived, and Courtney prattled, "We'll start with the appetizer sampler and then dig into the family feast." She tapped her fingers against her lips. "And, Lizzie, I hear you prefer simple." She smiled at me, which I think was meant to be friendly. "So can we also have the mac and cheese?"

"Of course. Drinks?" The waiter gripped his pencil, ready to jot down every word that came out of Courtney's mouth.

"Sarah, what can ya have?" Courtney eyed my wife as if she was on the appetizer sampler. Could the woman not control this side, or was she going into over-the-top-flirtatious mode to impress Maddie's friends?

"Water. Keep it coming."

"The beautiful lady will have your best house water."

Everyone laughed like Courtney was performing for a crowd in Las Vegas.

"The rest of us will have a margarita flight each."

I put a finger in the air to cancel mine, only to have Sarah smother it with a sweaty palm. Not drinking was one way to appease my guilt over Sarah carrying the babies. Besides, I tended to get drunk just by stepping foot into a liquor store.

Me, alcohol, and uncomfortable social situations were a deadly concoction.

Once the waiter left, Courtney placed her forearms on the table, the move nearly pushing her cleavage out of her shirt. "How far along are you, Sarah?"

Sarah's eyes boggled. Seriously? I wasn't jealous, since Sarah would be the last person on the planet to have an affair, but it would be safe to say I was stupefied.

"Five months." Sarah used a spoon to fish an ice cube out of her water and seductively popped it into her mouth—at least that was how it came across to me.

Usually, I wouldn't mind one bit; these acts were mostly for my benefit. Tonight, though, the show was for Courtney. I sized up Maddie, trying to gauge her pissed-off meter, but she was in her own world and didn't notice the antics my wife was putting on for the she-devil. No, not she-devil—succubus!

"No way! There's no way you're five months along. I would guess only a couple of months. What's your secret to looking so incredible?" Courtney leaned in further, and I prayed that one of her tits would spring out, jack-in-the-box style, and give her a black eye. They were even larger than Sarah's, and Sarah was pregnant.

"Oh, you know…" Sarah let the sentence trail off.

Courtney bobbed her head, understanding. Understanding *what*, I had zero clue, but I sensed this would be the trend for the entire evening.

"What do you do?" Sarah tugged on her shirt, revealing her own spectacular cleavage.

I sat back in my chair, hugging my girls close to my chest, unsure whether I should be pissed or just sit back and appreciate the battle of the boobs. How often did I have the chance to stare at four amazing tits?

"Advertising."

"Ah, like Don Draper."

"Kinda." She laughed. "But not as sexy."

"Don't sell yourself short." Maddie finally braved the conversation.

Courtney swiveled her head slo-mo style.

Was everything orchestrated with her?

"Oh, I never do. I meant that advertising isn't as sexy as it was back then. The Internet has been a significant game changer, and not in a good way. I could bore you to death about the downfall of pop-up ads and ad revenue dropping through the basement floor."

Maddie stroked Courtney's bare arm with a finger. "You could never bore me."

The intimacy of the touch made it clear the two of them had already hopped into bed, more than once.

I had the feeling most of Courtney's relationships were sexual ones that quickly became flashes in the pan. How did Maddie not see this? Or was this another sign of Maddie's angsty self-destruction?

"Here ya go. Margarita flights on the rocks." The waiter, wearing a Lone Star bandanna tied around his neck, set down four metal, semi-circular racks that each held four drinks ranging from blue to pink.

I grabbed the blue glass and shot it.

"Way to go, Lizzie!" Courtney devoured her blue concoction, too, and immediately seized the pink. She motioned for me to pick up mine. "All at once."

She didn't have to tell me twice.

Afterward, I blew out a mouthful of air, waiting for my peripheral vision to stop blurring.

Maddie downed one of the drinks, puckering her lips. "Gawd! What's in that?" She held the empty glass, squinting one eye as if its remnants might answer the question.

"Never ask. Just drink. Right, Lizzie?" The succubus nudged my arm.

"Right." I burped into my hand.

Sarah met my eyes, and then she casually nodded at my untouched water glass next to all the booze. I responded by sipping the pale yellow drink garnished with an orange slice instead. My wife's narrowed eyes warned me to pare down my behavior. Me, behave? She was the one who had been drooling over the sexpot at the table, and she was worried about my manners? What about my feelings? Two could play at this game—if it was a game. My brain was already slightly fuzzy.

"Lizzie, I hear you're a future stay-at-home mom." Courtney sucked on a lime wedge.

"I'm sorry? Stay-at-home mom?" I shook my head.

"Kit said you're not working." She discarded the lime peel off to the side of the bucket holding condiment bottles—right next to my ego.

"I'm an historian."

"Who stays at home?" She wouldn't let up.

"I write books."

"Really? What book are you working on now?"

Good question. I'd started my third book but quickly realized my thesis needed major retooling and more research—at least that was what I kept telling myself. However, I had no desire to spill the beans. "I've been offered a teaching position."

Sarah plunked her water glass down. "You didn't tell me that."

"It only just happened." Weeks ago, but I was an historian. Weeks didn't even measure up to a drop in the time span bucket. Even in my buzzed state, I squelched the urge to say it aloud.

"What? Where? Who?" Sarah's face flushed the color of confusion.

"Dr. Marcel wants to lighten his load. He's asked me to teach one or two classes a semester. I haven't decided whether I should accept."

I didn't mention I had led Dr. Marcel to believe I would.

"What's to decide?" Maddie pointed at Sarah's protruding belly.

Sarah's eyes softened, and she held up one palm. "Hold on, Maddie." She turned to me. "What do you want to do? I know you've been struggling working solely from home."

"That's an understatement." The tequila had loosened my tongue and my mind.

She smiled, giving me her full attention. "You've been losing your focus, even after your spurt of writing."

I nodded and sipped from another baby margarita glass. "I didn't want to tell you."

"Why?" Her voice didn't divulge any anger.

"Can we talk about this later?" I peeked at Courtney, who was latching on to every word, her expression hard to read.

Sarah straightened in her chair. "Of course. Just one more thing. I'm proud of you. I know how much you admire and respect Dr. Marcel. It's an honor to be considered."

Courtney hoisted a baby margarita. "To Lizzie!"

I had to join in.

Courtney flagged down the waiter and ordered three more flights. I remembered the first time I'd met Sarah's mother, Rose. She'd kept ordering drinks for me, despite Sarah doing her best to drink most of them to save me from embarrassment. Now that she was pregnant, she couldn't come to my rescue. I rubbed my eyes, trying to clear the booze mist that was settling in for the evening.

Sarah inclined her head to catch Maddie's eye, focusing on her with an intensity that briefly made me think she'd gone into labor. Maddie gave a quick nod, for Sarah's benefit, and I saw the crease in Sarah's forehead relax.

"So, Courtney, tell me more about the advertising biz. You mentioned pop-up ads crashing and burning." Sarah perched on her forearms once again, putting her goodies on display.

"Not a chance. It'd only bore the shit out of you. I'd rather learn more about you. What makes Sarah unique?"

Before anger had the chance to burble out of the pit of my stomach, Maddie swiped away my remaining mini-margarita and replaced it with one of her empties. Sarah was taking the hit for the team, offering herself up. However, the smile and sexy glow on her face made it clear she wasn't suffering all that much.

I put a hand over my mouth, restraining a giggle. Under the table, Sarah's foot slipped between my legs, resting on the chair. The poor thing was so swollen. While Sarah kept Courtney entertained, I massaged my wife's foot. When she glanced across the table at me, I motioned for her to switch feet.

"How long have you two been together?" Courtney actually seemed curious.

"Seems like ages." Sarah's eyes flittered toward me, causing the same sensation that had entranced me the first time our eyes locked.

"I can see it's true love." Courtney leaned back in her seat. "I didn't believe it could ever happen."

"When you least expect it," Sarah said. "Does that mean you haven't been in love?"

I was amazed by her boldness, but knowing her, she was doing her best to dig up as much intel as possible to protect Maddie.

"Here you are." Kit twirled through a family of six that was exiting the restaurant and leaned down to kiss his fiancée's cheek.

Maddie's eyes widened, clearly startled, which made Kit and Courtney bellow with laughter.

"Don't look so disconcerted." Courtney waved a hand in the air. "Odds are, if you're with one of us, the other will eventually show up. We've taken codependency to a whole new level. I don't think headshrinkers have a term for it yet."

Maddie mustered up a smile.

"Kit, how nice to see you." Sarah waved the waiter over and asked for another chair.

Kit gave her a peck on the cheek before taking a seat squeezed between Courtney and Maddie. "How are you doing, sweetheart?"

Sarah's condition elicited these kinds of sympathetic questions.

"At the moment, Lizzie is rubbing my feet under the table, so I'm in heaven."

"I'm next," Courtney purred.

I swallowed. Feet, except for Sarah's, were absolutely disgusting and on my *don't touch* list.

Kit slapped his thigh. "Oh, you Petries are such easy pickings. Don't ever play Texas Hold 'Em, at least not with us." He waved at himself and Courtney. "We'll eat you alive."

Sarah and Maddie shared a knowing smile.

"Take it easy on, Lizzie. She's nowhere near as much of an asshole as Peter." Maddie smiled at me, fluttering her lashes.

"Is that a compliment, though?" Kit's flushed face was hard to read. Was he teasing? Drunk? Or did he hate Peter that much?

"Oh, I mean it as a compliment most of the time." Maddie nibbled on a piece of cornbread that, unfortunately for me, contained chunks of jalapeno.

"But does she have Petrie moments?" Courtney asked.

"Of course," Sarah and Maddie chorused.

"Hey, I'm massaging your feet." I squeezed Sarah's foot, hard, but she closed her eyes, clearly enjoying the added pressure.

"Did you know Peter scheduled our wedding on Lizzie's birthday?" Maddie said.

"No way!" Courtney whistled. "So not cool. And we thought our families were bad." She smiled at Kit.

Courtney thought less of me for working from home… She was the one flirting—or rather screwing—Kit's sister's husband's ex. I cocked my head, wondering whether I'd gotten that right. Then shook my head, trying to clear the muddle.

Sarah snapped her fingers. "Hey, don't stop." She ground her foot into my lap.

"Whatever you say, dear."

Kit and Courtney shared a smile. "Maybe she isn't as bad. At least she's trainable," Kit said.

"Is Peter causing problems?" Maddie's expression tightened, no doubt with painful memories she usually preferred keeping in the past.

"He's a peach." Kit's top lip twisted, and his tone suggested the exact opposite. His eyes sharpened with a flash of rage I didn't think possible for the easy-going Otter.

Courtney glanced in my direction. "What was he like as a brother?"

I sniggered. "I wouldn't even know where to begin."

"They weren't close," Sarah offered.

"Can't blame you. He really planned his wedding on your birthday?" Kit's eyes softened.

I nodded. "I was usually an afterthought when it came to my family. There was one time, though, when he remembered my existence."

"When was that?" Maddie squared her shoulders.

"When my mom's brother was dying. Our uncle never married and stayed in Montana. He had a small inheritance that he planned on splitting between me and Peter. When Peter found out, he flew out to Montana and outed me to my uncle while he was on his deathbed. My mother actually gloated when her brother changed his will and gave all his money to Peter." I laughed.

No one laughed with me.

Kit's mouth fell. Courtney was suddenly absorbed in the trail of salt on the checkered tablecloth. Maddie rubbed her eyes with a thumb and forefinger.

"You never told me that." Sarah lifted her gaze to mine, concern in the dark depths of her irises.

I shrugged. "Happened years ago, before I graduated from college. But hey, it wasn't a big deal. It was only a few thousand." I shrugged it off.

My wife's eyes tapered nearly shut. "That's not the point."

I peered at my lap, wishing I hadn't disclosed that tidbit for all to hear. This was what happened when I drank.

"He hates gay people that much?" Kit sounded alarmed.

Maddie shook her head. "I don't know about that. Peter's an opportunist above everything else. I doubt he holds an opinion that isn't grounded in ambition or greed."

"So he tossed Lizzie to the wolves for a few thousand dollars, not for his principles?" Kit asked, although his face registered he knew the game Peter was playing.

Maddie and I both nodded.

"Well, my sister is perfect for him." He slumped back in his chair, crossing his arms over his narrow chest.

"Would Tie do the same to you?" Maddie asked.

"Would she out me?" He ran a hand through his hair. "I don't know about that. She's more cunning. She'd devise a way to destroy me completely, more than just a character assassination. Being a gay man, even in Colorado, doesn't hold the same cache for haters as it once did. No, she would conjure a no-holds-barred approach to destroy every aspect of my life."

"How'd you two meet?" Sarah nodded to Kit and Courtney, clearly trying to salvage the evening from slipping into dangerous territory. I'd already done my share of bringing the group down with my momentary lapse of judgment.

"Tie and I used to be best friends in high school." Courtney's smile dripped with malice.

"Never lovers?" Maddie asked.

"Gawd, no. Tie isn't the type. Once, when we were fourteen, I said we should practice kissing together, and the look on her face—no, we never ventured out of the friend zone."

"Are you still friends?" Sarah pushed.

"As much as anyone can be friends with Tie. By the time we'd graduated, I'd figured out Tie always has some devious plan going on. It's better to stay friendly, but not let her in, if you get my drift." For once Courtney was being sincere.

I tapped Sarah's foot under the table, and she flashed me a sad smile that implied it served Peter right. However, I felt conflicted. I wasn't fond of my brother, but did I want him to suffer?

Later that night, I settled under the covers in bed. Sarah was still in the bathroom. The room swayed. If Sarah and Maddie hadn't come to my rescue, helping me save face, I'd be puking my guts out right now instead of resting one foot on the floor to combat the spinning sensation.

Sarah, her silk robe completely open and fluttering around her like wings, entered the room, clutching a Nalgene bottle. "Here, drink." She hurled it onto the bed next to me and then slipped out of her robe and between the sheets.

"Thanks," I mumbled.

She plumped up some pillows behind her back. "Tell me about Dr. Marcel."

"Now? I'm exhausted." To prove my point, I yawned.

"Not going to work. You've been keeping this quiet, and I'm doing my best not to get angry, so step up and meet me halfway."

"Halfway? Not sure that makes sense." My tequila-foozled mind sputtered, trying to work it out.

She sighed. "Please, don't focus on my phrasing. Focus on not keeping a secret. It hasn't worked well for you in the past."

"That's what Ethan said. Even Casey agreed."

"You told Ethan and his daughter before telling me?" She frowned as if she couldn't decide whether she should laugh or be angry.

"She figured out I was keeping a secret. The kid is smart."

"Apparently smarter than you." She crossed her arms, allowing me to catch an eyeful of her tits.

"Is it wrong that I'm extremely turned on right now?" I made a point of ogling her girls.

Sarah followed my eyes to her cleavage and tutted. "Not going to work."

"Oh, it's working—for me, at least." I kissed her bare shoulder.

She shoved me off, but I moved back and peppered her neck with soft kisses.

Her breath hitched. "You're going to have to spill."

"I promise. First thing tomorrow. Right now…" I nuzzled my face into the crook of her neck. "I want to show you how beautiful you are. You were killing me all night, flirting with Courtney. You owe me."

She laughed guiltily and avoided my eyes. "I wasn't flirting."

I tugged her seafoam green slip up to stroke her belly. "And Hitler was never a Nazi. If you want complete honesty from me, all the time, you're going to have to step up as well." I shoved the covers off so I could nestle between her legs and kiss her expanding belly, working my way down. "This is a surprise. No panties."

"I had high hopes."

So did I, which was why I'd lit a few candles to set the mood.

I skimmed my fingers through her pubic hair. "That we'd have a heart-to-heart and then fuck? Or were you worked up after flirting with Maddie's date all night?"

She bonked my head with a pillow before tossing it onto the charcoal-gray carpet. It wasn't my favorite color, but Maddie had insisted it accented the dark red walls. Every room in the house had a theme; this one was love—or sex—and included several paintings and statues of naked women.

"Don't beat me now, not with my head between your legs." I looked up at her and winked. "What if you accidentally shoved my teeth into your love channel, causing permanent damage."

"Love channel?" She quirked an eyebrow.

"Given what I'm about to do, I decided against canal. Might spoil the mood, considering you're about to squeeze two humans out of your pussy."

She tossed her head back, laughing. "Do share. What are you about to do?"

"Eat your pussy. That is if you ever stop jawing and give me a moment's peace to concentrate."

"I need to stop talking. You're down there arguing like you're pleading your case in front of the Supreme Court."

She had a good point. I nibbled on her inner thigh, the top of my head rubbing against her wetness.

Sarah moaned. She was hot to trot, and I didn't want to waste this opportunity; such occasions had become increasingly rare over the past few weeks.

I turned my attention to her other leg, and her moans turned into demanding grunts. Admittedly, I missed playing with her breasts, especially considering their fullness, but the message was loud and clear these days: look but don't touch. The pain Sarah experienced outweighed any pleasure. However, as my mouth moved to her slick lips, I got a glimpse of her heaving mountains, and a satisfied warmth spread through my nether regions.

I slipped my tongue up and down her folds, separating them for a taste. She was wet and more fragrant than usual, her clit already engorged. I remembered reading about these changes in one of the pregnancy books. Was it constantly in that state now or only when aroused? Perhaps a question for later.

My fingers darted inside her easily, nearly slipping back out.

"Steady," she teased.

"You need a danger ahead sign down here," I mumbled into her pussy.

Sarah clamped my head between her thighs. If she was trying to punish me, she was failing. I flicked her clit with my tongue, and her legs went limp as her back arched. Focusing more than usual, I moved my fingers in and out of her.

Her movements rewarded my efforts. My tongue switched to double time, trying to keep up with her increasing verbal and physical commands.

Before she came, she rolled onto her side. "I'm sorry. It's so uncomfortable on my back."

I slanted my head to eye her position, trying to figure out the next step. "Do you want to be on top? Or stop?"

"No stopping!"

I clamped down on my lip to suppress a smile. I hadn't put the brakes on; she had.

Sarah smiled. "I'm sorry. This probably isn't much fun for you. The hormones, increased wetness, and it takes ages for me to come."

I moved up, placing my head on the same pillow as hers. Swiping some hair off her cheek, I said, "The last person you should be fretting about is me. Tell me what you want, what you need, and I'll do it."

"I'm sorry."

"What did I just say? You have nothing to be sorry about. We can spoon."

"Not that. You're right. I was flirting with Courtney."

"I knew it." I waggled a playful finger in her face.

"Every day, it seems like I'm getting bigger. I liked the attention. She made me feel sexy, even though I suspect she makes everyone feel that way."

"Don't I make you feel sexy?" I stroked her cheek.

"You do. It's not you. I've read all the books, and I know I shouldn't think I'm a blimp, but when I look down or feel the pressure on my back and knees, it's hard to stay in the right frame of mind." She placed a hand on my jaw, and I kissed the heel of her hand. "It felt good to have a stranger flatter me."

"A very sexy stranger."

"Hey!" She pinched my cheek.

"Oh, I'm not allowed to say it?"

"Not at all!" Her eyes twinkled. "But you came home with me."

"You never have to worry about that. No one else will put up with me."

She chortled. "We're a mess. I'm needy for a stranger's attention, and you're socially inept."

"Don't sugarcoat things for my benefit. Tell me what you really think." I kissed her lips.

Sarah pawed the back of my head, tugging me tightly toward her as if she wanted to shove my entire head into her mouth.

"Have you transformed into a black widow? You want to kill me now?" I panted.

She rolled me onto my back. "Don't be silly. We haven't finished yet." With that, she sat on my face. "I'm not squishing you, am I?"

"Are you kidding me? Don't even think of moving until you come. No matter how long it takes you."

"I like it when you talk to me that way."

I loved it when she sat on my face. I showed her that by getting her to finally achieve orgasm.

―――――――――――

The next morning, as soon as I stored my bike in the garage and stepped into the house, I knew I was in trouble. Maddie and Sarah sat on barstools at the kitchen bench, both with arms folded over their chests.

"What's this? The Spanish Inquisition?" I opened the fridge to grab an apple and a bottle of water.

"Ha! Much worse," Maddie crowed.

"Do I get a last meal?" I suspended the apple by its stem.

She shook her head.

I rolled my eyes and bit into the crunchy red flesh.

Maddie, annoyed, snatched my water bottle.

"If you want me to talk, you'll have to allow water. I'm parched." I cleared my throat and patted my neck with four fingers.

"Stop stalling."

The wrinkles around the corners of Sarah's mouth curled upward. I swear my wife loved watching Maddie call me out on my shit.

"I'm considering," I said to Sarah as I snatched the bottle from Maddie.

"Considering?" Maddie dragged out each syllable.

I took a much needed drink. "Yes. I think it'd be nice to teach again. They say you never understand something until you have to teach it. Maybe that's part of my problem. I've only taught Western Civ. Too broad. I need to teach the time period I study."

Sarah nodded thoughtfully.

Maddie waved a hand in front of Sarah's face. "You aren't buying this crap, are you?"

I crumpled against the counter on the other side of the kitchen island, my legs wobbly from a fifty-mile bike ride, and stared deeply into Sarah's eyes.

"I don't think she's selling anything." Sarah glanced at Maddie and then back at me. "I think she's lost."

"She's always been lost." Maddie swiveled to face me head-on. "A lost cause."

I closed my eyes and counted to ten.

"Maddie, please. Stop jumping to conclusions. You're always so hard on Lizzie. And I think a part of you has been waiting for her to flip out about the twins. She hasn't, really. You aren't here all the time. I couldn't ask for a more supportive partner who's there for me."

I smiled, remembering her sitting on my face last night.

Sarah winked as if in tune with my thoughts.

"Hello?" Maddie waved a hand in front of Sarah's face. "That's the point. If Lizzie takes this position, she won't be here when the three of you need her most."

Sarah gave me her full attention. "Will you start teaching this fall?"

"It's not set in stone, but I have the chance to teach one class this fall. Dip my toes in, so to speak. Two in the spring. None in the summer."

"One class." Sarah peered out the window above the kitchen sink, which was tucked into the corner.

I placed both hands on the counter. "If you want me to say no or you think it's a bad idea, I'll turn it down."

"You'd do that?"

"Of course. You and the twins will always come first."

"In that case, I say yes. But is one class enough to get you back into your groove?"

"What?" Maddie squealed, flapping her arms. "Why are you letting her off the hook? She kept this from you."

I reached across the counter and covered Sarah's hand with mine, ignoring Maddie. "Thank you."

"Don't thank me. One of us has to work to support our brood." Sarah laid her free hand on top of mine, and I playfully added another hand.

"Ha! What they pay adjuncts these days makes it seem more like volunteering."

"Who cares? I want you to succeed, so if this is what it takes to help you get back on track, do it."

Maddie sputtered under her breath, but Sarah and I kept our gazes locked on each other. We'd grown much closer during her pregnancy; more often than not, we communicated best by staying silent.

Maddie cleared her throat to break our trance. "I'm hungry."

"Does that mean you've given up trying to convince me to tell Lizzie to turn down a job that suits her to a T, working with one of the greatest scholars in the US?" Sarah broke free from my hands to pivot toward Maddie, hugging her arms over her chest, combative style.

"Yes. I know both of you. It's useless to talk sense into either one of you." I could tell by Maddie's softened shoulders that Sarah's words had sunk in. This was a once-in-a-lifetime opportunity. The timing stunk, but not everything in life worked like it should. My therapist would be so proud.

"Oh, don't be mad at her, Sarah. I think Maddie's freaking out. My life is on track, and hers is falling apart."

"My life isn't falling apart," Maddie said in a tiny, unconvincing voice.

Sarah and I both rolled our eyes.

"Says the woman who's dating Courtney. I trust Peter more than I do her." Sarah bit her lip, daring Maddie to contradict her.

"Not sure you can classify it as dating. More like fuck buddies. Last night was the first meal we've shared. At least she's better in bed than good ol' Petey."

I covered my ears. "Seriously, I could have lived a full and happy life never knowing my brother is bad in bed."

"I wouldn't say bad, just unimaginative." Maddie shrugged. "He wasn't like that in the beginning, though. Is that a Petrie trait? Try hard in the beginning, and then peter out."

I sputtered, "Don't even go there. I'm trying to curb my asshole tendencies, considering."

Sarah put a hand on Maddie's arm. "You'd be surprised; trust me."

Did my wife just vouch that I was a good lay? Maybe even a great lay?

Maddie's face fell. "Well, shit. Maybe Lizzie's right. We've switched roles. She has the perfect life, and mine is crumbling around my feet."

Sarah's tone softened. "Come now. It's not that bad. Your business is picking up. You have us, the greatest friends ever."

"And no one to go home to at night. Even before Doug split, I was so lonely. Do you know, before Courtney I hadn't had sex for months."

"Was that the reason you broke it off?" Sarah asked.

"Not the only reason. Doug's a great guy, but in the friend kind of way. Even though it sucks, I rather be alone than lonely in a relationship."

"How do you explain your liaison with Courtney, then? Won't that put you back in the lonely boat?"

"You don't think she's relationship material?" Maddie's face clearly showed she was grasping at straws. "Honestly, I have no idea why I'm drawn to her. She's beautiful, yes, but I know she's not good for me. She's like a can of Pringles. You know you shouldn't pop the top because you won't stop until the can is empty, but you can't say no."

Sarah blinked and turned to me.

Wasn't it enough that I was a good lay? Now she expected me to say the right thing to Maddie, of all people.

I sucked in a breath. "Whenever you feel lonely, you can come here and help us change diapers."

Sarah's lips thinned. She tried to curtail her *I can't believe that was the best you had* grin.

Maddie, though, belly laughed. "I wish I could say no, but that's the best offer I've had in months." She placed a hand on Sarah's belly. "Come on, little ones. I'm ready to meet you. Give Auntie Maddie some purpose in life."

— Chapter Eight —

"Please, Lizzie. Give Courtney a chance." Maddie wiggled my arm up and down. "You just don't know her all that well yet."

She was partly right, but I suspected Maddie also needed some convincing that the succubus was worth the effort. It'd only been a few days since she expounded on her Pringles' theory, and I had hoped that after some ruminating she'd see the error of pursuing a woman who didn't come across as someone who wanted to be pursued. Not in the relationship way. A roll in the hay, sure. Settle down—that was as likely as me scaling Mount Everest.

Not knowing Courtney wasn't the only reason I was uneasy. No matter what way I sliced it, Maddie was involved with Kit's fiancée. Even if she and Kit had some arrangement, as Sarah suspected, that knowledge still affected me on some level. My family situation had never been stellar. It wasn't like I was craving Peter's acceptance, nor his wife's. Still, I didn't want to rock the boat.

I yanked my arm free and crossed both against my chest, only lowering them when Sarah gave me the *you better behave* look. I could practically hear her: *Keep an open mind and let things be*. Because, throughout history, that has worked oh so well. Anyone remember Henry VIII? He wanted everyone to leave him alone, and he ended up beheading two women.

Maddie's eyes pleaded with mine.

"Fine. Invite her to lunch or something." My cell beeped, and I checked the message. "Sorry, I have to take this." I waved my phone like I'd just received a presidential pardon.

Sarah glared at me, but she said nothing. She didn't have to. I had never been the type to run off and answer a text, email, or carrier pigeon. My gut said she'd let it slide since she knew I needed to hole up in my cave, aka library, and deliberate. I could never move forward until I mulled something over. If I didn't, I made snap decisions, often resulting in a fight with Sarah. Years with Sarah taught me one thing: avoiding fights was key to happiness and a healthy marriage.

Courtney, clad in an expensive-looking black business suit and a scarlet silk blouse, breezed into the library on Maddie's arm.

"So glad you could make it." Sarah rose to greet our guest, who was supposed to arrive for lunch but hadn't managed to make it until after five in the evening.

"Please, sit. I'm so sorry about earlier. A major shit-storm landed on my desk this morning, and I had to set it straight or lose a million-dollar account." Courtney spoke as if everything she did was of monumental importance. She reminded me of Peter.

I eyed Maddie, trying to judge whether she'd caught on to that fact. Maddie gazed at her like a sycophant, as if she was about to bend over and kiss the Pope's ring. How had I missed this aspect of Maddie's personality for so long? Of course, I hadn't been around when Peter and Maddie started courting.

Sarah waved off her apology. "Please, no excuses needed. Now that I'm on summer break, I have loads of free time. What can I get you to drink?" She started to waddle to the bar.

I jumped into action. "It's okay. Have a seat." I directed my pregnant wife back to the couch. "Okey dokey, jamokeys— what can I get you?"

"Okey dokey, jamokeys?" Maddie echoed.

I shrugged. When I was uncomfortable, weird shit flew out of my mouth.

"Wine for me. You, Courtney?" Maddie laced her fingers through Courtney's with too much force.

"Wine works." Her smile was genuine. Unlike the night at the barbeque joint, her outfit didn't let her ample cleavage spill over. Secretly, I was disappointed. Did that make me a boob person?

"Lizzie, tell me about the Hitler Youth." Courtney settled onto the couch opposite Sarah.

It seemed odd that she'd opened with this thread before I had a chance to serve the drinks. Another sign she was desperate not to be pigeonholed even with everyday conversation.

"Tread carefully. Once she gets going, she doesn't stop." Maddie sniggered.

"No, seriously, I'm curious. How did you become interested in the Hitler Youth?" She slipped off a three-inch heel and tucked her leg under her body. Whatever stress she'd felt during the day seemed washed away with this simple act.

"If you're serious, let's talk about ordering some food first. Then we can unleash the hounds, so to speak." Sarah gestured to a stack of menus on the coffee table.

Maddie swooped in. "Do you have one for that Thai place I love?" She thumbed through a stack of about fifteen, finally locating the lime-green menu. "They have the best skewers," she insisted, patting Courtney's thigh.

"I do love a good skewer." She waggled her brows suggestively at Maddie. I wanted to get down on my knees and thank the gods I was no longer in the dating world. Had I made such an ass out of myself when pursuing Sarah?

The two of them huddled together, deciding their choices. It didn't take long for Courtney to pick out an appetizer and a main dish. At least she was efficient.

Maddie bounded off the couch. "I'm going to place the call. I already know what you two are getting."

I placed two glasses of wine on the table and poured ice water for Sarah and me.

Before I had a chance to sit down, Courtney pounced. "So, you and the Hitler Youth. How and why?"

Parking my ass on the arm of the couch, I sipped my water. "It just happened. Back in grad school, I had to write a research paper for my twentieth-century European history class. Everyone was picking obvious topics, like the origins of World War II, Nazis, Winston Churchill, the Cold War, the European Union—all things people had written extensively about. I wanted something different. I was already intrigued by World War II, especially the Nazi aspect, but I didn't want to focus on something everyone knew about."

Courtney nodded. "So not Hitler, Goebbels, or even Speer…?"

She scored major points for knowing about Speer, Hitler's architect and Minister of Armaments and War Production. Not that he wasn't known, but his name usually didn't pop up first thing.

"Exactly. However, coming up with a topic was a challenge. The afternoon before I had to write my proposal, I wandered through the aisles in the library, looking for a title that caught my attention. I found one about a young man forced into the

Hitler Youth, and that's how it came to be. Once I started studying it, I became more and more fascinated. Basically, I fell face-first into the Hitler Youth rabbit hole."

Courtney sipped her wine. "I'm jealous. You're doing something that interests you."

This piqued the teacher inside Sarah. "You aren't?"

Courtney, in mid-swallow, snorted. She quickly covered her mouth to prevent from spewing red wine all over her blouse. "Not at all. I work for an advertising company my grandfather started back before every house had a television. Choice was never an option for me."

Was that why she liked having choices, having flings outside of her professional life?

Maddie, who'd returned halfway through my spiel, rubbed Courtney's thigh. "Don't you like advertising?"

"I like the creative side to it, but a couple of years ago, I became part of the management team. I spend ninety percent of my time kissing the client's ass—like today. The guy wouldn't sit down and talk to me. He insisted we work through the problem by playing a round of golf. That's how he solves every one of his problems."

"That's what you were doing today? Playing golf?" Maddie stared wide-eyed.

"With my client, yes. If a client says jump, I say how high." Courtney turned her attention to Sarah. "What about you? Why teaching?"

"Oh, that's easy. I wanted to have my summers off." Sarah rubbed her belly. "Had I known one summer I'd be giving birth to twins, I may have found a different occupation." Sarah's smile and glow said the opposite.

"Did you always want kids?" Courtney's eyes laser locked onto Sarah.

"Nope."

"Really?" I blurted before I had a chance to think. It should have been a fact I'd always known about the person I was spending my life with.

Sarah laughed. "It wasn't until I settled down with Lizzie that I realized I wanted a family."

Maddie cocked her head. "I'm not buying that."

"I'm not lying. Before Lizzie, I liked dating and I had some relationships, but I always went in knowing it'd be short-lived. Fun for a time, but once it became work, I'd bail. Then I met Lizzie." She half-covered her mouth and stage whispered, "She was work almost right out of the gate, but I didn't run. And Lizzie didn't make it easy." Sarah lowered her hand and glanced over at me, smiling. "Falling for a commitment-phobe is a challenge, to say the least."

"Maybe she was the right challenge for you. I've been looking for that," Courtney confessed without any sense of unease.

Maddie, on the other hand, squirmed on the couch. If I were her, I'd take that statement to mean Courtney was still looking. Maddie wasn't a delicate flower, but I sensed she wanted what Sarah and I had: a loving relationship and a family on the way. It had taken me years to realize the things I'd chased after, and the things I'd chased away in pursuit of those things, didn't matter. What mattered was the woman sitting to my left and the two creatures growing inside her belly.

Courtney's cell phone lit up the room. "Ah, I was wondering when I'd hear from him."

"Kit?" Maddie's brow furrowed.

Did he always show up? Even when Maddie and Courtney were in bed? Threesomes had never appealed to me. Did they to Maddie? I tried to think back to whether or not we'd ever discussed that. Of course I hadn't detected any bisexual vibes from Kit. Then again, I'd missed the gay ones as well.

"Need to pinch off a load, Lizzie?" Maddie motioned to my scrunched face. My concentrated stare would scare most.

"Just thinking."

Courtney tucked her phone into her purse. "Hope you don't mind, but he's on his way over."

Maybe Courtney hadn't gotten the memo that Sarah and I owned this house and she should ask before inviting her fiancé over while she was busy courting our best friend. That was how it worked in my world, minus the faux engagement.

"Shall I order more food for him?" Maddie attempted to sound perky and welcoming.

"Nah, we're used to sharing." She stood. "May I use your restroom?"

"Of course." Sarah gave her the lowdown of where to find it.

Courtney was barely out of the room when Sarah quirked an eyebrow at Maddie. "Do you ever get her to yourself?"

Maddie's spine stiffened. "That's an issue, for sure," she said, collapsing into the back of the couch.

"Even, uh, during sexy time?" I rubbed my chin thoughtfully.

Her eyes bugged. "Did you just ask me whether I've had a threesome with Kit and Courtney?"

"I think I did." I rubbed my chin more thoroughly, as if that made the situation less awkward.

The doorbell rang.

"Food's here," Maddie said needlessly, darting out of the library to the front door.

Sarah met my *Now what?* glare and shrugged. "It's not ideal."

"I don't see this ending well."

"I don't know... I think it'll peter out before it really has a chance to foment. Courtney isn't playing coy."

I'd always hated the phrase "peter out" because it made me think of my sibling.

"Did I hear something about Peter?" Courtney waltzed in, her face slightly damp.

"What do you really think of Peter?" Sarah motioned for me to refill Courtney's wineglass, which I did.

"He's interesting. I admire his business drive. He's actually sent some business our way." Courtney slipped her blazer off and laid it over the back of the couch.

"Really? That was kind of him." Sarah blinked rapidly. Was she struggling to associate Peter with any act of kindness? Or was she, like me, trying to figure out Peter's angle?

Maddie returned, laden with white plastic bags.

"I'm curious what you think of..." Sarah paused as if mulling over the proper word choice before shrugging and saying, "his marrying Tie."

Courtney continued, "Peter has no idea what he got himself into when he tied the knot with that one. However, I'm not sure he had much choice in the matter."

That caught my attention.

"Shall we eat on the back deck? I'm roasting." Sarah didn't wait for an answer, standing to lead our odd group outside to congregate around the black iron table under a large oak tree.

Maddie divvied out the takeout containers and rounded back to the conversation Sarah had tried to stall. "What about Peter's cheating?"

I accidentally dropped my veggie spring roll into the duck sauce. Sarah handed me a recycled paper napkin, grinning at my clumsiness.

"I see Lizzie takes after her brother some. Never discuss the things people like to keep hidden." Courtney scooped Pad Thai into her mouth.

I focused on a blue jay intent on retrieving a peanut that had slipped into the cracks of the flagstone patio. Each peck lodged the shell further into the crevice.

"Does Tie know?" Maddie nibbled on a beef skewer, corncob style.

"Of course. She knew before their first date."

"How?" Maddie's tone suggested she didn't really care, but the way her sapphire eyes zeroed in on the food implied the opposite.

Courtney set her chopsticks down. "You really don't know?"

Maddie shook her head.

"They met briefly while Peter was engaged." She spoke softly and slowly. For the first time, Courtney seemed uncomfortable in her own skin.

Maddie sucked in a breath. "Engaged... to me."

It was hard to tell whether she was stating it or asking. Courtney must have thought the same thing; she opted not to reply.

"I see." Maddie stood. "I need..." She left the rest unsaid and disappeared inside.

"Should I go after her?" Courtney asked Sarah.

Sarah folded her napkin in half and then into quarters. "No. Give her some time."

"I thought she knew. Did you two know?" Courtney peeked at me and then gave Sarah her full attention.

We shook our heads. "Peter and Lizzie aren't close. During the first year of our relationship"—Sarah motioned to me and then to herself—"she wasn't in contact with her family. It wasn't until Peter and Maddie moved back that Lizzie reconnected with them. Maddie was the instigator."

I closed my eyes, not wanting to see the hurt in Sarah's eyes. The reason I'd allowed Maddie into our lives was the fear of committing to Sarah. I hadn't liked it when she called me a commitment-phobe earlier, but her assessment was dead-on. It nearly made me laugh out loud to think I'd been judging Courtney for how she lived her life while I was guilty of my own transgressions. Was that why it bugged me that Courtney played with Maddie's emotions? Because I knew the toll it had had on Sarah? Because I knew what I'd nearly lost?

"I see. Another fucked-up family." Courtney's smile revealed more than she probably intended.

"Is yours as bad?" Sarah asked softly.

"Hard to define, but it wasn't great. And we're all in business together. Greed and families are never a good mix. Having board meetings with family members—a deadly combination." Her steely eyes showed her steadfastness.

"There you are. I rang the bell, but no one came. Luckily the front door was unlocked." Kit sashayed onto the deck and patted the top of Courtney's head, then Sarah's, and finally mine. Were we playing Duck, Duck, Goose? He took the seat Maddie had vacated, and his face zagged up. "Uh-oh. Did I miss something?"

"Maddie found out about Tie's affair with Peter." Courtney sipped her red wine.

"Where is she? I should talk to her." Without awaiting a reply, he pranced back inside our home in search of Maddie. These people had no issues invading anyone's privacy.

I took a fierce, noisy slurp of water.

Sarah squeezed my thigh under the table, as if reassuring me Kit had no intention of stealing my books. Still, a simple, "Do you mind if I search your house top to bottom for a woman I hardly know?" would have made me feel loads better.

"I'm curious. How do you and Kit keep it together?" Sarah asked.

"Pretending to be in love?" Courtney arched a brow. Sarah nodded. "It's easy, really. I've been pretending one thing or another all of my life. So has Kit. Besides"—Courtney leaned back in her chair—"I do love Kit. He's the brother, best friend, and confidant I never had until now. I can't imagine my life without him."

"Do you really plan on marrying?"

I admired Sarah's determination to keep pushing.

"That remains to be seen. I think both families suspect it's a farce, to some extent, but it's a farce they like to maintain publicly." Courtney cradled her wineglass close to her chest, like a child does a teddy bear. "It's not that our families are so opposed to homosexuality. It's us they don't like. Neither Kit nor I are conventional in any way, shape, or form, and neither one of us—after watching our parents', grandparents', and siblings' disastrous marriages—has any desire to really settle down." She plunked her glass down on the table and eyed Sarah and then me. "I see you two have a strong relationship, and I don't mean that can't happen, but the odds are ninety-nine to one, and you're the one."

Sarah's laughter tickled my eardrums. "Are you saying that since Lizzie and I are happily married, your odds are zilch? That's absurd."

"Are you saying the marriages around you are happy?" Courtney's smile signaled her belief in the ninety-nine to one theory was rock solid.

"Lizzie's friend Ethan has a great marriage."

I was in mid-swallow and nearly choked.

Courtney waved a hand. "You see; even Lizzie sees things my way."

Sarah gave me the hairy eyeball, a phrase I picked up from the Urban Dictionary. "Their marriage isn't *that* bad."

"They don't have sex. They had to adopt Casey because of Ethan's aversion to 'fluids.'" I made quote marks in the air.

Sarah's face reddened. "Pffffft — you're still a commitment-phobe at heart."

I smiled and laced my fingers through Sarah's. "Not when it comes to you and our little buns in the oven."

"So you buy Courtney's theory?" Sarah's voice softened.

"Not sure. Before I met you, I would have said the odds were one hundred to one that any marriage would fail." I raised her hand to my lips. "Luckily, I was wrong." I turned my gaze to Courtney. "From one commitment-phobe to another, don't give up. Love is worth it."

Courtney cocked her head to the left and nodded. From the tightness in her shoulders, I had a feeling my words slid right off.

Kit ushered Maddie back outside, one hairy arm flung around her shoulders. "Found her in the nursery." Her eyes were puffy, and she held a Kleenex to her nose.

Sarah stood and hugged her. "I'm so sorry. We didn't know."

"Apparently, we're the only three in the world who didn't." Maddie collapsed in the chair wedged between Sarah and Courtney. The latter reached out and gave Maddie a supportive squeeze on the shoulder. It did not have the desired effect; Maddie edged her seat closer to Sarah.

Kit pulled up an extra chair beside me, smiling his usual chipper smile. "News like this takes time to sink in."

One look into Maddie's grief-stricken eyes nullified his optimism. Was Maddie still in love with Peter? I'd never understood her feelings for him. Of course, my own feelings about Peter were off-the-scale negative. That certainly clouded my judgment when it came to their relationship. Love was a funny thing. It was supposed to make a person happy, yet more often than not, it tortured individuals. One look at Maddie proved that.

I stole a glimpse at Sarah, who was watching me with soulful eyes. How in the world did I get so lucky?

— CHAPTER NINE —

"WHY'D WE AGREE TO GO TO DINNER WITH THEM?" I USHERED
SARAH TO THE SUV in the garage, my arms out protectively in
case she stumbled. Lately, it seemed all we did was have one
awkward family meal after another. Was this part of raising a
family? The kids hadn't even popped out yet!

"Stop that!" She yanked one arm down. "Just because I'm a
blimp doesn't mean you have to direct traffic."

"I'm not directing traffic. I'm being cautious. You can't see
your feet, and I want to be prepared in case you slip." I eyed
her nearly eight-month-pregnant belly, wondering how she
was able to walk at all. It seemed to smash all of Newton's
theories.

Sarah's tone grew nostalgic. "I haven't been able to see my
toes since the twenty-sixth week."

I glanced at her puffy feet spilling out of leather flip-flops.
"They look lovely. I like the shade Maddie picked out."

Maddie had been dragging Sarah out regularly to get a foot
massage and pedicure. Sarah's toenails were a soft shade of
lilac, matching her soft jersey skirt and fitted maternity top
that provided ample room to stretch over her even more
ample stomach.

We finally made it to the car, which was only four feet from the door that led to the kitchen. I opened the car door for her, unable to stop myself from taking a cautious stance while she hoisted herself into the passenger seat.

"Comfortable?"

"It's almost August, it's over one hundred degrees in the shade, and I'm bursting out to here"—she held her hands in front of her to emphasize—"with two babies in my belly. What do you think?" Her dark eyes warned me not to try saying anything clever.

I sucked in my retort of, "Hey, you're the one who wanted a baby." Instead, I replied, "Right. Stupid question. However, if there's anything I can do to make you more comfortable, just let me know. I'm at your service." I leaned over and gave her a peck on the cheek. "I love you."

Lately, I'd been saying I love you about twenty times a day. Technically, I wasn't the one who'd knocked-up Sarah, but I still felt guilty as hell that she was carrying our babies.

When I took my seat at the wheel, Sarah swiveled to face me. "You know, you may be catching on to this relationship thing. Only took you five years."

I smiled. "And you said I was a slow learner." I cranked the AC to high and positioned all the vents toward my wife.

Her melodious laughter trilled through my body. Even at this stage in her pregnancy, she was the most beautiful woman in the world.

"Let's hope you're faster when it comes to raising your demon spawn." She rubbed her stomach tenderly.

"I'll try." I sighed. "Let's go have dinner with the fam first." I put the car in reverse and backed out of the drive.

"Don't let Peter get to you tonight."

"Get to me? I would never let such a thing happen," I said as cheerily as possible as I turned onto the road heading east toward the I-25 highway entrance.

"Keep using that tone and you might convince yourself." She rested a hand on my leg and then winced.

"You okay?" I checked the rearview and side mirrors and pulled over.

Sarah bit down on her lip, taking a second. "Yeah. I'm fine." She exhaled through her mouth. "Just ready to get these babies out."

"Hey now, they aren't quite done baking yet." I spoke to her belly, "Another couple of weeks, little ones, to make it to thirty-eight weeks."

"Are you kidding me? Most twins are born before that. Are you that competitive?"

I thought it wise to avoid looking in her direction.

"Remember when I said you were learning?"

I nodded.

"Forget I said that. You're unteachable." She inclined her head against the seat and blotted her sweaty forehead with the back of her hand. "A couple more weeks. Gawd."

I swallowed my response that a teacher should never tell someone they're unteachable, chalking her words up to "baby brain." Scouting over my shoulder to ensure no one was in my blind spot, I eased back into traffic.

The highway entrance signs approached. "What do you say? Fancy going to Cheyenne instead? Get a good steak, listen to country music, maybe buy some shit kickers?"

"Shit kickers. Since when did you start calling boots that name? I can tell you've been hanging out with Maddie too much."

"She's a bad influence. You sure we should let her hang around the twins?" I rested a hand on Sarah's stomach.

"Lesbian parents of twins can't be too choosy." She cradled her hand on top of mine.

"Did you feel that?" One of the babies tried to boot my hand off Sarah's belly. "Do you think that was Olivia or Frederick?"

"My guess is Olivia. Hopefully I can teach her to be like the women in my family, even though we used your egg."

"Which is?"

"Spitfires."

"I'll be outnumbered completely. You, your mom, Ollie..." We'd decided Olivia's nickname should be Ollie, since Liv was too similar to Lizzie.

"Oh, I'm sure Freddie will join forces with us to survive," she said without a trace of humor.

"Four against one. That's not fair." I wormed my hand onto Sarah's thigh.

"Ah, you'll be fine. Just stay out of our way." She smiled with her eyes closed. "What do you think tonight's announcement will be?"

"When it comes to the Petries, I think it's best not to assume anything. We'd just be wrong. Besides, usually the announcements are about Peter's next wedding, and so far, Tie hasn't divorced him yet. Dad never has anything to say."

"I doubt Tie will ever divorce Peter. It's not in her man-trapping DNA. I think she plans on making his life hell just for shits and giggles. She's related to Kit, another pot stirrer. Rich kids with too much time on their hands are trouble. Maybe Peter will divorce her."

"And admit he made a mistake? No way."

"Care to make a friendly wager?" Sarah rubbed her hands together. "I love winning money."

"Let me get this straight. You want me to place a bet on my brother's marriage?"

"Yes." She bobbed her head for emphasis.

"Okay. But how do we figure out the terms?"

She laughed. "Why do you have to complicate things? Think kiss."

"You want to kiss?" I glanced over my shoulder to see whether it was clear to pull over.

"Not that type. K-I-S-S. Keep it simple, stupid. This is simple. If Peter asks for a divorce, I win."

"And if they stay married, I win."

"Yep. That's the gist." She patted my knee. "See, that's not so hard to understand. God, sometimes I forget I'm married to a PhD."

"Says the woman who loves to mention I'm a doctor when introducing me to friends and colleagues."

"Now I can officially call you Professor Petrie." The pride in her tone was unmistakable.

"Ugh. Sounds awful. Having that last name hasn't been easy. The only thing that makes it bearable is having a jackass brother named Peter Petrie." Sarah's laughter confirmed she agreed. "Back to the bet, it could take years to find out who won."

"Patience. We'll know when we know."

"What happens if we don't remember the bet, though? He's seven years older than I am. Odds are he'll die first, but—"

"But you're so competitive you'll want payment even if you're six feet in the ground." Sarah stared out the side window. There wasn't much to see along the stretch between Fort Collins and Denver, hardly a turn in the road, let alone anything of interest. Occasionally some cows, horses, or a lone tree broke the monotony of sunbaked dirt.

"Of course! Glad you're seeing the flaw in the arrangement." I smiled, sure she was rolling her eyes even though I couldn't see her face.

"Or maybe you're missing the obvious. I believe Peter will ask for a divorce well before he's dead."

"Why do you think that?"

"He picked her because he thought she'd be easy to control. After the whole Maddie thing, he wanted a wife who was dumb as a post. But she isn't. She played him from day one. Your brother is a business genius—or thinks he is. He has to know by now that he got conned. Tie is many things, but she isn't stupid or controllable."

"Are you saying she got her hooks into Peter right from the start, even before Peter considered her as his future wife? That's some serious planning."

"Women like her are born schemers. That's how their mothers brought them up, and their mothers did the same." She circled her hand, indicating and so on.

"Thank God Rose didn't train you from the cradle."

Sarah shifted her upper body, with great effort, to look me in the eyes. "What makes you think she didn't?"

"Uh…"

Shit, had I been played from the start? Not that I was complaining. Sarah was a knockout in every way: great wife, lover, companion, and mother-to-be. But to know I'd been played stung.

"But you love me, right?" I needed clarification, even though I was 95.63 percent certain our marriage was on solid footing. Kicking my insecurities to the curb completely wasn't possible, apparently.

"An unintended but delightful consequence."

My entire body went cold.

Sarah continued to stare me down.

"Please tell me you're kidding?"

She didn't move a muscle in her face for what seemed like well over sixty seconds, not that I could stare at her that long while passing two semis in the left lane.

When I merged back into the right lane, she broke out in hysterics. "Of course I'm fucking with you. I'd have to be in love with you to put up with your idiocy."

"Is that supposed to make me feel better?" It did, somehow. Not that I would confess that to her. Why let her know she was completely in control? She had been since day one, although it had taken me years to realize and accept it.

"I like to keep it real. Besides, you're my idiot, and I love you more than I ever thought possible. Please don't ever doubt that. I know you didn't grow up with the best examples of happy relationships, but you and I were made for each other." Sarah placed both hands on her swollen belly. "And I would never bring children into a loveless marriage."

I stroked her stomach again. "Children—never thought I'd say this, but I like the sound of that."

"Get the lead out. I'm starving." Sarah chomped her teeth for emphasis.

———————

"Whoa. Are we in the right place?" I helped Sarah to a chair at the bar, conveniently located next to the restrooms, where Sarah had already made one pit stop upon arrival.

Sarah's eyes grew three times the normal size as she gazed around the steakhouse. Every square inch of the scarlet red walls featured some type of animal head mounted on it. "This isn't the usual place for your family; that's for sure. What's that?" She pointed to a rabbit with antlers hung to the top left of the bar.

"Jackalope." The bartender placed both hands on the bar. "His name is Blackberry."

"Blackberry, like in *Watership Down*?" Sarah asked.

He nodded. "What can I get you, pretty lady? Ice water? Or something with a bit more pizzazz? Virgin cocktail, perhaps?"

"Ice water, but I won't turn down a lemon slice or two." Sarah looked as if she'd just ordered a snow cone in the middle of the African bush. "I can't believe how hot it is." She tugged at the neck of her top.

The bartender eyed me as he filled Sarah's glass with more ice than water.

"Coke, please."

Sarah sipped the water through a straw. "Never heard of a jackalope."

"That's because they aren't real. It's a jackrabbit with antelope horns, but this one has deer antlers." He shrugged off the inauthentic creature.

"So it's a jackadeer," I joked.

Neither of them cracked a smile.

"Tough crowd," I muttered. Sarah motioned to the seat next to her.

"What brings you out on a hot day that's not fit for the living?" he asked, glancing at her massive belly.

"Family dinner. Not mine—hers." She jabbed a thumb over her shoulder in my direction.

"Ah," was all he said, but his meaning was perfectly clear.

"Hey, it was your idea to accept. I would have been perfectly happy staying in."

He laughed. "Family. Gotta love them or kill them."

Before I had a chance to study his face to determine whether he was serious, I heard, "Good Lord, Sarah, you're"—Peter's eyes ballooned, and he sputtered—"so large."

I shot a withering look at my brother—needlessly, it turned out. Tie whacked the back of his head as if she'd been waiting all day to pounce.

"Nice wallop," Sarah said as she gave Tie a welcoming hug, to the best of her ability, while remaining in her seat.

I would never say this out loud, but hugging a beached whale was not an easy feat.

Tie grinned triumphantly. "He never thinks before he opens his stupid mouth."

"Oh, I think that's a family trait. Except for you, Charles." Sarah kissed my dad's proffered cheek. "Did you three drive together?"

As usual, Dad nodded but stayed mute. However, the jovial glimmer in his eyes was different. All the years he'd been married to my mother, I'd never seen his eyes show any hint of happiness. Today, though, he was practically rupturing at the seams—for him.

Peter cast his gaze around. "Where's Glenn Close?"

"What?" I checked the patrons in the bar.

"I'm assuming Maddie is in Fort Collins." Sarah's tone suggested Peter shouldn't push his luck when it came to our best friend.

"I'm not making the connection." I scratched my head.

"*Fatal Attraction*," Tie explained before informing the bartender she needed an ice water stat.

"Oh, that." I mimed a lightbulb going off, pretending I got it.

Sarah placed a hand on my leg and gave me an *I'll explain later* squeeze.

"Mrs. Petrie, your table is ready." The hostess motioned for us to follow.

Sarah and Tie led the way. I shadowed Sarah vigilantly, noticing Peter put his arms out a bit, as if readying himself in case Sarah took a misstep. Maybe he wasn't such an ass after all. Or maybe he feared he'd get hurt if Sarah fell on him.

I pulled out Sarah's chair, and Tie harrumphed until Peter took the hint. He started to say something but seemed to think better of it. Maybe that was what Peter needed all of these years, wallops to the back of the head to keep his inner asshole in check. And maybe he liked having a woman put him in his place.

Peter immediately ordered two bottles of wine.

"Are you sure you want two? Neither of us will be drinking." I motioned to Sarah's condition.

Sarah shook her head. "I think aliens on Mars can see me. No need to point out the obvious."

Tie laughed, and the trace of a smile materialized on my father's face. My cheeks tingled with the beginnings of a blush.

"You can have some. Sarah can drive home," Peter said as if Sarah hadn't made a joke. It wasn't the first time I'd wondered whether Peter had a sense of humor.

"I don't think the seat will move that far back. Even if it did, she'd never be able to reach the pedals." I feigned trying to grab the steering wheel from the backseat.

Sarah shot daggers at me over the rim of her water glass. Mental note, only Sarah can make jokes about her size—no one else, including me.

Tie caught her eye, and Sarah nodded swiftly. Before I realized what was coming, Tie smashed her hand into the back of my head.

Peter laughed—a positive sign my brother wasn't a complete robot. Not that I had any illusions of trying to develop a close relationship with him. Just enough. Was that the right example to set for my children?

"Tie, I'm hereby electing you to the role of family enforcer."
Sarah beamed.

I rubbed the tender spot on the back of my head. "How
many hours do you spend in the gym?"

"Not enough. She had to buy new swimsuits for the
summer." Peter smirked at his own joke as he buttered a roll.
Tie smacked his head with hurricane-like force, causing him
to drop the bread, which rolled across to the next table.

Tie turned in her chair to apologize to the couple sitting at
the table behind us. "Sorry about that." Her tone was one of
such easy-going charm that I had to remind myself she'd
already whacked Peter twice and me once. Three whacks in
under five minutes. Was abuse a new habit of hers? If so, I
didn't like it.

"Don't be. If my husband said that to me, I'd hit him, too."
An older woman, who probably hadn't worn a swimsuit in
twenty years, glared at Peter.

"Shall we call a truce?" I offered.

Sarah and Tie grinned, knowing they had the upper hand.

"It's a simple rule. Don't say shitty things. Think before you
speak." Sarah shifted in her seat and grimaced.

"Jesus. You aren't going to pop out Elizabeth's offspring at
the table, are you?" Peter ducked this time, which Tie had
anticipated. Despite the movement, she managed a direct hit.

"I'm buying a helmet," Peter whined, yet there was an odd
sparkle in his eyes. Had they been experimenting with BDSM
or something? The thought nearly made me spew the contents
of my stomach.

I turned to Sarah. "You okay?"

"Yeah, I'm fine. Just Braxton Hicks." She eyeballed Peter. "I
wish I could pop these babies out today. No one tells you how
miserable the last weeks are. Or if they did, I didn't believe

them. And the hot flashes… If they're any indication of what's to come, I don't want to go through menopause."

"I'm starting to question this whole pregnancy thing." Tie fanned Sarah with a menu.

"What do you mean?" Peter asked his wife.

"No offense, Sarah, but it looks like hell."

"But you want kids, right?" Peter pushed.

"Yeah." She hefted a shoulder. "Maybe we'll have a surrogate. Not sure I'm made to give birth." From the disdain in her eyes, Tie wasn't kidding, not at all.

"Well, we wouldn't want to ruin your Sports Illustrated Swim Suit Edition body." I couldn't decipher Peter's plastic smile. Was he being sincere or mocking?

Neither could Tie, apparently, since she didn't whack him again.

"What's good here?" I asked in an effort to ease the tension.

Petrie family meals were usually fraught with tension, but with Tie and her new penchant for whacking, a hint of violence permeated the air.

While the four of them studied the menu, I studied Tie, thinking over Sarah's words. When I first met Tie, I'd written her off as an airhead, but I was starting to see the light. Courtney was right: there was no limit to her conniving.

The waiter arrived with the wine and took our orders.

"Now that the food's on its way, what's the big news?" Peter asked me. "Besides the obvious."

"I thought *you* had an announcement," I said.

Peter shook his head.

I almost blurted out, "Then why the hell did I have to drag my pregnant wife all the way to Denver?"

Dad cleared his throat, shifting in his seat. He had big news. Was he retiring? Good Lord, what would the man do?

Sarah's soft smile melted my heart and, from the relaxed look in my father's eyes, paved the way for me to hear his announcement.

"I'm getting married," he said.

"Married?" I squinted at the man across the table, a man I barely knew.

"To whom?" Tie asked.

"Helen."

"*Helen* Helen?" Peter asked in a tone that implied he'd already met the mystery woman.

Dad nodded.

I queried Sarah's face, but she gave an almost imperceptible shake of her head.

Peter balled up his napkin. "No. You can't."

Dad didn't say anything, just cocked his head slightly to confront his firstborn.

"You don't marry your mistress. It just doesn't happen," Peter continued.

"Prince Charles did," Tie said without a trace of irony.

I was surprised she didn't mention that Peter had, too, if Courtney was to be believed. More than likely, she never wanted us or anyone else to know that juicy morsel. The glare she gave her husband to zip it was as close to a death threat I'd ever been witness to.

Mistress? Helen was Dad's mistress? It didn't seem like an appropriate name for a mistress. During Mom's final years, I'd discovered my father had frequently stepped out of the relationship. But I'd never heard his mistress's name. Actually, I'd assumed it was a string of women, not a relationship. Did that make it better or worse?

Sarah nodded, agreeing with Tie's observation as if we were having a completely normal family conversation about my father marrying his mistress. The meals hadn't even arrived yet.

Dad remained mute, although the vein in his forehead pulsed.

Peter glared at a cougar's head on the wall above Tie's formidable face.

I needed to do something. "Hey, did you know the jackalope over there"—I pointed to the bar—"is named Blackberry, after the rabbit in *Watership Down*?"

Sarah wasn't in my direct line of sight, but I sensed the shock on her face. Diversions weren't my specialty. But I couldn't stop. "Do you think BlackBerry the phone is also named after the character?" I gestured to Peter's cell. It wasn't a BlackBerry, but I had already crashed into the desperation zone.

"Elizabeth, what the fuck are you talking about?" Peter asked.

I had absolutely no idea.

"I think BlackBerries were called that because they thought the keys looked like seeds." Tie sipped her wine. "I remember reading that somewhere."

This little nugget that slipped out of Tie's mouth reinforced Sarah's point, and I was starting to wonder whether I'd lose the divorce bet.

"I remember reading *Watership Down* when it was published, before you were born, Lizzie." Dad shifted in his seat again, blocking Peter from his sight completely. "I'd read a review in *The Economist* when it came out, and I wanted to know what the fuss was about."

My dad read books? I wasn't sure what was more shocking: that my father was marrying another woman less than a year after my mother's death or that he read novels. I'd only ever seen him read the *Financial Times*.

"My students don't complain too much about that book." Sarah placed a hand on my thigh. Did that mean I'd done an okay job steering the conversation away from the pink elephant in the room?

Peter bolted upright in his seat, breathing heavily through his nostrils like an eighty-year-old man who'd just climbed a flight of stairs. He eyed Tie, who sipped her wine with a mystifying smile that almost dared him to make some kind of declaration. The waiter approached with our salads. Peter glanced at his wife and then at Dad, who was still ignoring him, before staring at his fork liked he wanted to stab someone with it.

The waiter, perhaps sensing the drama, placed the plates on the table and scurried away.

I was curious about Helen but wasn't sure now was the time to ask how they met or how long they'd been together. Did I really want to enter that realm of my father's relationship? That would send Peter into another fury.

Sarah and Tie chatted about the impending arrival of the twins, the safest topic at the moment, until the waiter returned to remove our salad plates and replace them with our main courses.

Tie wafted the aroma from her plate to her nose and then kissed her fingertips, releasing them with a flourish like an Italian gangster in a movie. "Oh, this smells so good. Reminds me of my childhood."

"Did you eat a lot of elk?" Sarah asked without an ounce of ridicule in her tone.

"Never at home. But we used to come here once a week for family dinners."

That explained why we were here this evening. I was starting to see the hunter in Tie, though I doubted she wasted her time pursuing elk. I blinked. Was I dreaming or actually hallucinating? Did people get delirious when it was over 105 degrees? I yanked on the collar of my shirt.

Peter forced a smile, baring his unnaturally white teeth. If he ever decided to get out of the finance biz, he had a great future in politics, probably only at the state level, though. Smarmy and Peter went hand-in-hand. He grabbed his knife and fork and tucked into his fifty-six-dollar T-Bone, topped with sautéed mushrooms and onions, each an additional seven fifty. Was that why he hadn't scrammed earlier when it was obvious he'd wanted to? His seventy-something dollar meal? Surely, Peter, the finance whiz kid, could afford to skip out on a steak dinner without batting an eye. He was probably more concerned about his inheritance.

Coward. I wanted to circumnavigate the table, flapping my arms about, kicking up dirt, and squawking like a chicken, "Bock, bock, bock."

Sarah nibbled on her quail, while I sat dumbstruck. Was everyone going to pretend Peter hadn't just had a major temper tantrum? What about the news that my father was getting married for the second time? How old was he anyway? Sixty something? Or closer to seventy? How in the world did I not know this?

"Have you and Helen set a date?" Tie carved into her elk with precision.

Dad shook his head and finished up a mouthful of steak. After taking a sip of red wine he said, "No. We want to wait until my grandbabies are here." He motioned to Sarah. "My guess is one week."

"One week." Sarah's voice cracked, and she set her fork down. "The doctor thinks two, but one sounds... so... much sooner."

I squeezed her leg under the table.

"I better clear my schedule, so I can meet my niece and nephew as soon as possible." Tie turned to Peter. "And you're going."

Tie and Peter planned to be at the hospital on the day the babies were born? Now I was terrified, and I wasn't the one squeezing watermelon-sized babies out of my twat.

"When do the rest of us get to meet Helen?" Tie's question hinted she was displeased that Peter already had.

"Do you want to meet her?" Dad directed the question to me.

Sarah dug her nails into my thigh before I had a chance to open my mouth. "Of course."

I gripped my water glass tight and took a long guzzle of the cool liquid.

— Chapter Ten —

"Lizzie." Sarah shoved my shoulder.

I rolled over in bed. "What?"

"I—" She grunted in pain, snapping me wide-awake.

"It's time?"

Sarah emitted a groan as confirmation.

I hopped out of bed in one motion. "Battle stations." For the past few nights, I'd had jeans and a T-shirt ready to go by my bedside. In less than seven seconds, I dressed, donned a baseball hat, and slipped into flip-flops.

"Help me out of bed." Sarah held out one lethargic arm.

I dashed to her side and eased her into an upright position.

"Jesus fucking Christ!" she screamed, clutching her stomach.

I didn't know what to say. I couldn't say, "It's okay. Everything's going to be fine." How did I know what she was going through? It wasn't like she'd stubbed a toe. She was in early labor, and she had to go through it twice—hopefully in a relatively short span of time. I tried to recall what the Lamaze coach had drilled into my head about what to say. "Remember to focus on your breathing."

The heart monitors *thump, thump, thump*ed. Sarah, her eyes closed, rolled her head from side-to-side on the delivery table. The pain was kicking into high gear, mocking the discomfort she'd felt so far, leading up to D-Day. I had no clue how she could bear it. Two hours earlier, I'd been convinced she had reached the maximum pain threshold one human being could endure, but the obstetrician had insisted she wasn't about to deliver. We had arrived at the hospital yesterday, which now seemed like weeks ago.

For many hours, Sarah had tried different positions to help alleviate her discomfort. Standing, walking, lying on her side, and even getting down on all fours. She, however, didn't take to the birthing ball. Never before had I realized the importance of gravity. Now that she was fully dilated and had been pushing for more than an hour, Sarah was on the bed, hopefully ready to pop out the twins. The storming of the beaches on D-Day took less time.

The epidural, recommended for multiple births just in case of an emergency, had kicked in, but didn't wipe out her pain completely.

"Keep breathing through it, Sarah," the OB instructed.

The OB tech in green scrubs scurried around, prepping machines and setting up instruments in the operating room, another safeguard the birthing team insisted on, much to Sarah's annoyance, who wanted to deliver both babies vaginally. Odds were with her, since the babies were in the vertex/breech position, meaning the first one was head down, the other would have to be turned.

At one point, Sarah gazed at me, shook her head, and smiled to let me know everything was going to be fine. The smile didn't last. One arm reached behind her head to fist the pillow. She concentrated on her breathing again. "Okay, okay, okay," she said, even though no one had asked her a question.

"Breathe, Sarah. Breathe." I encouraged her, holding one of her hands in both of mine.

Her breathing intensified, punctuated with guttural moans.

"Little pants, Sarah." The obstetrician smiled encouragingly.

Delivery nurses stood on each side of the bed near Sarah's legs, her knees up in the air. The OB sat on a stool, like a baseball catcher. I would have giggled at the scene, if not for Sarah's pain.

The crown of the baby's head appeared, and I stared into Sarah's eyes. "Oh my God. You're doing this!"

She smiled—or grimaced—it was hard to determine. More of the head emerged, and a woozy feeling washed over me. "Oh my God. How in the fuck are you doing this?" I rubbed the top of my head with both hands.

Sarah belted out another scream. One of the labor nurses who had been with us the entire time gave me an admonishing glare that simultaneously said *You're a fucking idiot* and *Snap out of it.*

"You're doing great." I said. "I love you so much. Oh my God…"

Her face, contorted in agony, wrenched at my insides. Her moans subsided to a lull, and we all waited breathlessly until her face jagged up in pain again.

"Push, Sarah," the OB said.

Behind me, someone on the delivery team counted to ten. It seemed like the room now swarmed with hospital staff, and I couldn't keep anyone or their roles straight.

Another pause followed before the process repeated itself.

"The head's out," I said to Sarah, practically jumping up and down, wanting her pain to end.

A bluish shoulder appeared.

"It's almost here." I squealed like a little girl, probably for the first time in my life. "There's an arm." Everything happened quickly after that, and the next thing I heard was a cry.

A baby's cry.

Our baby.

The obstetrician briefly placed the wrinkled, bluish bundle covered in grotesque slime on the bed in between Sarah's legs before whisking it up to Sarah's chest. "It's a girl," she announced.

Maddie had been coaching me for weeks not to scowl at the sight of the babies seconds after their birth. "For the love of God, Lizzie, don't say anything stupid or pull a face," she'd scolded me over and over. "Labor is a messy business."

A pair of scissors was thrust into my hand.

"Cut between the two." The woman pointed to two clip-like things on the baby's umbilical cord. "Right there."

I cut the cord in a daze.

"Olivia," Sarah cooed, tears sparkling in her eyes.

Someone placed a blanket over Olivia, while another was working down below, gearing up for Freddie. My gaze returned to Sarah and our daughter.

Grinning, I swiped both eyes with the back of my hand.

"Straighten your legs, Sarah," the OB prompted.

Sarah was remarkably calm, while everyone else roved around the room, completing their tasks. My eyes never left Olivia. I was transfixed. It was as if time had stopped for me and no one else.

The babies' nurse swooped our miniscule daughter to the side and placed her on a sci-fi-looking table surrounded by a plethora of machines and gadgets. Another team member joined her and started patting Olivia down with a sheet while the other shoved something into the baby's mouth. She cried out. I wanted to tell the person to stop, but I was too stunned by their efficiency. They worked on our tiny baby with quick, robot-like urgency. I was awed and annoyed in equal measure. My daughter wasn't a thing to be treated in such a manner.

Sarah gripped my hand, and I turned to her.

Our second child was on its way.

Sarah's grip tightened, and she peered into my eyes with an intensity I'd never seen before. "I don't know if I can do it. I want to go home. One is plenty."

I kissed the top of her head. "You're doing great."

"I'm so tired. I want to go home now!"

"Look at me." I hunched down. "You are the most amazing woman I've ever known. You can do this." I squeezed her hand. "I love you."

Sarah made a move to get out of bed. "If you love me, you do it. Please." Her gush of energy dissipated, and she sank against the padded headboard of the bed. "I just don't know if I can do it again. Not so soon." She clenched her tear-streaked eyes closed.

I smoothed her sweat-soaked hair and peppered her forehead with kisses. "It's almost over. Afterward, all of this"—I waved to the room—"will be wiped from your memory. Focus on Olivia"—I nodded in the crying infant's direction—"and on Freddie."

Tears streamed down her face. "Why did you insist we have twins?"

I grinned. "Is that how you remember it?"

"No rational person would volunteer for this. This is torture." The weak smile on her face gave me hope that her sanity had returned.

"You got this—"

Sarah's nails dug into my flesh.

"Okay, Sarah." The OB hunched down between Sarah's legs. "Freddie wants out."

"I'm not ready!" Sarah shouted.

"Sarah, listen to me. You can do this." The obstetrician's voice was firm but supportive.

I stayed at Sarah's side, clutching her hand.

"Can I have a warm towel?" the OB asked one of her team members.

Sarah winced.

"Push, push, push, push," the OB coaxed.

"You're doing well," agreed the delivery nurse in a comforting tone.

The one on my left mumbled, "Wait for the next contraction."

"Got a heartbeat for the baby?" asked the OB.

I sucked in a breath. Was something wrong?

There were more barked orders, but I could no longer decipher who was saying what, so many were talking at once.

The doctor reached inside Sarah, causing my wife agonizing pain. Clearly, Fred was in extreme duress. The anguish on Sarah's face reached deep inside, making me feel as if the floor was swallowing me whole.

Suddenly, there was a flurry of activity, including a drape being yanked over to block Sarah's view. I remembered reading approximately ten to twenty-five percent of twin births resulted with one being born vaginally and the other by emergency C-section.

The drape meant even though the odds were on our side, statistics had let us down.

When they had insisted I wear sterile garb, I thought it was just a hospital regulation for delivering in the OR—I never thought for a moment they'd actually have to cut Sarah open.

Please God, let him be okay. I didn't want to leave Sarah's side, and I couldn't discern how much she was hearing.

Heidi Murkoff's book stressed it was important to stay calm, even though everything would start to move quickly. She advised in the case of an emergency not to worry. Was the woman mad?

I willed myself not to enter panic mode. Holding Sarah's hand, I said, "Everything's going to be fine."

"I feel something, I think," Sarah said as if in a daze.

I peered over the drape and saw the horizontal incision. Serious mistake. Yet, I couldn't stop watching. There was graphic, and then there was seeing your wife's stomach slit open like some perverted medical experiment.

Forcing my eyes to Sarah's worried face, I reiterated, "Everything's going to be fine." I never thought acting was in my future, but maybe I should give it a go, because right now I deserved a fucking Oscar for pretending to be cool, calm, and in control. I leaned down and kissed her forehead. "I love you. You're doing great."

Unlike Olivia, Fred was eased out of Sarah's belly.

"Here we go, Freddie," said the OB.

Our son was here and was deathly quiet.

The OB clipped his cord, not even bothering to offer the scissors to me.

He was bustled away to a side table. Three pairs of blue-gloved hands pounced on him. A tiny oxygen mask was put over his mouth. A neonatologist, a man whose name I couldn't remember, had been waiting in the wings in case he was needed, and he now joined the group.

"Come on, Freddie," one of them urged.

I glanced over to the other bed where someone was measuring Olivia's head with a tape measure. She was so tiny and fragile. I dabbed a tear on my cheek. She was turning pink, as if coming to life, but Freddie remained blue.

The man placed a stethoscope on Freddie's chest. Others patted him and wiggled him about.

A machine beeped, and the male doctor chanted, "Come on. Come on, come on, little one."

Please God, I know I never talk to you, but if you're there, please help my son.

The neonatologist continued repeating, "Come on."

Four individuals waited anxiously at our son's side, fierce determination on all of their faces.

I glanced at Sarah. The doctor was stitching up the incision. Someone was messing with her IV. Concern showed through the exhaustion in her eyes. I forced a confident smile, which she reciprocated. Shit, Sarah deserved the Oscar, because I knew she was in hell worrying about Freddie, but more than likely didn't want to alarm me.

"He's beautiful," I said, trying to convey everything was A-okay.

She didn't take her eyes off me, unable to see Fred. *Stay calm, Lizzie. For Sarah. And your son.*

"There… he's perking up." The man cradled Freddie's head in one giant palm.

Olivia was swaddled up in a blanket, and before I could process what was happening, I was cradling my daughter, both eyes still glued on Freddie.

Freddie started to pinken, and Sarah called me over to her side.

Everything was happening so fast. I had hoped Sarah hadn't heard the commotion surrounding Freddie, considering the burst of action and the drape blocking her view. At least I prayed she didn't.

"Hi, Olivia. I'm your mom." I slowly walked to Sarah, afraid I'd break the fragile creature in my arms, and held her out for Sarah to see. "This is your other mom. She's your super mom, considering what you and your brother just put her through." I kissed the top of Ollie's head.

Sarah cried and motioned that she wanted to hold her. I handed her off as if I was transferring the most delicate object on the planet. Sarah nuzzled her. "Is Fred okay?"

"Of course he is." I glanced across the room. "He's turning the most beautiful shade of pink."

I wasn't lying, much to my relief.

After being transferred to the room, and what seemed like an eternity, Freddie was placed in my arms. "Hi, Freddie." Tears trickled down my face.

Thank you, God. I owe you one.

Olivia wailed, and Sarah beamed.

"Boy you have a set of lungs," she whispered. "Look at your brother—quiet as a mouse." Sarah nearly tripped over the last part but forged on. Was it for her benefit? Olivia's? Mine?

"I want to hold him." Sarah made room, and I placed Freddie into her cradled right arm. "There you go."

Freddie seemed peaceful, nestled into Sarah's warmth.

Olivia's tiny mouth opened and closed, her pink tongue poking in and out.

"I think we know which one will be the troublemaker," I joked.

Sarah smiled. "They're perfect. I can't believe they're here."

"Where the hell are they?" Tie's voice echoed down the hospital hallway.

"If we don't find them soon, I'm leaving." I could practically picture Peter's pout.

"Oh, are your niece and nephew interrupting your golf game? 201… 203." Tie's cheery face appeared around the doorjamb. "We're here!"

Maddie stifled a laugh. Sarah's grin showed her true feelings, but it had nothing to do with Peter and Tie. She was exhausted from having given birth to two babies less than four hours ago. I sat in a chair next to Sarah's hospital bed, with Freddie cradled in my arms. Maddie, standing by the window, held Ollie. Sarah and I had decided not to have anyone else in the room during the delivery, but Maddie and Sarah's mom, Rose, had been at the hospital the entire time.

"Oooh… I want one." Tie made a beeline for Maddie, her arms outstretched.

Maddie caught Sarah's eye, as if to ask permission to hand over the innocent bundle. Sarah gave a slight nod.

"You're so tiny and beautiful," Tie cooed.

Maddie looked Peter up and down. "Does Gordon Gekko know you're raiding his closet and hair gel?"

Peter was clad in a blue-and-white striped shirt, red suspenders, and a polka-dot tie. His hair was slicked, as if he'd dipped a wide-tooth comb in super glue and brushed straight back. If Peter were caught in a category-5 hurricane, not one hair would budge.

He snarled at Maddie.

Tie jiggled Ollie in her arms, smiling. "Don't pay him any attention. I pulled him out of a meeting." She nuzzled her chin against Ollie's fuzzy head.

"Not just any meeting. A board meeting." He straightened his tie and fiddled with a silver monogrammed cufflink.

Tie rolled her eyes and turned her back on him. "What are their names?"

Maddie inched next to her and tugged on Ollie's fingers. "This is Olivia, and Lizzie's holding Frederick. They already have nicknames. Ollie and Freddie."

"Hello, Ollie. I'm your aunt Tie-Fannie."

It was hard not to laugh at her pronunciation.

Not missing a beat, Maddie said, "But you can call her Aunt Tie."

Tie bounced on the balls of her feet. "Yes, you can. And Freddie." She glanced over to me, indicating she wanted to hold the delicate child in my protective arms.

I didn't want to let go, but Sarah's forced smile and determined eyes demanded I let the spaz hold my son, even if he hadn't been able to take his first breath on his own.

Maddie scooped Ollie from her hands, and Tie waited expectantly with open arms.

"Be careful with this one." I reluctantly handed off Freddie.

Maddie studied me in that way of hers, trying to suss out the reason behind my comment, but she soon shook it off and attempted to thrust Ollie into Peter's arms. "Hold your niece."

Peter backpedaled. "Uh, I don't know how."

"You don't know how to hold a human being?" She scoffed.

Peter bent forward. "It's so tiny."

"It's a she. Ollie." Maddie smiled at Olivia and hoisted her up to get an eyeful of Peter. "Ollie, this is your uncle Peter. He acts like he owns the world, but he can be a nice guy about as often as you witness Halley's Comet." Maddie placed Ollie in Peter's arms.

He frowned at Maddie and then stared down at my daughter. "Hi... Olivia." Peter looked as natural as Attila the Hun might look holding a baby on the battlefield.

Sarah and I exchanged a look that communicated, *Good grief*. Would it kill Peter to call our child by her nickname?

"Hello." My father's voice was softer than usual as he edged into the room.

"Hi, Charles," Maddie and Sarah said in unison, causing my father to smile, sort of—what passed for a smile.

A smiling woman in her early fifties stood next to him, her arm looped through my father's. Her other hand held a gift bag with two teddy bears poking out.

"You must be Helen," Sarah said. "Thanks so much for coming."

"Thanks for having me." She put a hand out for me to shake. "Lizzie?"

I nodded, confused as to how she'd recognized me so quickly, and clasped her warm hand. Maybe she noticed the family resemblance, or had my father shown her pictures of his children? Quite possibly my wrung-out appearance screamed I was the other parent in the delivery room.

"It's nice meeting you." I waved to the bed. "But Sarah is the hero of the day."

Sarah motioned for them to bring it in for a hug. I glimpsed a look of relief on my father's face. Leave it to Sarah to put everyone at ease, even after the trial she'd just survived.

Dad sidled up next to Peter and asked, "Who's this?"

"Olivia," Peter's tone softened, and his stance grew more relaxed. Maybe there was hope for him after all. "Here." He handed Ollie to her grandfather.

Dad, much to my surprise, full-on smiled. Helen grinned, too, making me wonder how long she'd wanted to be a part of the Petrie family. Should I warn the poor woman?

Freddie started to fuss in Tie's arms.

"Come to Mommy, Freddie." Sarah waved Tie over.

Nestled on Sarah's chest, Freddie opened his mouth and clumsily licked his hand for a moment, as if searching for something.

A lactation consultant in zoo animal print scrubs entered the room, taking in all the people, balloons, and stuffed animals before setting her sights on Freddie. "Oh, good. He's hungry." The woman stood by Sarah's side and untied Sarah's gown, exposing a full breast.

I stood in the middle of the chaos, dumbfounded.

Maddie and Tie migrated to Dad and Olivia, joined by Helen. No one seemed flustered by the feeding taking place five feet away.

The consultant gave Sarah instructions and encouraged Freddie to latch onto the nipple.

Rose entered without much ado, nodding to those whom she knew before hightailing it over to her daughter and grandson. She and the woman exchanged a few words and continued to encourage Sarah and Freddie.

I glanced around the room. Only Peter's mouth was forming an O. We locked eyes briefly.

"Can I get anyone anything?" He scouted the room frantically, and I considered that it was probably the first time I'd ever seen him wanting to be ordered about.

"Coffee for me." Tie smiled knowingly. "Anyone else?"

Everyone but Sarah nodded.

"Uh, I'll join you," I said.

"Cool," he said. Then I think the situation sunk in, and he straightened. "Elizabeth." He motioned for me to walk ahead of him.

We walked in silence for several minutes until we located a coffee cart near the hospital wing entrance.

"How many do we need?" I asked.

"You've always been terrible at math." He shook his head, but his tone lacked its usual condemnation. "Let's see. Tiff, Dad, Hel—" He held three fingers in the air, as if hesitant to utter her full name. "Maddie, you, and me." He continued to hold six fingers in the air. "Sarah can't, right?"

"Correct, but don't forget Rose. And I prefer chai. Six coffees and one chai." I whirled about and rattled off the order to a teenage boy with floppy hair and acne.

Standing to the side, waiting for the orders, Peter shifted on his feet. "How does it feel, being a parent?"

"Surreal. I know I had months to prepare for it, but today, when it was happening, it was…" I didn't finish, not knowing how to describe what had occurred hours before. How could I tell my brother, whom I wasn't even close to, about Sarah's legs in the air, the blood, the amniotic crud, the screaming, pushing, crying, and moaning? It was like a war zone, with my wife and babies in the midst of everything. And all I could do was stand by, helpless.

"A little late for cold feet." He laughed, stopping abruptly.

I shrugged. "Sarah was absolutely amazing. I could never do that."

"Well, you're on the hook now. Save your pennies for two college funds." He laughed again, but his stare drifted to the sliding doors at the entrance. I remembered Tie's comment that she'd prefer a surrogate. Was she kidding? It was hard to tell what to believe when it came to Tie—and to Peter, for that matter. However, considering the expense for us getting pregnant, I wondered whether he would worry about the cost of a surrogate. The bottom line was the only line that mattered in Peter's world.

His iPhone buzzed, and he glanced at the screen. "Uh, congrats." He ran a hand over his hair, which made a crunching sound.

Had Tie texted to remind him to congratulate me? Or had Maddie? My money was on Maddie. I put a hand on his shoulder. "Thanks, Peter."

How Tie managed to drag him out of the office on a Monday morning was a mystery. It shocked me, although it was a shock I probably could have lived without. Despite that, for Peter, he was being relatively pleasant. Would becoming a parent and Peter becoming an uncle shift our relationship into different territory?

"Here you go. Six coffees and one chai." The pimpled teen gestured to the cups crammed into two cardboard carriers.

When we returned to the room, Ollie was latched onto Sarah's nipple. Helen held Freddie, with Rose clasping his fingers. My father had an arm ringed around Helen's waist. I'd never seen him do that with my mother. I blinked several times before I let my eyes focus on what mattered.

Sarah smiled down at our daughter.

Daughter.

Son.

Wife.

How did this happen to me, an independent woman? Yesterday we were two, and now we were four.

A shudder ran through me.

As if her sixth sense had kicked in, Maddie flung an arm around my shoulder. "You look exhausted," she whispered.

"Don't be silly. Sarah did all the work." I handed her a coffee and motioned to the sugar and cream packets in the middle of the carrier.

She leaned closer. "Sarah said you were amazing. I'm proud of you."

My nostrils burned, and my vision blurred. Sarah watched me from the bed, smiling, at peace amid the chaos of our complicated family and the roller coaster of emotions that came with over twenty-four hours of labor. I smiled back as a sense of calm suddenly whooshed through me.

Tie plucked Freddie from Helen's arms and cuddled him to her chest. "That settles it, Peter. I want one."

Peter tugged on his collar and sipped his scolding hot coffee. I could tell he was holding back a venomous sneer. "I already gave you your coffee. Do you need another already?"

She shook her head. "Not that. A baby. I want a baby. Now."

Peter's facial muscles didn't budge, but I sensed he was experiencing the sensation of the ground disappearing from under his feet. Aside from Tie's baby talk, everything else in the room fell silent, making it clear I wasn't the only one to notice his panic.

— Chapter Eleven —

A FEW WEEKS LATER, I WOKE AT THREE MINUTES AFTER TWO IN THE MORNING IN an empty bed. I yawned and dragged my body to the nursery. Sarah sat in a rocking chair, feeding Freddie and humming softly to him. Not wanting to wake Olivia, I waved at her and parked my butt on the window ledge by the chair, patting the top of Freddie's head.

"Why are you up? The next wail is all yours," Sarah whispered, covering her mouth to mute the sound and stifle a yawn.

"I missed you," I whispered back.

"Aw, that's sweet, but don't even think of getting out of your slot."

I leaned over and kissed the top of her head. "Wouldn't dream of it."

Weeks before the twins arrived, Sarah and I had plotted out several different scenarios and arrangements for nightly feedings to make things fair. Sarah was concerned about my sleep on the nights before I had to lecture, but it wasn't acceptable for her to be the only one to get up at night. Rose had purchased a top-of-the-line breast pump and hospital-worthy cozy recliner for nursing mothers.

Mostly, the schedules we devised were utterly useless. We finally agreed to taking turns whenever we could. Having twins meant both babies often needed attention at the same time. Some nights, I pulled more shifts; other nights, Sarah did. We finally admitted defeat and hoped that in the long run, everything would even out. Our ultimate goal became surviving one night at a time.

In twenty-one days as a parent, the only thing I'd learned about babies was that they didn't care about the time of day, schedules, or anything. Pissing, pooping, crying, and eating took precedence, and both of our lives now revolved around those actions. Yet, I loved it. Who knew twin chaos would suit me, the über freak whose watch required seven daily alarms to keep me on schedule?

Rose came over every morning at eight to help. I had once mentioned that she didn't have to; I could hire help in the mornings. My ears were still ringing from her scathing response. The Petrie family had never been afraid to hire people: cleaners, nannies, chauffeurs, landscapers, personal shoppers—you name it. We had phone numbers to cover all bases.

The Cavanaughs wouldn't hear of it. Sarah had grown accustomed to Miranda, my cleaning lady, even after a minor bump in the road when she thought Miranda was moonlighting as a prostitute. Miranda, of course, never did such a thing. Actually, it was my evil ex, who was prostituting herself to support her drinking, combined with one of my fibs that led Sarah to believe such a thing about the ever-devoted Miranda.

Another Petrie coup involved yard work. Our lawn wasn't massive, but I still hated mowing it and pruning the bushes. Sarah had broken down last March and permitted me to hire a high school kid, who was saving for college. During the winter, the kid, who lives two doors down, shovels our sidewalks and drive whenever it snows. When he graduates from high school next year, I'll have to search high and low to find another kid who's saving for college, so Sarah can't say no.

Childcare was a whole different ballgame. No stranger would ever suffice. Sarah was taking the entire school year off, but there was already talk about her staying home until the twins were of school age. Even then, she'd probably only work part-time. Luckily, we could afford for her not to work. Rose didn't have a job either, so she was our go-to babysitter and helper during the day. Maddie popped by most nights. We were extremely fortunate to have both of them.

Sarah gently placed Freddie back into his crib. We stood and watched him settle, before she grabbed my hand and led us to our bedroom. After climbing under the covers, she snuggled her head on my chest. I tapped the screens of both baby monitors to ensure they were working properly, something I couldn't stop myself from doing several times a night.

"You're going to break them." She laughed quietly.

"Do you think I did?" I swiveled my head to check the screens.

Sarah patted my chest. "It's fine. You need to get some rest before your big day. You nervous?"

"Nah," I lied, ignoring my frazzled nerves. "It's not my first time teaching."

She sighed. "I thought we talked about this. No more lying. It's okay to be nervous. You've been out of the classroom for a few years. Besides, the first day is always nerve-racking for the students and teacher."

I shrugged. "I'm trying not to think about it."

She draped her arm over my shoulder and dropped off to sleep. I held her tightly in my arms, keeping my eyes on the baby monitors, waiting for my shift.

"I see you've been on baby duty." Dr. Marcel placed a hand on my rumpled shoulder.

I smiled sheepishly. That morning, when I'd looked in the mirror, I spied large black circles under my eyes. "With two, it's all hands on deck 24/7."

He chortled. "I know. My identical twin boys had me tied in knots. I'm not sure I've had a good night's rest since then, over forty years ago. Being a parent changes you. For the better, of course." His kind eyes put me at ease.

Dr. Winterspoon stood outside Dr. Marcel's office door and motioned that he needed to talk to my mentor.

"Good luck with your first class today, Lizzie. I know you'll be fine. Glad to have you officially on board."

"Thank you, sir. It's an honor."

His face broke into a grin. "No more *sir* business. Call me Frank. All the professors do." Dr. Marcel waddled toward his office and greeted Dr. Winterspoon with a handshake, ushering the American environmental historian into his office.

The main office overflowed with students, all badgering the three admins with a barrage of questions. I pirouetted through the crowd to my mailbox and flipped open a manila folder stuffed with papers I'd requested one of the admins print out for me. I glanced at the top copy of the syllabus, satisfied that it was ready for me to hand out at my ten o'clock class.

In my office, I slipped a navy blazer off a hook on the back of my door and put it on. Sarah and Maddie had insisted on a pantsuit for my first class of the semester. I grabbed my leather satchel, which contained my laptop and handwritten notes on the off chance my laptop failed at any point during the lecture.

The classroom was empty the hour prior to my teaching slot, allowing me to get accustomed to the technology and space. I didn't like to stay put behind a podium. I preferred to roam in the front, jotting dates and names on the whiteboard.

Unlike my teaching days during grad school, the class size was much smaller—only thirty students were enrolled in the history of the Weimar Republic. The room was one of the older, more neglected ones on campus. It was in the Animal Science building, and the lingering stench of embalming fluid or whatnot was testimony to what usually occurred in the labs. During my grad days, I'd taught in one of the larger lecture halls next door to the human anatomy room and could never help peeking at the cadavers, even though I told myself it was disrespectful. The brown carpet in today's small room had seen better days, and the walls were scuffed with random black marks. However, the podium had been recently installed, and the whiteboards behind and to the side gleamed. There were six rows with six desks in each row.

I plugged in my laptop and flipped through the PowerPoint slides, mentally ticking off all the points I wanted to make. My cell phone vibrated, and I read Sarah's text: *Good luck. I'm so proud of you!*

I dashed off a thank-you and asked whether the twins missed me and how she was doing. All I got back was a smiley face. I understood. She had her hands full, but I'd hoped for a bit more information. I didn't want to perpetuate the Petrie family misery by having a disconnect between my work and home life.

A handful of students strolled in, putting a halt to my parental worries. Probably a good thing since I was imagining things that hadn't happened.

Show time, Lizzie.

"Dr. Petrie?" A young woman with a timid smile approached. "I'm hoping I can register for your class even though it's full."

I nodded, expecting at least one last-minute student who was desperate to get some much-needed credits to graduate. "You're the first to ask. I can't make any promises, but I might be able to approve an override. If you can sit in on class today and Thursday, I'll do my best." I transcribed her details.

"Thank you, Dr. Petrie."

"Lizzie, please. Dr. Petrie is too clinical for my liking."

She laughed heartily, which bolstered my confidence, but deep down I knew she wanted one thing from me: three credits to graduate.

Moments later, the clock and more students in their seats indicated it was now or never. I said, "Welcome, everyone. Just to make sure, this is the History of the Weimar Republic. Everyone in the right room?" I scanned the thirty something individuals, noting only a few empty chairs. No one made a move. "Great. Let's get started."

The hour and fifteen minutes flew by, and the rush I normally experienced after a successful lecture flooded my body. It was good to be back.

Several students bum-rushed to the front, hoping to be first in line. The first few classes always required a little handholding before the routine settled in for the rest of the semester.

"Lizzie," called a student to my right.

"Lizzie," said another from my left.

"Lizzie," a student called from behind me.

I laughed. "Don't worry. I have time. Let's head to my office and see how I can help."

A gray-haired professor made his way to the podium to prepare for his class as my small troupe, now five strong, plodded outside with me. We made it to my office, three buildings down. I'd forgotten how youthful and energetic college students were. I was willing to bet none of them had three-week-old twins at home.

The thought of my two babes put extra pep in my step as well since I wanted to finish up early and be home by lunch, if possible.

Inside my office, I rubbed my hands together. "Who's first?"

They all jabbered at once.

I walked in the front room to find Sarah, Maddie, and the twins all there. Freddie slept in a roomy clay flowerpot, surrounded by roses and other blooms I couldn't name, and Ollie was napping in a red wagon that was stuffed with fresh daisies, fake bees, and butterflies.

I stopped in my tracks. "What's going on?"

"We're taking photos." Maddie held a brand-spanking-new Canon Rebel to her eye as she hovered over Freddie, clicking away.

Sarah, sitting on the floor and rubbing Ollie's back, smiled at me. "How was your first class?"

"Is he okay?" I motioned to Fred, who didn't seem that uncomfortable in the reddish pot, but I'd never napped in one myself, so what did I know?

"Nope. I'm allowing Maddie to torture my babies while I sit idly by." Her tone was teasing, but her eyes spoke the truth.

I threw my hands up. "Just checking." Leaning down, I kissed the top of Sarah's head. "My class went well, I think. It's been a long time, so who knows? Kids these days probably expect me to speak in hashtags and abbreviated text speak." I shrugged.

Maddie lowered her camera. "Hashtag Weimar history rocks."

I smiled. "Not sure I got that point across yet. Early days. And I may need to come up with a more believable tagline concerning the Weimar Republic, considering what it led to." I sank into the couch, resting my head against the back, eyes closed.

The couch cushion listed to the left, and I sensed Sarah straddling me. I reached out and put my hands on her ass right as the click of the camera snapped my eyes open. I was fondling Maddie.

"Shit, Maddie!"

She waved away my alarm. "Close your eyes like you were." She focused the camera, explaining why she was so up-close and personal.

"Don't they have lenses for close-ups? What are you photographing, anyway? My eyelashes?" I groaned, and craned my neck around her to gauge Sarah's reaction to my accidentally grabbing our best friend's ass.

Sarah, now cradling Freddie, shook her head with an absent smile that communicated *I haven't slept in days, so let's pretend that didn't happen.* "Maddie is taking a photography class. She wants to be the next Anne Geddes."

"Maybe next time Ms. Geddes could warn me when she climbs into my lap."

"You have no appreciation for art," Maddie said.

"You have no appreciation for personal space." I smooshed my eyes closed again.

"Poor Lizzie. Beat from teaching one class. How will you cope next semester when you're teaching two classes?"

"I'll cross that bridge when it comes." I yawned.

"Stop fidgeting." Maddie tapped my forehead with an ice-cold finger.

I complied, not for her benefit but out of sheer exhaustion. I'd had maybe three hours of sleep last night, an hour less than my new norm.

The peace was shattered by Ollie letting out a howler monkey screech. I shoved Maddie, and she laughed, still snapping photos as she rolled on her side on the couch. "Action photos. I love it!"

"It's okay, Ollie." I scooped my daughter into my arms. "I won't let Maddie torture you anymore." Sure enough, she stopped crying and settled into my arms. I eased into a leather chair across the room from the mad photographer and nuzzled Olivia onto my shoulder, all the while giving Maddie the stink eye. More than likely, Ollie's crying had nothing to do with Maddie, but my sleep-deprived brain wasn't completely operational.

Freddie started to fuss, so Sarah instinctively unbuttoned her shirt and helped him latch on to a nipple. "Ouch!" Her face contorted. "Take it easy, shark boy."

The click of Maddie's camera continued, but neither Sarah nor I said anything, resigned to her new hobby.

"Someday, you'll thank me for capturing these moments," Maddie crowed.

"What would we do without you?" I closed my eyes again.

"Well, aren't all of you a barrel of monkeys today?"

"Says the woman without two screaming infants to care for." Sarah laughed. "Oh, Lizzie, before I space out and forget this, my mom and Helen are coming for lunch on Sunday."

That grabbed my attention. "Your mom is friends with my father's mistress? When did that happen?"

"Helen isn't your father's mistress." Sarah's narrowed eyes didn't intimidate me.

"Only because my mom is dead. Who knows how long they carried on while Mom was alive?"

"Roughly twenty years," Maddie said.

"You've got to be joking." Ollie stirred in my arms, and I murmured, "Sorry, munchkin. Mommy will be quiet."

Maddie tapped her index finger against her thumb several times. In case I didn't understand the movement, she added, "Zip it."

"I think Helen's a lovely woman. Your father is a lucky man."

I flashed back to how they'd interacted at the hospital. They had seemed like a happy, loving couple, but I was still having a hard time accepting it at face value—unlike Sarah, who was so determined to be surrounded by family for the twins' sake that she was willing to stick her head in the sand.

Sarah stood. "Time for Freddie's nap."

I motioned that I'd follow with Ollie, but my wife shook her head. "She seems cozy with you. Me, I'm dying for a shower."

Maddie tagged along after her to the nursery.

I rubbed my cheek against the soft, sparse hair covering Olivia's head, inhaling her wonderful baby scent.

The *click, click* of Maddie's camera intruded on my quiet time with Ollie, and I sighed.

"Sarah wouldn't let me take photos of her in the shower," Maddie said. "I thought you'd appreciate them." She giggled. "She wants to wait until she's in better shape."

I would appreciate naked photos of my wife, but I'd rather take them myself. "Please tell me you didn't just try to photograph my wife in the shower."

She shrugged as if it was no big deal.

"Maybe we should discuss boundaries, if you plan to continue with photography."

"What do you mean *if* I continue?" Her tone was razor blade sharp.

I didn't have the energy to remind her about her cooking classes. "I'm only saying you can't take any opportunity to get a shot."

"I wonder if Annie Liebovitz faced this much hate when she started out?"

"Liebovitz? I thought you wanted to be Geddes."

"I don't want to be like anyone. I want people to associate me with my own art."

"May I make a suggestion?"

She nodded eagerly.

"Take after Ansel Adams. We have a few Aspen trees in the backyard you can start with. Work your way up to waterfalls."

"Why do I even talk to you?"

"I wonder that all the time." I winked at her. "How many classes have you had?"

"None. First class is this Saturday."

I laughed. "I wish half of my students were like you—doing homework before there's any homework to do."

"Photography is cool. History is in the past."

"Technically, you got the concept right."

She rolled her eyes. "How do you feel about Helen?"

I'd only met Dad's love interest once, but she was quickly inserting herself into my life. "For a mistress, she seems nice."

"I think you need to get out of that mindset. It's not fair to her."

I shook my head, careful not to wake Ollie. "How is it not fair? You're the one who said they'd been together for two decades. All that time, Dad was married to my mother."

"Who was a miserable woman." Maddie put up one palm and let the camera dangle around her neck on a strap. "Don't even try to convince me otherwise."

"I thought you'd feel differently about this."

"Why? Because Peter cheated on me?"

I nodded enthusiastically.

"Don't act so excited about it. Sometimes, I really wonder about you." The serene expression on her face said the opposite.

"I didn't mean it that way. I just meant I thought you'd be on my side."

"Your side? This isn't about taking sides. This is about life. About your parents' marriage. And let's face it; that wasn't on strong footing, even without the Helen factor."

"I never said my mom was pleasant or easy to get along with. But if he loved this other woman—?"

"Helen."

"This *Helen*. Why didn't he divorce Mom?"

"Life isn't always black and white."

"Like photography?" I joked.

She huffed. "Are you going to act like an adult now?"

"Is it so bad that your dad is marrying Helen?" Sarah returned, having showered and dressed in record time.

I stroked my chin. "I don't know how to answer that question."

"Charades? I'd love to see you act out your answer." Maddie waved for me to give it a go.

"You know, I think you missed your true calling. Stand-up comedian." I shifted Ollie's head into a more comfortable position.

"It's not too late for me. If one video goes viral on YouTube, I'll be rolling in it."

"I'm sure you can find a class. You've been a whiz at signing up for random things."

Ollie stirred in her sleep. I wanted to kiss her precious head, and I would have if I wasn't enjoying the peace and quiet so much. Someone once told me that the "lump" stage of babies was the best one.

Sarah sat at my feet, resting her hands and chin on my thighs. "They're so sweet when they're sleeping."

"That they are."

"What do you mean you don't know how to answer?" she whispered, ruining my hope that the conversation was over.

"That's exactly what I mean. I don't know how to answer."

"Methinks she's hedging." Maddie stared at me.

"How come Maddie can get away with things, but I can't?"

"Because you're avoiding the conversation." Sarah's expression dared me to rebut her claim.

I slumped further into my chair, careful not to jostle my daughter too much. "I don't know how to answer, because I truly don't know how I feel. Part of me thinks I should be outraged that my father cheated. Part of me doesn't give two shits, making me feel like the world's worst daughter. These polar opposites are swirling in my head. So when you ask me to explain, I can't."

"You're conflicted." Sarah cut to the heart of the matter.

"Very much. It'd kill me if you cheated. I didn't know Mom well, but my Spidey sense tells me she'd have been pissed."

"Spidey sense?" Maddie quirked a brow.

"Lizzie's been brushing up on lingo to communicate better with her students and with the babies." She waved a hand at Ollie. "So you want to begrudge your father his happiness because your mother would be pissed if he got married? Doesn't Charles deserve some happiness in his life?"

I massaged my forehead. "I don't begrudge him anything. I just don't know how to accept it without feeling like I'm betraying my own mother."

"Who hated you." Maddie took a stuffed bumblebee from the wheelbarrow and jabbed it into her chest.

"Nice action there." I smiled, and she mimed bowing in her chair.

"Hey, I'm as shocked as the rest of you," I added. "Mom doesn't conjure up many warm, cuddly feelings."

Sarah inhaled deeply. "I think you should sit down with your father and talk this over."

"Uh, no." I tried to sink even further into the chair.

"Why?" She tossed her hands up. "It's called communication. I know you and your therapist have been working on it for quite some time."

"With the people in my life. Dad isn't—"

Sarah's face immediately reddened, registering fury. "—a part of your life?"

I put a finger to my lips. "Steady. I wasn't going to say that." Maybe I was, but it was best to change course—fast! "Dad isn't the best at communication. If you think I'm quiet, he hasn't carried on a conversation since… ever."

Sarah bobbed her head to concede the point.

"But why didn't he divorce my mother? At least give her a shred of her dignity back."

"Why do you think it was your dad who didn't want a divorce? Have you forgotten what your mother was like?" Maddie boosted the strap over her head and placed the camera on the coffee table.

"I'll never be able to forget what she was like." I rubbed Ollie's cheek.

"Exactly." Maddie leaned back on the couch. "You're asking questions that only one person can answer, and if I know Charles at all, he'll take his secrets to the grave unless you ask him."

"Not all of them. He plans to marry one."

Sarah glanced at the baby monitor on the side table. Freddie was making cooing sounds, but he wasn't completely awake.

Sarah squeezed my leg. "I understand this must be hard. I do. But your reaction scares me some."

"Why would disgust at my father cheating on my mother scare you? Shouldn't it make you feel secure?"

Freddie belted out a primal scream that made all three of us turn toward the baby monitor.

Maddie hopped up. "I'll check on him."

"Thanks," Sarah said, watching as Maddie disappeared up the staircase. When she turned back to me, she shook her head sadly. "It's not that. It's how you act when people make mistakes. Humans aren't perfect. Sometimes we have to remember to judge a person not by what they've done but by how they recover from their mistakes." Her eyes lingered on Ollie, still sleeping in the crook of my arm. "It's easy to write off a person when they've disappointed us. Accepting people as they are takes love, patience, and forgiveness. But you already know that. I've forgiven your mistakes, and you've forgiven mine. I just wish you could use what you've learned in therapy and extend it to your father. You only have one—you're lucky he's still around." Her eyes were moist. "I wish my father could have met our children."

I reached for her hand. "I know, sweetheart. He would be so proud of you. You're a wonderful woman, wife, mother, teacher, and all-round great person with such a big heart." I sighed. "I'll try to come around and fast. I promise."

"I know you will. You're stubborn, and I tease you all the time about being an idiot when it comes to relationships, but you really are amazing, Lizzie. Let others see what I know. Let more people into the inner sanctum."

We laughed, both relieved the conversation had ended on a positive note. It was the most we'd said to each other since the twins' birth.

Olivia wriggled and rubbed an eye with one small fist.

"Lunchtime, sweet girl?" Sarah lifted Ollie from my arms, letting her gaze rest on my face for a brief moment.

"Well, that was the most disgusting diaper I've ever changed," Maddie said, still rubbing sanitizing lotion into her hands. "What are you feeding him?" Nodding at Ollie, who was now firmly attached to Sarah's breast, she added, "I don't recommend sucking on Sarah's nipples anytime soon. You'll be on the shitter for days."

My mouth fell open.

Sarah grinned. "After having these little sharks feed on me every hour, I don't think I'll ever let anyone so much as look at my breasts. I've never felt sorry for cows before. Now I doubt I'll ever drink another glass of milk. This is inhumane." She lovingly brushed the top of Ollie's head, blunting her criticism of breastfeeding.

Maddie's cell buzzed. She inspected the screen and then stashed it to the side, disappointed.

"Not who you wanted?"

"Just Kit inviting me for drinks later."

"How's that situation going?" Sarah asked.

"About as you two suspected, I think."

"And how's that?"

"Miserable. Not sure how much longer I can stand it."

CHAPTER TWELVE

SATURDAY MORNING, SARAH STAGGERED INTO THE KITCHEN, HER HAIR ASKEW. Even the bags under her eyes had bags. "Why in the world did we have twins?"

"Seemed too cruel to cull the herd when they were still inside." I pushed a cup of herbal tea across the kitchen island to her as she plunked herself down on a barstool and supported her head on her hands.

"If you had to choose to put one up for adoption, which would it be?"

I clamped my mouth shut. Sarah was beyond exhausted, but once some life started to coarse through her weary body, it was possible she'd make me pay for answering honestly. "I'm going to get the paper."

"Coward," she called after me.

Birds twittered outside, our quiet street serenely tranquil so early in the morning despite the chill that hung in the air. The cold worked its way through my lungs, perking me up even more than my cup of chai had. Placing my hands on my hips, I tilted my face to the low-hanging sun, soaking in the vastness of nothing. No crying babies. No whining spouse. No students. No administrative assistant shrieking that getting thirty-five copies of a handout by the following morning was impossible. Just me and the stillness.

Fuck, I felt alive. Happy. But I didn't want to leave Sarah alone for too long with the twinkies.

I strolled down the end of the drive to collect my paper, still enchanted by the calm—until I saw the puddle under my paper. While Sarah and I had recently welcomed twins, George from across the street had brought home an adorable Yorkie. Seriously, the thing could fit into the palm of my hand. How could such a tiny creature create such a massive puddle of piss? And why on my newspaper?

I plucked the paper up by a corner, hoping I could salvage some sections. Alas, it was hopeless. With a groan, I let the pee-soaked newsprint splatter to the ground.

The exhaustion that had been welling in the pit of my stomach exploded into rage. "Goddammit, Gandhi! I'm going to kill you, ya little rat bastard!"

Betty, the old woman from next door, had slipped outside, ninja-like, and gasped at my outburst.

As my own words hit me, I wondered why George had named his Yorkie Gandhi.

I waved awkwardly to Betty, who was still clutching her chest as if Satan himself had said hello.

"And I thought I was being unreasonable this morning." Sarah stood on our front stoop with Freddie on her hip.

"That damn dog pissed on my paper. Again." From the look of amusement on Sarah's face, my defense was flimsy.

George had been the first neighbor to officially welcome our children to the Whipple Street club. The curtain in his front room shifted an inch. "Shit. He heard."

"I think the astronauts in space heard you. Honestly, I didn't know you had it in you." She flicked her head, beckoning me back indoors before I could cause more trouble.

"I didn't mean… I mean, I'm not happy about the paper, but I didn't mean… I'm just so tired."

"Spit it out." Sarah's smile irked me. "Gandhi got your tongue?"

I cringed.

Fortunately, Ollie wailed, and I trudged upstairs to the nursery. More than likely, Sarah was already concocting a plan for me to apologize to George. Hopefully, I didn't have to apologize to Betty, who was sweet as pie, too. Just the thought made me nervous. No one was that sweet, unless she was a brilliant psychopath.

By the time I'd changed Ollie and taken her downstairs, Sarah had buckled Freddie into his bouncer and opened the *New York Times* on her iPad for me to read. "Maybe if you read the newspaper on the iPad, we could avoid having neighbor issues."

"I like the feel of newsprint. What can I say?"

"More than I think you should. Shall I refresh your memory about what occurred less than ten minutes ago?" She sipped her tea, which was surely tepid by now. "I think a gift basket will do the trick."

"He's diabetic." I bounced Ollie on my hip.

"No. A basket full of dog toys. You didn't threaten to kill George, just Gandhi—the only thing he has in his lonely life. The man's wife hasn't been in the ground for a year yet."

I put up one palm. "Please stop. I feel bad enough."

Sarah turned to Freddie. "You see, Fred. This is what happens when you and your sister don't let us sleep. Now I have to spend the morning shopping for a gift basket for a dog that's a third of your size." Freddie cooed at Sarah as if he'd understood everything she said. Ollie, on the other hand, spit up on my shirt.

"Can you order me some more T-shirts?" I asked.

"We have a washing machine. Why do you insist on tossing out every shirt that gets a little puke on it?"

I whirled around to show her the damage. "You call that a little puke? You gave birth to the exorcist child."

"Come here, baby girl." Sarah held her arms out. "You should shower." She nodded for me to take my leave while I could.

———————

Ethan sat at a table for two in the coffee shop of Barnes & Noble, his eyes on the door. "Well, look what the cat dragged in."

I rubbernecked over my shoulder.

"Nice try. You look like shit." His grin was a weak attempt to camouflage his *I told you babies had a way of running even the most organized person ragged* expression.

"Thanks, buddy. How are you?"

"One thousand percent better than you. Have you slept at all since bringing the poop machines home?"

"Sleeping? What's that?" I drummed my fingers on the table, and then added in a robot voice, "Does not compute."

He chuckled. "I don't miss the first year. It does get easier, though." He shifted in his chair. "Okay, not easier, but you'll start sleeping again in about"—he glanced at his bare wrist—"seven months."

"That's one of the things I love about you. You always keep it real." I eyed the six-person line at the register and exhaled in frustration, my breath rustling the loose strands of hair around my face. "You know, I had this foolish notion that because I've suffered insomnia since high school I wouldn't be affected by sleep deprivation. That I'd be used to being exhausted." I leaned over the table. "I had no fucking clue what I was getting into."

He broke into a belly laugh. "So, all the alarms on your fancy sports watch aren't helping?" He paused. "Trust me. No one knows what it's like being a parent until they become one."

The line at the register shortened. "What can I get you?" I asked him.

"My usual, please."

Several moments later, I returned to the table with his regular cup of joe, fresh fruit, and a new concoction I hadn't tried before.

Ethan set his book down and peered at my espresso con panna, which came in a fancy clear coffee glass. "No chai today?"

"I thought I'd try an espresso. Knock the cobwebs out of my head." I tapped my temple. "The dude suggested this as an introduction for espresso virgins. The dollop of whipped cream is supposed to make it more palatable."

"That's so like you, to jump into a hardcore drink after drinking a wimpy one for years. This I can't wait to see." He steepled his fingertips together.

"Geez, you make it sound like I've only ever had chai."

"I've never seen you drink coffee. Black tea, yes. But espresso—no way. Not even in grad school when you pulled all-nighters all the time." His eyes widened, and a slight smile twisted his lips. "Go on. Wait…" He fished his phone from his pocket and held it with both hands. "Now, go."

Cautiously, I elevated the harsh smelling drink to my lips. I hesitated.

"You can do it," Ethan urged.

"Um…"

"Don't overthink it." His expression tried to convey support.

"Fine. Here goes nothing." I sipped it, immediately spitting the vile fluid into a napkin. "Oh my God! That's hideous!" The barista had tried to talk me into a latte, but I'd been adamant I needed more kick.

Ethan's shoulders shook with laughter, but he never lowered the phone. His cell bounced up and down as his body jiggled. "Try it again, now that the shock has worn off."

I did, with nearly the same result. At least I was able to forcefully swallow this time.

Several people turned, their mouths hanging open as Ethan panned to the crowd.

"Enjoying yourself?" I wiped my tongue with the napkin and popped two grapes into my mouth in a weak attempt to extinguish the taste.

"Oh, yes!" He continued filming. "Children, animals, and idiots make the best YouTube videos." He winked.

I dumped two packets of raw sugar into the drink and motioned for him to put the camera away.

"No way. Come on. Give it another try."

I really didn't want to. But neither did I want to throw out a drink I'd already paid for. The third sip wasn't as bad.

"It's like beer, really. Takes some getting used to." Ethan tucked his phone away now that my antics had subsided. "You might want to keep trying though, just in case Sarah ever decides to have another kid."

For a moment, I stopped breathing.

Ethan palm-slapped his forehead. "Damn, I put the camera away too soon. Your face right now is priceless."

"I think my heart stopped." I took a healthy slug of the still bitter liquid.

"Shall I get you another?"

His jovial tone annoyed me. "A chai would be great."

He groaned as he stood to get in line. "Wimp!" he sniped over his shoulder.

"That's rich coming from the man who orders the same drink every single time. At least I'm trying new things."

"How's it working out for you?" He stepped up to the cashier, not bothering to wait for a reply.

I continued to sip the espresso. Although both Sarah and I had trust funds and I now had a part-time job, I was racked with financial worries. Babies were expensive. They were growing so quickly that half their clothes would only fit for a few more weeks. Sarah and Maddie kept insisting on buying cute little shoes to complement every outfit, never mind that they were babies and neither of them could walk, rendering the shoes useless.

"Here you go." Ethan plopped the chai down on the table.

"Shall we find a quiet spot behind a stack of books?" The café was tucked in the front of the store, by the magazine racks, and the noise from customers and registers rattled my overwrought nerves.

"What? This isn't romantic enough for you?" He gestured to the overall messiness of the jostling crowd.

I motioned for him to grab his drink. "Come on. There's usually a few chairs in the home improvement section."

Sure enough, we located four empty chairs and a small table.

I collapsed into a seat and immediately took a long sip of my chai. "You're the best BFF ever." I chugged the scorching liquid again to nullify the lingering taste of espresso and chased that with an apple slice.

"BFF? Text speech? You must be delusional. Soon you'll know what AYSOS stands for?"

I took a stab in the dark. "Ah! You! Help!"

He laughed. "Not quite. Try: *Are you stupid or something*?"

"You've been keeping that one in your back pocket, haven't you?"

He grinned sheepishly. "Maybe."

"Sometimes I think my only reason for existence on this planet is for my friends' amusement."

"It's not your sole purpose. You're teaching again, remember?"

"And changing diapers."

Ethan pinched his nose and waved a hand. "Oh, I don't miss that stage at all."

Sarah appeared around the corner, pushing the twins in a stroller. "I thought I'd find you here."

"Where are Lisa and Casey?" I asked.

"Still attending story time. Ollie started to get fussy." Setting one hand on the stroller, she rocked it back and forth.

I peered inside. "She's sleeping now."

"She settled down as soon as we left. Now I'll never know what happens to Pete the Cat and his white shoes." Sarah shrugged, clearly unperturbed by the mystery. "How are you, Ethan?"

"Better than Lizzie. Check this out?" He retrieved his phone and played the video of my espresso taste test.

Sarah covered her mouth. "Oh, my. Can you send me this?" She turned to me, shaking her head. "You didn't know you'd hate espresso?"

"Never had it before." I tossed my hands up.

"Such a waste of delicious caffeine. I'd kill for a cup. Or even a good whiff."

"I can buy another and let you sniff it all day, if you'd like." Caffeine was allowed for nursing mothers within moderation, but Sarah had been avoiding it at all costs in case it kept the babies awake.

"You would do that?"

"For the mother of my children, yes." I stood up. "Shall I get Lisa and Casey something?"

"Nah. They have to head out right after for dance class. It's ballet this month. We came in separate cars."

I returned with an espresso for Sarah, another plain coffee for Ethan, and a steaming chai. "I think the government should pass a law making caffeine free for parents."

"Geez, too many people who should never have kids already make too many. Don't add to over population by tempting caffeine junkies." Ethan stirred in white sugar.

Sarah held her espresso under her nose, inhaling deeply.

"Go on, have some. Heidi Murkoff says it's okay in moderation." I encouraged Sarah to take a sip.

"She does?" Sarah's eyes grew sevenfold.

"Yes. I can grab a copy of *What to Expect When You're Expecting* if you don't believe me."

"Oh, I believe. I'm so fucking tired I'd believe it if you told me you were descended from alien leprechauns."

Ethan cocked his head. "That would explain some things."

"Hardy har har, Ethan." I turned to Sarah. "Did you know you can eat up to five hundred calories more a day because you burn that much breastfeeding?"

"But I'm feeding two. Does that mean I'm burning a thousand calories?"

I rubbed my chin. "Logically, that makes sense."

"But illogically?" Ethan pitched an eyebrow over his black-framed glasses.

"I don't remember reading that it automatically doubled."

"And if it's not completely black and white, Lizzie doesn't understand." Sarah grinned.

I shook a stuffed giraffe in Freddie's face. Ollie was still out cold; otherwise we'd be hightailing it out of the shop. Freddie observed wide-eyed, with curious caution. He clearly took after me. "I'll do more research for you."

"If I asked you to research what a hippo fart smells like, would you?" Sarah crinkled her nose, and I wondered if she did so subconsciously.

"I think we can only accept firsthand observation." Ethan's sincere expression failed to mask his derision.

"All right. As much as I'm enjoying bantering with adults, I think we should get to the heart of the matter. I'm guessing we have about twenty minutes before Olivia wakes up." I nodded to Sarah to get the ball rolling. Today's meet-up was always intended to be more than a casual chat.

Sarah stared, as if wondering why I had to mention that, but she seemed to accept it was best since these kinds of conversations were difficult for me.

"Lizzie and I have been talking about the twins, what would happen to them if—"

Ethan teetered forward in his chair. "You're not sick, are you?"

"Oh, no. Unless you count sleep deprivation, we're in great shape. We just want to know that if something does happen, our kiddos will be taken care of. My mom is getting up there in years, and Lizzie's family—"

"Is in a class of its own," I let fly.

Sarah frowned at me. "We've talked with Maddie, and she's game, but you know Lizzie, she likes to have a back-up plan for every back-up plan, and I would too in this case." She stopped to smile at our twins.

At the moment, they weren't a handful. But when they awoke, all bets were off. "Would you also be willing to help out with the kids if we... weren't around?" I asked.

Ethan stared open-mouthed at Sarah and then at me. "Really?"

"If it's too much—"

Ethan waved Sarah off and rested his hand over his heart. "No, I'm honored, and I know Lisa would feel the same way. Why, Lizzie, I didn't know you trusted me this much."

"I don't. We just don't have many options." I winked at him.

"Don't listen to her." Sarah's tight smile chided me.

"I never do." Ethan swiped at one eye with his index finger.

They laughed together, and I feigned being offended. I couldn't put my finger on exactly when my wife and best friend had become so friendly. They even texted on a daily basis now. Ethan rarely texted me—albeit I abhorred texting, but still.

A wail from Olivia quieted their merriment.

Sarah sighed. "Give her to me."

Before she could undo her top, I said, "Why don't we take them outside? Fresh air helps with digestion, I hear."

"Walking outside after eating helps with digestion." With one hand, she motioned for me to hand her over, while her other freed one of her massive breasts.

I reluctantly handed Ollie over and then pulled Freddie onto my lap.

Ethan gawped. He was clearly surprised Sarah intended to feed Ollie right there in the store.

An older man and woman moseyed by, the woman tutting after taking her sweet time to get an eyeful of my wife's bosom. She whispered something unintelligible to her companion. It was hard to decipher whether she was more outraged by Sarah's exposed boob, even covered with a muslin blanket in a weak attempt to provide privacy, or her decrepit husband's leer. Ethan, squirming in his seat, flipped the woman the bird behind her back. It seemed like a futile gesture, but Sarah seemed to appreciate it.

I bobbed a happily cooing Freddie on my lap while Ethan rattled the giraffe in his direction. Freddie's tiny arms flailed above his head. "I'm certain he's inherited my sporting skills, or lack thereof."

"Hey, you're lucky. Casey is a whiz at dance, basketball, soccer, and God knows what else. Lisa and I are constantly taking turns ferrying her to one activity after another." He motioned he wanted to hold Fred.

After a while, Sarah buttoned up her shirt and handed Ollie back to me. "I'll be right back." She made a beeline for the bathroom.

"Feeling better, Ollie?" I followed, pursing my lips and making baby sounds I'd previously sworn I'd never make, not even for my own child.

"Motherhood has made you soft. Isn't that right, Fred? She's a softie woftie. Yes, she is."

"Because you're the paragon of manhood."

Ethan stuck out his tongue. "Whatever."

I leaned back in the chair, positioning Ollie sideways on my lap in an attempt to get her to burp. I patted her back, working up and down. Occasionally, I mixed it up by rubbing her back the way the nurse had shown me.

"I always had more luck with the over-the-shoulder method. Don't forget the burping cloth, though."

"I always forget that. You have no idea how many shirts and pants I've thrown away in the last few weeks." I reached into the diaper bag hanging on the back of the double-wide stroller.

"You actually throw clothes away when your baby spits up? All this time you've been teasing me about my dislike of fluids, and you're worse than I am."

"At least I like sex."

He scrunched up his face. The older couple returned just in time to overhear that nugget. The woman didn't tut this time, but the look of horror on her face was priceless. Served her right for getting worked up about Sarah breastfeeding our child in public.

Ethan waited for them to totter out of range. "Do you still like it after—?"

"After?" Of course Sarah and I hadn't had sex since the births. She was still sore, and neither of us had any extra energy to expend.

"After seeing—you know, the babies, blood, and..." He pantomimed etcetera with a grossed-out look on his face.

The experience would be hard to erase from my memory bank, not that I would admit that aloud—not even to my best friend, who'd just agreed to be a father to our children in case I wasn't around. "Oh, that. It's completely natural." I stood, placed the cloth on my left shoulder, and repositioned Ollie.

"That's it. Pat her a bit more." He stood, rocking Freddie in his arms. "Yeah, like that. So tell me the truth. Have you felt like getting your groove back on with Sarah?" He fixed his eyes on mine. "I know it's hard for some."

I glanced over my shoulder. Sarah was nowhere in sight. "It's different now, somehow. Besides being exhausted, I keep getting visions of—it was like a war zone."

Ethan nodded thoughtfully. "Just so you know, Sarah's talked about it with Maddie, who in turn told me."

I knew Sarah had been worried about that before the births: that I'd place her solely in the mom box. "What should I do?"

"You're asking me?" He grinned. "The deed. Do the deed. Trust me; it won't be bad."

"How am I supposed to trust you when it comes to sex?"

"You know what they say… Those who can, do; those who can't, teach."

Ollie spat up.

"Ah, perfect timing." Sarah took our daughter from my arms and secured her in the stroller. "Time to roll."

Ethan caught my eye. I had a feeling he was still communicating what we'd been discussing.

Time to roll… in the hay.

— Chapter Thirteen —

"Helen, would you like a cup of coffee?" Rose stood next to the dining room table, waiting for an answer. "We have a lovely lemon sponge cake for dessert."

"Yes, please."

Sarah followed her mom to the kitchen, leaving me alone with Helen. We didn't dine often in the formal room. The mahogany dining set, antique hutch along the back wall, fringed Oriental rug on dark hardwood floors, crystal chandelier, and cinnabar walls made me uncomfortable in my own skin. Sarah was well aware of my feelings, but this was the first time we'd hosted my future stepmother, and her desire to welcome Helen properly usurped my dislike of formality. Also, I showed no interest in decorating, so in her book, I didn't have any room to complain.

Helen eyed me from across the table, her head tilted expectantly.

"So…" I started and quickly faltered.

She reached over and patted my hand. "I know this must be awkward, to say the least. Cap—"

"Cap?" I interjected.

"Oh, that's what I call your father." She smiled innocently.

Cap—his initials Charles Allen Petrie. Never in my life had I heard anyone call my father anything other than Charles. For two decades, my father had been involved with this woman, and she had an endearing nickname for him. Puzzle pieces in my head started to click together, initiating a wave of queasiness.

"Coffee's on." Sarah and Rose breezed back into the room.

Sarah placed a tender hand on my shoulder before retaking her seat. "Mom was telling me about your shop, Helen. I have a mania for fresh flowers."

Helen nodded. "Yes, I've been fortunate to survive. Not many florists made it through the Great Recession."

"Our friend Maddie had a tough go of it with her design business. It's slowly coming back to life."

"Maddie—she was at the hospital?" Her voice hitched at the end as if she was asking a question she already knew the answer to. Had she met Maddie before then? Surely she had heard the name from my father.

"She used to be engaged to Peter."

Helen glanced down at her laced fingers on the table. "That's right. I remember the name."

The temperature in the room seemed to have dropped several degrees.

"How long have you owned the shop?" Rose shifted in her seat, blocking me from her view.

"Oh, gosh. Almost thirty years."

Was that how she'd met my father? Did he hop into the store to buy my mother flowers and… boom? Love at first sight? I wanted to ask, but I wasn't sure it was the right time to put her on the spot. Also, how would I handle knowing the whole story?

"According to your website, you have a branch here."

Was Rose conducting a job interview: position Lizzie's new mother? What was next? *So, Helen, tell us in three words why you'd make a good mother for Lizzie, who, according to all who know her, is special.*

"Really?" Sarah said much too enthusiastically. "I'll need to put in a standing order. Do you deliver?"

"We do. My son—" Her voice stilled, along with my heart.

"I didn't know you had a son," Rose said, clearly not jumping to the conclusion I had leapt to. Judging by Sarah's fingers gouging into my thigh, my wife had as well. "How old is he?"

"Twenty-eight. He's working on his MBA. He has grand plans of becoming like Amazon, but in the flower world. Although, right now we own shops only in Denver, Boulder, and here."

Rose laughed, and I exhaled my first breath since hearing Helen had a child. If Maddie was right, my father and Helen had been together a little over twenty years, not twenty-nine, which meant her son wasn't my half brother.

"Do you have any other children?" Rose asked, oblivious to the tension hanging in the air.

The color instantly disappeared from Helen's face.

Realization must have crashed into Rose's mind, because she puffed out an apologetic sigh.

Helen studied me carefully. "I have another son who's graduating from high school this spring."

No one spoke. Not a sound could be heard. Not even the birds outside the three-paned window squawked.

"Would you excuse me?" I stood and discarded my napkin on the tablecloth. "I think I hear the twins fussing in the nursery."

I sank onto the third step of the staircase, out of view of the infernal dining room. My vision blurred, and my breathing grew rapid, like I'd just run up and down the staircase for an hour.

Sarah stuck her head around the corner and approached cautiously.

"Not now." I shook my head. "Please, not now."

She eyed me before agreeing with a nod. Then she sat next to me quietly, one arm draped around my shoulder.

Moments later, she said, "I should get back. Do you—?"

I cut her off with a vehement headshake.

Much to my surprise, Sarah didn't drag me kicking and screaming back in there.

Hours later, my wife found me in my library, sitting on a cushion in the bay window. Twilight settled along the horizon, tingeing the sky over the foothills a purplish gray.

"Would you like a drink?" She motioned to the bar.

"Do I need one?"

"After that bombshell, I'm surprised you aren't already snockered." She laughed and half-heartedly added, "Of course, it hasn't been confirmed that you have a half brother." Without waiting for my reply, she prepared a gin and tonic, thrusting it into my hands as she took a seat next to me in the window.

I sipped the fizzing concoction, not tasting a thing. "I don't know how, but I feel it in my bones that he's my brother."

"Want to talk about it?"

I was surprised she was giving me the option. "Nope."

She smiled her smile that meant she'd only give me a reprieve for so long.

"Mom feels awful."

I took another tug of my drink.

"To find out that way—she didn't mean it."

Hank wandered in, meowing, and jumped between us with his back arched. Sarah drew a hand away to stroke his shiny black fur, head to tail.

I waggled his tail. "How would it have been better to deliver the news?"

Sarah's eyes went blank, and she shrugged.

"I mean, for twenty something years my father carried on with this woman—and that's been enough for me to adjust to—and now I find out they had a child together."

"Allen."

I sucked in a breath. "He has my father's middle name?"

"Yes."

I shrouded my eyes with one palm. "Jesus. Am I wrong in thinking you don't name a son after you when it's with a mistress? You do that with a woman you love. How am I supposed to process all of this? I'm not equipped—"

Hank kneaded my thigh with his paws.

Sarah waited patiently in the darkening room.

I glanced out the window. "I don't even know what to think, what to say. My father had two families—and from the looks of it, I got the short end of the stick when it came to mothers. Helen's a sweet lady who owns a flower shop, for Christ's sake. My mother—" The back of my throat tingled, and I swigged my gin and tonic. "Why did I deserve that? Deserve her?"

Sarah remained quiet.

"And not only that, I feel guilty as fuck for wishing I had a mom like Helen, rather than the Scotch-lady who tormented me from the moment I made my appearance in this oh-so-wonderful world." I slumped against the window. "I'm going to be in therapy until I'm eighty."

One of the twins cried out, and I started to get up.

"Stay here," Sarah said, patting my thigh. "I got it."

Hank followed her out of the room.

The purplish light turned inky black, and an odd sensation overcame me and forced me into action. I stopped briefly in the kitchen to pour the contents of my gin and tonic down the drain.

Next stop, the nursery.

When I stepped into the room, Freddie, still in his crib, squirmed happily. "Hey there, little man." I scooped him into my arms.

Sarah was rocking Olivia, smiling. "Shall we order Chinese for dinner?"

"Do you think they're ready for Moo Shu Pork?" I raised Fred over my head. "Do you want a Pu Pu Platter?" He didn't giggle, but his face radiated happiness.

"I'm so hungry, I could probably eat poo." Sarah stood and patted Ollie on the back to burp the eating machine. "You feeling better?"

I cradled Freddie to my chest. "TBD. I just didn't want to miss this."

"So I shouldn't invite Helen, your father, and her two sons for dinner just yet?" Her eyes twinkled.

"By all means. The twins and I can stay in a hotel."

"A night alone. That idea isn't half-baked." She bumped me with her hip.

"Come on, dear. Let's get some food in you before you really do eat…" I couldn't reference poo aloud. The neat freak in me stopped that conversation cold.

"I feel like we're drowning in shit—literally and figuratively." Sarah wasn't kidding.

— Chapter Fourteen —

"Elizabeth." Peter's voice drifted out of the speaker on my cell phone and made my stomach shudder.

"Peter. What's up?" I glanced at the clock on my nightstand. It was a little after eight on Monday night.

"Uh… do you have time for lunch on Friday? I was hoping we could talk about *things*."

Was *things* code for Dad and Helen?

"I do, if you make the trip up here." This was an interesting turn of events. Peter and I never met privately for lunch.

A clicking sound on the other end of the line suggested he was checking his calendar. "Friday, say around two?"

"Sounds good. Come by the house. I'll order in. Would you prefer sandwiches or pizza? Or something fancier?"

"Pizza is fine."

"Is Tie coming?"

He sucked in a lungful of air. "She can't make it, unfortunately."

"Too bad. I'll see ya Friday."

The phone went dead.

Sarah breezed into our bedroom, wearing pajamas she'd lived in for three days straight. "Who was that?" She settled under the covers and rested her head on my shoulder.

Holding her close, I replied. "My brother. He's coming over for lunch on Friday to discuss things."

Sarah remained quiet for a moment, much to my shock. I peeked to see if she'd fallen asleep, which was not unusual these days, but she met my eyes. "Hell's frozen over."

I laughed. "Lately, you've been full of one-liners."

"I'm too tired to form complete thoughts. It's easier to steal a line or cliché to communicate." Her eyes wandered to the baby monitors. Freddie wiggled on his bed, but he didn't need attention. "What do you think Peter wants? Do you think he's learned about Allen?"

"Who knows? My gut is telling me it's about Dad's November wedding, considering the invitation we received in the mail today."

"Weddings do bring families together." She slipped her hand under my shirt and tweaked my nipple.

I kissed the top of her head. "Hmmm… I think just as many, if not more, have torn families apart. History—"

One of the twins squealed.

"Saved again." I wiggled out from under Sarah, relieved. "My turn."

"I need to start adding a dollar to their college fund every time one of them saves me from a history lecture." She yawned. "Ivy league schools aren't cheap."

"So funny. Get some rest. The next shift is T minus forty-five minutes." I tapped my watch.

She groaned and smothered her head with a pillow.

That Friday, ten minutes before two, my cell phone rang. I pounced on the phone, motioning for Sarah to pay up. We'd made a bet whether or not Peter would actually show for lunch.

"Elizabeth?"

"What's up, Peter?" I couldn't keep the smile out of my tone.

"I can't remember which house is yours, and I neglected to add you to my contacts."

Crestfallen about losing the bet, I handed the crisp five-dollar bill back to Sarah. "1815."

"See you soon." He disconnected.

Sarah clapped her hands together, attracting both of the twins' attention. "Mommy made money."

Ollie reached out a hand.

"Yes, get used to that. Your other mommy is horrible at bets. You can supplement your income by betting with her. And here's a tip—she's so competitive, she'll make bets on anything."

Both twins sat in their individual monkey chairs on the kitchen island.

I placed my cell phone down on the counter. "Are you teaching our children to take advantage of me?"

She nodded. "Someone has to."

"Are you serious? It seems like every time I blink, someone wants me to pay for something. My debit card hasn't gotten this much action ever."

"At least something is getting action."

"Hey, now. These"—I motioned to Olivia and Freddie —"were your idea. Don't blame me if we're exhausted. When's the last time you showered?"

She tapped her chin. "Yesterday, maybe. Is that why we haven't had sex? The doctor has cleared me for action."

I covered Freddie's ears.

"What about Ollie?" Sarah asked.

"Oh, it's clear she takes after you."

"What does that mean?" She crossed her arms.

"Ten bucks I don't have to explain."

Sarah put her hand out. "You see, Ollie. That's how it's done."

"You see, Freddie. That's how you wiggle out of a conversation with a woman."

The doorbell rang. "Ten bucks it's Mom," Sarah said.

"Nah. It's the pizza for Peter."

Both of us were wrong. Peter stood in a three-piece suit on my front stoop, squirming in his custom-made Italian shoes. "I thought for sure you'd just left Denver."

"I'm never late, not even for inconsequential appointments."

"Glad to know where I stand." I waved him inside. "Come into the kitchen and see your niece and nephew."

His expression wasn't receptive, which was why I didn't give him a chance to refuse.

"Peter. How was your drive up?" Sarah gave him a hug.

Peter eyeballed her pajamas and robe, casually conferring with his Rolex. "Fine. How are you and the babies?"

Sarah smiled. "Best not to ask." She turned to me. "I'm going to hop in the shower. Let Mom in for me, please."

"Of course." I kissed her cheek. "Take your time. There are two of us."

She beamed. "I might do that. What a luxury to have a shower that lasts longer than sixty seconds."

"Two?" Peter scanned the kitchen for another adult.

"It's okay. You aren't afraid of a baby, are you? You might want to take off your jacket and vest, though. They tend to spit up more regularly than Old Faithful."

He flinched, removing his layers and rolling up his shirtsleeves.

"Sarah and her mom will be heading out soon, so we'll be hanging out with the twins. We wanted to give them a chance to see you." I relished his look of revulsion, which he tried to bury with a nod and a forced smile.

"Hello!" Rose called from the front of the house.

"In the kitchen with the twinkies," I answered.

"Where are they?" Rose entered the room, nearly stopping dead when she saw Peter's perfectly styled hair and expensive suit, sans jacket and vest. "Hello, Peter. How are you?" Her tone could refreeze glaciers that had melted centuries ago.

"I'm well. You?" He put a hand out to shake, business-like. And Sarah thought I was the awkward one in the family.

She nodded, in Rose fashion, causing Peter to glance at me out of the corner of his eye. It was oddly reassuring to see him uncomfortable in his skin.

"There they are." Rose squealed and made gobbling sounds as she pretended to eat one of Freddie's bare feet. Freddie wriggled in his rocker, loving every second. Ollie demanded she be included in the game by letting out a loud wail. Rose repeated the performance with my daughter. "Is Sarah ready?"

"Not by a long shot. She just went upstairs to shower. Can I fix you something to drink?"

"Tea would be lovely." Rose unclipped Ollie and cradled her close. "How's the big bad world of finance treating you, Peter?"

Since I wasn't the one in the hot seat, I admired Rose's carefully crafted expression, which simultaneously showed interest and condemnation. Sarah had the same touch, but she hadn't reached Rose's mastery—not yet at least.

Peter ran a hand over his hair, careful not to rustle his "do" too much. "Okay."

Just okay? Usually he loved to opine about how hard it was to be a slimy robber baron.

Rose's eyes widened, no doubt taking note. "Trouble?"

"What? Oh, no." He waved a diffident hand.

The teakettle whistled, much to Fred's dismay, and he wailed. "Peter, would you mind holding him?" I asked as I poured hot water into a china cup.

Peter stared at me as if I'd just asked him to eat a live scorpion, tail first.

"Here, take Ollie. I'll get Freddie." Rose handed my innocent daughter straight into the viper's arms.

Peter's eyes narrowed, and his arms were stiff.

"Go on, cuddle her to your chest and rock on your feet. Like this." She demonstrated with a red-faced Fred, who started to settle. Unlike his sister, his moods shifted quickly once in someone's arms. Ollie was the terror of the two.

Peter followed her lead, Herman Munster-like, but Ollie didn't seem to mind. Spit bubbles burbled from her lips, dampening his blue and white striped shirt. Inwardly, I smiled.

"Hi, Mom." Sarah pranced in, fresh as a daisy, her hair still slightly wet.

Peter's face shone with relief… until he realized Sarah didn't plan on rescuing him.

"Can you make the tea to go?" Rose's smile conveyed it wasn't a request.

"Of course." I poured her tea into a travel mug. "Would you like one to go as well, sweetheart?"

Sarah nodded.

It wasn't long before the two of them skedaddled, leaving me alone with Peter and the twins.

"Is Sarah's mom always—?"

"Yes." I cut him off.

"You're a better ma—person than I am. How do you put up with her snootiness?"

That was rich coming from my brother. "Years of practice."

His face remained blank.

Usually, I let out a sigh of relief when Rose left, but this time I'd wanted to go with her. However, I strode to the chairs with confidence. "Let's move these two into the library." I took Ollie from him and refastened the safety straps in her seat. Rose had already secured Freddie. Without being prompted, Peter grabbed Freddie's chair and followed me. Funny how everyone picked up on Fred's chill vibe. "Come on, Ollie Dollie."

The doorbell rang moments after we arrived in the library. "That's the food. I'll—"

Peter jumped off the couch. "Let me!" He darted to the front door, reaching for his billfold from his back pocket, like Doc Holliday at the O.K. Corral.

"Uncle Peter's funny, isn't he?" I wiggled a foot of each twin as they sat side-by-side in their chairs. They loved being in our presence most of the time, and we found it cut down on outbursts. Maybe it was a twin thing. "What a silly uncle."

"Order enough?" Peter stood in the doorway, holding four large pizzas.

I shrugged. "Food is rare around here these days, except for the twins, of course." I motioned to the side table, which already had plates, napkins, and silverware in case Peter didn't eat pizza like a normal person. "Let's dig in. I'm starved." Also, I was procrastinating. I wasn't too keen on beginning our conversation.

"Still have bourbon?" He loosened his tie and undid the top button of his shirt.

"Aren't you driving?"

"Not far. I'm meeting a client in town for golf. Two birds, one stone, you know."

"Help yourself." I motioned to the bar.

"Would you like something?" He poured a robust portion into a tumbler.

I widened my eyes. "No thanks.

He continued to pour.

I chomped into a slice that was burdened with pepperoni, sausage, and Canadian bacon. Peter opted for the barbeque chicken, which Sarah had ordered. Barbeque and pizza didn't sound right to me.

On couches facing each other, we ate in silence but much too quickly.

Peter jettisoned his plate and grease-smudged napkin on the coffee table and locked his cold eyes on mine, not speaking.

"What's on your mind?" I prodded. Might as well get this over with.

"Dad."

"I assumed. Did you get the invite?"

He nodded gravely. "The day I called."

"Me too. When he announced his engagement, you weren't shy about voicing your objection."

Peter rolled his tumbler between his palms. "I know. He took me by surprise; that's all."

"This family has a way of doing that."

He snorted, avoiding my eyes.

"I take it you've known about Helen for some time." I tapped Freddie's giraffe, which I'd found wedged into the back of the couch, against my thigh, while the theme song to *Jaws* played in my mind.

"Correct. You?"

"I didn't know about Dad and—not until Maddie told me on your wedding day."

Peter bolted from his chair, silently fortunately, so as not to upset the twins. "She had no right—" he whispered.

"That's neither here nor there." I flung my hands up in a *what gives* motion. I failed to mention that Maddie had also informed me of Peter's indiscretions and his proclamation to his bride-to-be that it was normal. From the fire shooting out of his eyes, he knew I knew. Was he really meeting an associate or his mistress? If I asked, would he bother telling me the truth? "Are you going to the wedding? Is that what this is about?"

Peter collapsed onto the arm of the sofa and ran a hand over his hair again. "He asked me to be his best man."

"Really? I'm surprised, considering."

He nodded. "I don't know what to say."

"Do you want to refuse?"

Peter shrugged. "I don't know the right thing to do. He's my father and it's an honor, of course. But what will people think?"

Interesting that he hadn't referenced our mother at all. I wondered whether he knew he had competition in the son department. If he didn't, I was of the opinion that Dad should break the news about Allen, not me.

I leaned forward. "Are you asking my advice?"

Peter's face softened, hardened, and then acquiesced. "I guess so. You know... the family."

If he meant I knew what it felt like to be the one on the outside, he nailed it. "My advice is that you can't say no. Jesus, when Tie asked me to be in your wedding, it was the last thing I wanted—but I said yes."

He took no offence to my saying it was the last thing I wanted, since I suspected he'd been of the same opinion. "That's what Tiffany said."

He never pronounced her name in her preferred Tie-Fannie manner. Not surprising, since he never called me Lizzie. Perhaps that was a form of endearment.

"Were you hoping I'd say it was okay for you to refuse?"

He actually smiled, shyly. "Yeah, I was. You were my last hope, really, considering."

"Considering I'm not much of a family person?"

He nodded.

"Sorry. Sarah has rubbed off on me. And now that I'm a parent, well, I see things differently."

"Do you like it?" He jerked his chin in the babies' direction.

"Thinking differently? Or being a parent?"

"Both?" His face displayed genuine curiosity.

"Thinking differently takes some getting used to. It throws me for a loop. Being a parent… that's totally different. I've never experienced something that made me feel this complete, happy, and terrified." I gazed at the twins, now both happily snoozing. "I don't want to fuck them up like I was."

Peter's spine stiffened. "Do you blame Mom?"

"Interesting question and one I've discussed ad nauseam in therapy."

"You're in therapy?" His face tightened with concern.

I nodded.

"Does it help?" He avoided my eyes.

"Most of the time. It can be infuriating depending on the session." I hefted one shoulder. "But it helps keep me sane, and it's improved my relationships, especially with Sarah."

Peter stood and walked to the bay window. "I've known about Dad and Helen for years. I wasn't sure why Dad introduced me to her, but I wish he hadn't. I thought it was normal, and that ended up costing me."

Even with his back to me, I could sense the pain on his face.

"Can you fix it?" I asked. "My therapist likes to say, 'It's never too late.'"

He remained quiet, lost in his own thoughts. Finally, he let out a snort. "I never realized how miserable Mom was... until Maddie..." He left the rest unsaid.

"I didn't either, really. It couldn't have been easy, for either one of them." If we were going down our family's rabbit hole, I needed a drink, but I was in charge of the babies. "You need a refill?"

He nodded.

When I handed him another full tumbler, he peered into my eyes with a sadness I'd never seen before.

I retook my seat on the couch. "I knew Mom was unhappy, but I never suspected about Dad and Helen. How long did it go on?"

"Years," he mumbled over the rim of his tumbler.

"Always Helen?"

"As far as I know." He gripped the glass, and his knuckles whitened. "I suspect there weren't any others. Dad has honor on some level."

Did his wry smile mean he himself wasn't honorable? Was he regretting his decisions, regretting losing Maddie?

"Does that make it better or worse?" I meant for the question to be rhetorical.

He shrugged and took a gulp. "Now that she's gone, I guess it's a moot point."

"What about you? What do you want from all of this?" I felt like my therapist.

"Ha! What'd your therapist say, 'It's never too late'? That's bullshit." He slugged his bourbon. "Tiffany's pregnant." His stony eyes made it impossible to guess his feelings. Was this the real reason he'd sought my opinion? As a new parent?

"Congratulations." I coughed. "Is that what you want?"

"I didn't even know we were trying. Do you remember that dinner, when she said she wanted to use a surrogate?"

I nodded.

"I actually believed her." He palmed the top of his head.

"Are you implying she's trying to trap you?" I spoke softly, unsure whether that was the right phrasing. Peter and I weren't the type to talk about ordinary topics like the weather, let alone personal topics like marriage and family woes.

"I don't think so. At least I hope not. It's just… the timing couldn't be worse." He looked over my head at the books stacked on the floor-to-ceiling shelves behind me.

"Do you want to be a father?"

"Maddie and I always talked about it."

It was becoming clearer to me that my brother was still in love with Maddie.

"What's wrong with the timing now?"

Peter massaged his eyelids. "Work—it's killing me."

Neither of us had to work, but both of us had an incessant drive to succeed. Our mother had drilled that into us.

"There you are." Sarah breezed into the library, smiling at the still-sleeping babies. "Any trouble?"

She meant the twins, of course, but I nodded in Peter's direction. He still had his eyes covered, so he didn't notice.

Sarah sat down on the couch next to me.

"How was lunch?" I asked to give Peter a few more moments.

"Good. It was nice to get out, even if only for an hour." She motioned to the babies. "It's hard to stay away."

"I bet. You've been holed up here for days."

She questioned me with her eyes.

Peter smoothed his suit pants and started to get up.

"Wait, Peter. Stay. Talk." I motioned for him to retake his seat.

He hesitated but soon eased back onto the couch, rubbing his eyes. Did he want to stay and talk, or was the bourbon kicking in? Either way, I was glad. I wasn't sure I'd let him behind the wheel at the moment.

"Would anyone like another drink?" Sarah marched to the bar.

"Please," I said.

She returned with a gin and tonic, which she thrust into my hand, and the Blanton's bottle, which she set on the side table next to Peter. "So what's going on?"

Peter remained mum, but he gave a *go ahead* hitch of his shoulders.

"Two issues, I think. One: Dad asked Peter to be his best man. Two: Tie is pregnant."

Sarah nodded thoughtfully, tapping a finger against her water glass. "Congratulations, Peter. How far along is she?"

"Ten weeks." He slugged his bourbon, simultaneously tugging on his already loosened tie.

"A spring birth, then. She did it right. Being eight months pregnant in the summer is hell." Sarah's laughter was more forced than normal. "Are you happy?" Her tone was soothing, like a therapist's.

"Yeah." His face was deathly pale. "It's normal, right? To be nervous?" He peeked at Freddie, who stirred quietly. The faint trace of a smile curved on my brother's lips.

"Of course it is. I fainted when Sarah told me she wanted to have a baby."

"Really?" he asked with obvious relief.

"Dead away. Lizzie has a habit of doing that." Sarah rose to get Fred. "Have they eaten?"

"Nope. Slept the entire time. Maybe because both were up most of the night."

"So it's true? Parents never sleep?" Peter's eyes narrowed.

"Not a wink. I gave a lecture yesterday, and ten minutes afterward, I couldn't remember whether I'd actually shown up for it or whether the whole thing was a hallucination. I'm leaning toward the notion that I actually gave the lecture, since I haven't had a phone call demanding to know where I was."

"Lizzie! Let the man find out on his own." Freddie latched on to Sarah's nipple, and she placed a soft blanket over her shoulder, providing some semblance of privacy.

I wanted to fire back, "Says the woman who's constantly flaunting her boobs." Even in my sleep-deprived state, I was wise enough to keep this to myself.

I wiggled in my seat, wondering whether I'd ever get used to Sarah feeding the twins in front of people, even if Peter was my brother. Peter, to his credit, didn't react, unlike the time in the hospital. Maybe he was distracted by his situation. Or maybe he was becoming used to outrageous behavior; he was raised by our mother, after all, and married to Tie, not to mention that he'd been engaged to Maddie. It dawned on me that all of his life, my brother had been henpecked. The thought almost made me laugh out loud. Was that the reason behind his bravado?

"So, the wedding," Sarah jumped right in. "You're going to accept, right?"

"That's what everyone keeps hinting at."

"Oh, I'm not hinting. I'm stating you can't refuse." Sarah's voice was soft, but her face was hard with a fierce determination. She smiled sweetly. "One problem solved."

"Is it that easy for you?" Bafflement was etched into my brother's brow.

"When it comes to family, yes. Let's face it; the majority of people phone it in when it comes to family situations. All you have to do is show up, give a toast, and be yourself—" She shifted in her seat, leaving me to wonder whether she actually wanted to say, "Be yourself but not completely."

He turned to me. "Would *you* be his best man?"

"Uh—"

"Hypothetically, of course. I'm not trying..." He left the rest unsaid.

I stifled a smile. Was he taking a dig at me or not? The Peter sitting on my couch was not the Peter I was used to.

"Of course. Like I said, when Tie asked me to be in your wedding—I didn't want to."

Sarah's laughter trilled. "It was masterful how Tie set that up."

Peter met her eyes. "I didn't even know until the rehearsal."

"What's your objection to Charles and Helen marrying?" Sarah asked.

He bristled. "My mother, of course. She'd never approve."

Sarah blinked as if trying to ignore Peter's hypocrisy. Peter the Cheater, who had betrayed Maddie and married Tie.

Interesting that he'd mentioned Mom to Sarah and not me. Regardless, he was dead-on. Mom would not approve of Helen. And she sure as hell wouldn't want her husband to have an ounce of happiness without her. Not that she'd provided any happiness while they were together.

"Your mom isn't here." Sarah bravely stared him down.

"I know that. But she's been in the ground less than a year, and he's already planning a November wedding." He stood and paced the room.

I glanced to Sarah for guidance, and she motioned that we should give him a moment. The fact that he was opening up was a minor miracle.

"Hello!" Maddie shouted from the entryway.

"In the library," Sarah and I shouted back. Ollie fussed, and I rushed to the baby's aid.

Peter froze.

"Hello, Peter. I didn't know you'd be here." Maddie breezed in. "Can I have some?" She didn't wait for a response, flipping open the box and snagging herself a slice of barbeque chicken pizza.

Peter still hadn't moved, except his eyes, which followed Maddie's every move.

She sat on the couch and tucked her legs under her. "What'd I miss?"

I snorted, and Sarah laughed.

Maddie's eyes scrutinized her former fiancé. "I take it this isn't a casual family get-together."

"Yeah, right. Because these two are so close." Sarah yanked her head to me and then to Peter.

Peter flinched, but I just shrugged.

"So lay it on me. From the look in Peter's eyes, he needs help." Her face filled with a tender expression.

"Tie's pregnant, and Dad wants Peter to be his best man." I handed Ollie to Sarah and took Freddie to burp him.

"Jesus, Elizabeth. It's bad enough you told Sarah." Peter marched to the window, turning his back on us.

Maddie's face blanched, and she set her pizza aside. "I need a drink for this conversation." She levered herself off the couch and swished Peter's bottle of bourbon on her way to the bar. "This may not get us through." The bottle was less than half full.

Sarah and Maddie both turned to me with expressions that implored me to make a bourbon run. I groaned and muttered that the bar was fully stocked with other booze. It was hard to tell whether Peter had heard or whether he was even listening. I'd only had two sips of gin and tonic, so I couldn't use that as an excuse not to go. Then again, did I want to stick around with Peter and Maddie in the same room?

"Anything else while I'm out?" I asked.

Maddie draped an arm over my shoulder and walked me to the front door. "Arby's."

"We just ate an hour ago."

"Trust me on this. Otherwise I'll have to send you back out. We can keep it warm in the oven."

I pulled away. "Since when did you start liking Arby's anyway?"

"Not me. When he's stressed, Peter loves the Bourbon bacon and steak, curly fries, and orange-cream shake. Oh, jalapeno poppers and a cherry turnover."

"You're joking, right? My brother, who wears three-piece suits and custom-made shoes, dines at Arby's?"

"Crazy for it. Order a lot. This is going to be a long day." She plucked Freddie from my arms. "What about you, Fred? Will you be an Arby's man like your uncle?"

By the time I returned, arms laden with Arby's bags and two bottles of Blanton's, Sarah was alone in the library with the sleeping babies.

"Great," I whispered. "I bought all this for nothing."

Sarah put a finger to her lips. "They're in the breakfast nook. Drop off the loot and come straight back."

I threw her an incredulous look. Of course I'd dash for cover! If Maddie wanted to swoop in and play Peter's therapist, by all means.

We left them to it, and the next morning, when I retrieved the paper from the driveway, I wasn't all that surprised to see both of their cars still parked on the street.

So much for Peter's golf meeting. And possibly his marriage.

I sighed. My newspaper hadn't been pissed on today, at least, but there were some bite marks. That I could handle. I spied George in his driveway and waved exuberantly, letting him know there were no hard feelings.

Sarah wandered into the kitchen, looking like hell. "I don't think Arby's agrees with me."

"The ham and cheese wasn't bad. Next time, maybe you shouldn't scarf all the jalapeno poppers. Just so you know, I'm not on diaper duty today. Who knows what that's going to do to the twins' stomachs?"

"Nice try."

I grabbed a water bottle from the fridge and shook it. Sarah nodded, and I lobbed it to her and extracted another from the back of the stainless steel Kenmore Elite, which had cost more than an average used car.

"I'm almost afraid to ask, but where did Peter and Maddie sleep?"

Sarah hitched a shoulder. "I went to bed ages before them. Did you bump into them at all during the night?"

I shook my head.

"Me neither."

The guest bedrooms were upstairs, but I had only seen one door closed on my way down this morning.

The kitchen looked like a cyclone had swept through: Arby's wrappers, empty wine bottles, and a half-empty Blanton's bottle. Hopefully, that was only the second bottle, not the third. Could a human drink a full bottle of bourbon and survive? Surely Maddie had consumed some of it.

"Let's get the babies up. I have a feeling our guests will be in rough shape." Sarah tugged the tie on my bathrobe to get me moving. We padded upstairs in our slippers, still yawning.

When we reached the floor above, we found Maddie hugging a wide-awake Freddie. I quirked an eyebrow as Sarah quietly closed the guest bedroom door. For someone who'd stayed up most of the night, drinking and commiserating with Peter, Maddie was coping well.

After disappearing into the nursery and reappearing with Ollie, Sarah wrenched her neck in that bossy way of hers, to instruct me to collect the monkey chairs.

When I arrived in the kitchen, I immediately turned my attention to Maddie. "How are you even upright?"

"Coffee. Now!" Maddie buckled Fred into his chair.

"Do I even want to know what happened last night between you and my brother?" I scooped organic Guatemalan coffee grounds into the filter and filled the maker with water.

"You aren't seriously asking me whether I slept with Peter, are you?"

I tilt-a-whirled around. Maddie's arms were defensively folded across her chest.

"You know, the way things are going in this family, nothing would shock me anymore. So did you?"

"I'm not going to dignify that question with an answer."

Her cageyness troubled me.

Sarah set out a coffee cup for Maddie—Peter's new mistress. I was almost certain of it.

"He's still in love with you, ya know." I retrieved lemon yogurt from the fridge, yanked the plastic lid off, and dipped a spoon right into the container.

Maddie hijacked the container and scooped a mouthful. "And I'll always love him. Leaving someone doesn't stop you from loving them."

"Even if he's married and a father-to-be? First Courtney, now Peter."

Maddie glared at me. "Courtney doesn't count—she and Kit have an arrangement."

"Are you still seeing her?"

"Not often. Only when one of us gets lonely and we can find the time."

"And Peter? Does he have an arrangement with Tie? Or were you getting even with her?"

"Lizzie!" Sarah stretched a finger toward the deck, implying she wanted a word in private.

Outside, she tapped her slippered foot on the deck. "What's wrong with you? Interrogating Maddie?"

"I'm only trying to find out what happened last night."

"Why do you care so much?"

"Why don't you? They slept together—in our home."

"What bothers you more? That they slept together? Or that they did it in our home?"

I rolled back on my feet. "Aha! So you agree they did the deed." I cringed and glanced up at the guest bedroom window, which was open an inch at the bottom. A slight breeze ruffled the curtain and sucked it briefly outside.

"What happened or didn't happen is none of our concern."

"Has everyone gone insane?" I tossed a hand in the air. "Is it perfectly normal for everyone associated with the Petrie family to hop in and out of people's beds, no matter who gets hurt?"

"You've known for years that Peter's a cheater."

"Exactly! And it was Maddie who told me, right before she ditched him at the altar *because he cheated.* Now she's doing it to Tie—"

Sarah gripped my shoulders. "Stop it. This has absolutely nothing to do with you."

"Nothing to do with *me*? He's my brother. And she's our best friend, who agreed to take care of our children if anything happens to us. What kind of example would she set for the twins? You can't tell me this isn't a sticky situation. What was Maddie thinking?"

Sarah chewed on her lower lip. "I don't know… I really don't. But—"

"But what?"

Sarah was speechless.

Gandhi wandered into our fenceless backyard and took a crap on the lawn. In his mouth was a squeaky toy in the shape of a newspaper—part of the apology gift basket.

"I just don't get it. If Peter and Maddie still have feelings for each other, why don't they—?" Sarah stopped abruptly, lost in thought. Perhaps the mere suggestion of divorce made her squirm. "Maybe Peter doesn't want to admit marrying Tie was a colossal mistake, considering she was the cause of Maddie leaving him."

Knowing my big shot brother, that made sense, but the cost—was it worth it?

"Maybe you should go for a bike ride. Let me talk to Maddie. It's probably best if you don't see Peter right now."

"This is the perfect example of why I stayed away from anyone with the last name of Petrie—they give me a headache!"

———————— ⸻ ————————

Two hours later, when I returned, Peter's and Maddie's cars were nowhere to be seen. I punched in the garage door code and waited while the door creaked upward. The SUV was gone as well.

Inside, everything was quiet. Sarah had left a note that she and the twins were visiting Rose.

As I rummaged in the pantry for food, my cell phone vibrated in my pocket. Dad's number flashed across the screen. "Hello," I said quietly, even though there wasn't a chance in hell I'd wake the twins, who were blocks away at Grandma's house.

"Lizzie. How are you?"

I stood in the middle of the kitchen, the phone jammed to my ear, not hearing another human being. After weeks of continuous crying, squawking, giggling, and cooing, the silence was off-putting. "I'm good. You?"

"I think we need to talk."

"Um, okay."

"I know you have your hands full."

Did he have his suspicions about Peter and Maddie, or did he just mean the twins?

"Can you make a late lunch today?"

I nodded needlessly. My father was intelligent, but he didn't have superpowers that allowed him to see my head nodding through telephone wires. "Yeah, I'm sure that'll work."

"Great. Half past two at Three Amigos?"

"See ya there."

We hung up.

How in the world did my father so casually know the name of any restaurant in Fort Collins? I remembered Helen saying her florist shop was here in town.

I dialed Sarah's number.

"You cooled off?" she answered.

I didn't bother replying. "I know I ditched you with the twins all morning, but my dad wants to meet for lunch today. Is that okay?" My voice came out frostier than I intended.

"Fine with me. Shall the babes stay at my mom's tonight?"

"Do you think they should?" I softened my tone.

She breathed into the phone. "Of course I don't want them to, but I don't want them to pick up on—"

"I get it."

She heaved a sigh. "I don't. My mind is still reeling about the whole situation."

"I'm right there with you. But I promise not to pout and throw things in front of the twins."

She belly-laughed. "Stop by after you shower, okay? Seeing the twinkies will probably perk you up a bit before your powwow with Charles. We're trying to pick out Halloween costumes. Fred makes a beautiful princess, but Ollie wouldn't have a thing to do with the purple dress."

I curbed a retort about putting a dress on our son, knowing Sarah was adamantly opposed to adhering to strict gender norms. Instead, I said, "She takes after me." I sat on one of the barstools in the kitchen and doodled on the notepad.

"Hurry up. I miss you."

I rushed through my shower, and within thirty minutes I'd made it to Rose's living room and was holding a squirming Ollie, who was dressed in a daffodil costume.

"You going to confront your dad?" Sarah asked. Rose and Fred were in the nursery Rose had set up in her home for when the twins stayed over. It was almost identical to the one in our house.

"Nope. I have a feeling he's going to confront me. Funny how my family forgot all about me for years, but now that everything is crumbling, my brother and my father suddenly want to open up. I don't know how much more crisis control I can take. And now Maddie too... I mean, I knew she was struggling, trying to find a hobby or whatever, but not in a million years did I see this coming."

"I don't know what to do or say either. I might adopt the stick-your-head in-the-sand routine."

"Finally seeing the allure of my method? And to think of all the times you've pleaded with me to open up." I laughed.

"I know you didn't have the best childhood, but please tell me it wasn't this drama-filled." She plowed on to a different topic. "Or maybe all families are like this. I don't know. I only have my mom."

"You're asking the wrong person."

"Don't worry too much. I'm sure everything will work out eventually." She studied my face, her eyes darkening with concern. "Maybe it's time for our family to take a trip to the zoo."

I smiled. "Aren't they a little young?"

"Never too young. And I think it will do their mommy good to spend some quality time with the otters—not the Kit version."

I laughed. "If Peter divorces Tie, at least we won't have to deal with Kit and Courtney either."

"They'd still be Peter's child's aunt and uncle, if they marry, and could pop up on special occasions, like graduations or weddings."

"Good grief. Is there no end to the Petrie tangled webs?"

CHAPTER FIFTEEN

DAD SAT IN A BOOTH SITUATED BY THE KITCHEN OF THE SMALL, FAMILY-RUN restaurant. He rose and smiled awkwardly when he spotted me. "So glad you could make it," he said.

I slid into the booth across from him. "I've never been here. Is it good?"

He eyed me. "It's my first time. Gabe recommended it."

"Gabe?" I shook out my folded napkin and placed it on my lap.

"Helen's oldest son. He lived here in Fort Collins back when Helen first opened up a shop in Old Town."

"I see."

Dad glanced toward the kitchen, where a man in a chef's hat was busy grabbing a pan off a sizzling burner and dramatically shaking the contents. The scent of grilled peppers, onions, and spicy beef permeated the room.

"Ever since I've known Gabe, he's wanted to go into business. He pestered his mother for months to get the shop up and running here."

"Is Allen business-oriented, like Gabe and Peter?" I decided the best defense was offense.

"No. Allen… Allen isn't sure what he wants to do. He likes history."

Did I get the history gene from Dad?

"Really?"

"Yeah." He motioned for the waiter. "What would you like to drink, Lizzie?"

The waiter smiled expectantly, his pen hovering over a notebook.

"Coke, please."

Dad ordered a Corona with a lime wedge.

Seriously, it was like I'd never met the man. "No bourbon?"

I remembered what my brother's recent bourbon spree had led to. At least Dad had a driver, so he wouldn't have to stay at my house and get into mischief.

"They only have margaritas, beer, and wine. The fajitas smell good. I think I'll go with that."

I set my menu to the side. "Me too."

The waiter returned with our drinks, and we placed our order for steak fajitas and watched as he whisked the menus out of sight, leaving me nothing to distract myself with. I fidgeted with the fringe of the colorful tablecloth, which matched the small curtains bunched at the top of the restaurant's windows. A fake palm tree with faux margarita glasses dangling from the fronds sat behind my father's head.

Dad cleared his throat but didn't say anything.

Awkward silence followed. Or rather, there was awkward silence, and then there was the awkward silence of lunching with your father days after finding out he'd had another secret family for decades—a family he was obviously close to, despite ignoring your existence for years.

"I didn't want you to find out that way." His shoulders drooped. "I should have been the one to tell you. Helen feels awful about it."

I nodded. "She seems nice."

"She is."

Another silence slipped between us, and I tried to imagine what Sarah would say in this moment.

"Did Mom know?"

He shifted in his seat. "Not everything."

"Why didn't you leave? Tell her the truth?"

"Never figured out a way to leave." He glanced down at his hand, gripping the beer bottle. "It was complicated."

"And Helen was fine with that?"

He grunted almost inaudibly. "It wasn't the ideal situation, but she had her own life with her business and—"

"Two sons."

"I was going to say her family and friends."

The waiter appeared, carrying a tray over his head. A billow of steam followed him. "Here you go." He arranged our plates, two tortilla containers and side dishes of shredded cheese, black beans, sour cream, guacamole, salsa, and Spanish rice.

The tortillas were toasty warm, but that didn't stop me from loading one up to the point I could barely fold it into my mouth. Dad committed the same error.

After we'd both finished our second gut-stuffing fajita, he leaned back in his seat and lifted his gaze to mine. "I can't apologize for the past. I can only move forward."

"With your family, with Helen."

Dad cupped a hand over mine. It was the first time I think he'd ever touched me like that, as far as I remembered. "It doesn't have to be like that. I want you and Peter in my life."

"*Now* you do. What about all those years I never heard from you?" I traced my fork along the lines in the tablecloth.

He leaned back. "I don't remember you banging down my door, either."

"Never thought I was wanted."

He sighed. "Neither did I."

It was true. I ran from all of them. I kept my own secrets, good and bad. Maybe it was time I didn't. "I have Graves' disease," I blurted out.

He blinked. "Is it...?"

"Fatal?"

He nodded, open-mouthed.

"Without treatment, yes. But I've been in remission. It's easy to manage, fortunately."

"How long have you been in remission?"

"Years, now. Sometimes I forget I ever went through it."

Dad rested his chin on steepled fingers. "I see. Was Sarah there for you?"

I shook my head. "It was before I met her. She was present for the tail end of it. She celebrated with me when I no longer had to take all the pills. In the beginning, they made me sick as a dog."

"I always assumed... You were so successful in school. I never thought..." His quivering voice trailed off.

"That I needed you?"

He remained stone-faced but took a generous swig of Corona.

I shifted in my seat. "She told me that once. That she hated me because I didn't need her."

He blinked. "Who told you that?"

"Mom. Near the end. I asked her why she'd never loved me."

My father stiffened, sucking in his lips as if he was carefully mulling over his words. "I don't think that's true. I think your mother hated herself for not being the mother she wanted to be for you. Even at a young age, it was clear you were—quiet. She didn't know how to handle quiet." The trace of a smile brightened his eyes. "I always liked that about you. Today's world needs more thinkers. You were the complete opposite of Peter. He was talking about all the things he wanted to accomplish."

"Mom doted on him."

"Only to needle you. Peter figured it out, I think. That stung him more than you'll know. Your mother was a… difficult woman. If I could go back, I would have left, no matter what. To save both of you."

"No matter what? What do you mean?"

"She made threats." He waved a dismissive hand, his eyes downcast, focused on the tablecloth. "It doesn't matter now."

"Yes, it does. What threats?"

"To destroy me, my company. That I could have lived with. But she also threatened to destroy you. Peter. Never let me see either of you. After she found out you were gay, she wanted to cut you off financially."

It was hard to believe he'd stayed solely for Peter and me. "And Helen? Did she make threats against her?"

His eyes understood my implication that there was more to the story. "Yes. She swore black and blue that she'd destroy Helen. I couldn't let her do that. I couldn't let her go after any of you. And if she'd ever found out about Allen, I don't know what she would have done."

"How did you keep it—Allen—from her?"

He sighed. "Your mother never really wanted to know the truth. She asked, and I denied, denied, and denied. The thing that mattered most to her was that no one in our circle knew. That there wasn't anything for the ladies at the club to gossip about."

I thought back to Peter asking what people would think if he was Dad's best man. So much bother, keeping people quiet—people who didn't matter anyway.

I swallowed. "I had no idea."

"It doesn't matter now." His shoulders relaxed.

"Do you think Peter will turn out like her? He stole Uncle Jerry's money from me."

He bolted upright. "What do you mean?"

"You didn't know?"

His fierce headshake suggested he didn't.

"When Peter found out Jerry was dying, he visited him and outed me. Uncle Jerry changed his will days before he died. Mom gloated over that. Peter's triumph, I guess."

The vein on my father's forehead bulged. "No, I didn't know." He folded his hands on the table. "I don't even know what to say."

"I think that's why I always stay quiet when it comes to family stuff. I never know how to explain all the... the—"

"Bullshit."

"Yeah, the bullshit. Is Allen like Peter?"

Dad's face softened. "He takes after Helen, but he reminds me a lot of you. Quietly determined. Maybe someday you two can get to know each other."

"I'm assuming we'll meet at the wedding."

He laughed. "Well, there's that. But I meant on a different level."

He meant on a *sibling* level. Well, that hadn't worked out so well for me in the past.

"Why did you introduce Helen to Peter and not me?"

"You know about that?"

"Peter came over for lunch yesterday. We had a heart-to-heart."

"I wanted him to know that not all mothers were like yours. I realized later that it was a mistake, so I didn't repeat it with you." Dad motioned for another beer. "I love your brother, but he makes life so much harder than it needs to be."

You're telling me. And Dad didn't even know about the Maddie situation. "Have you spoken with him lately?"

"Briefly. Everything okay?"

I coughed into my napkin. "Not sure, really. My guess is no."

"I'm surprised he talked to you."

I laughed. "Me too. Must have been desperate."

Dad's face relaxed. "You know I didn't mean it like that. He keeps all his cards close to his chest."

"I think we all do. Does he know about Allen?"

"I haven't figured out how to tell him... yet. Peter thinks differently than you do."

"Inheritance."

"Exactly. Learning about Jerry makes things even thornier."

Indeed.

"Maybe becoming a father will change him. I know being a mother has changed me for the good. I hope at least."

Dad sat upright. "Is Tiffany pregnant?"

Crap. I slapped a hand over my loose lips for a moment. "That slipped out," I said eventually. "I should have let him tell you."

He waved off my concern. "I'll act surprised."

That made me laugh since the man hardly ever showed any type of emotion.

"Oh." I perked up in my seat. "Speaking of babies, I almost forgot. Sarah thought you'd like a recent photo of the twins." I scrounged in my messenger bag and withdrew the gift.

He stared fondly at the photo Maddie had snapped of me juggling a baby on each hip.

"They're getting so big," he said, smiling.

"Monster-sized. We can go see them if you'd like."

"I would like that. Very much."

"How you hanging in?" Sarah climbed into bed after putting the twins down for the night—or for a few hours, hopefully.

"That depends." I bundled her into my arms.

"On what?" She nuzzled into the crook of my neck.

"If anyone plans to dump more of their shit on me."

"Does that mean it's a good time to mention—?"

I smothered her mouth with my palm. She pretended to wave a white flag, and I released her.

"You going to meet Allen?" she asked in a tone that didn't lend any insight into her feelings on the subject.

I emitted a troubled sigh. "Dad wants me to. After all these years, I think he wants everything to seem normal."

After my lunch with Dad, I'd spent several hours filling Sarah in on the conversation, particularly about my mother's threats.

"I can't blame the man. So much to keep hidden." Sarah rested on her elbow and propped her head on her hand. Her other arm was draped over my stomach. "And so much for you to accept at face value."

"Rome wasn't built in a day."

She smiled. "Do you ever run out of history references?"

"I hope not. Wouldn't say much about my teaching abilities."

She whacked my chest.

"Hey, what'd I say about adding more woes to my life? The last thing I need right now is a broken rib."

"What's the first thing you want?" Her eyes narrowed.

I examined the monitors. The twinks were sound asleep. "Do you think we have the time and energy?" I did my best to flash a seductive grin. "It doesn't seem right that Maddie and Peter got busy in our home and we haven't done that since before the twins popped out, months ago. You said the doctor gave you the all clear."

"Wow! Your powers of seduction are severely lacking. You managed to reference Maddie, Peter, *and* the birthing process."

"I'm out of practice." I leaned into a kiss that was met with vigor. "But I think it's time to get back on the horse." I shoved all thoughts of the messy birth to a far corner in my brain, doing my best to lock it up for good. Sarah didn't want me to put her into a mom box, and the last twenty-four hours had taught me a lot about life: cherish the one you love, because more than likely, even your best friend will disappoint you.

"Still not wooing me," she teased.

"Shut up and get naked."

She shimmied out of her silk nightgown, her smile widening with sinful guilt.

I rolled her onto her back. "It's been so long since I've had a taste." My knee separated her legs.

Sarah stripped my T-shirt off in one motion. "God, I've missed you," she murmured, capturing my mouth with a sensual intensity. "Giddyup."

— Chapter Sixteen —

THE NEXT MORNING, ROSE CAME OVER TO WATCH THE BABIES SO SARAH AND I could go to breakfast together before my class. I wasn't sure how much Rose knew about the events that had occurred the day before, but her sympathetic expression clued me in to Sarah's real agenda for breakfast.

Since time was always short these days, we ate at a café across the street from campus. The place buzzed with caffeinated energy.

I stirred brown sugar into a steaming cup of Earl Grey, one eye squinted.

Sarah laughed and folded her arms. "You know, don't you?"

"That I'm about to be reamed? Kinda."

"Reamed." She laughed harder. "I thought I did that last night."

"I think I prefer your definition over mine." I winked but then signaled with a flick of my hand to get it over with.

"I'm just worried. You have so much on your plate right now, and I don't want you—us—to destroy the relationships that matter."

"Maddie?"

"That's a big one."

I stared at a grove of trees across the street, near the oldest part of the campus. "How should we handle it?"

"Good question. I know a significant amount of alcohol was involved—"

"You know, if you get drunk and commit a crime, you'll still be prosecuted for it."

"True, but it's probably best not to lead with that." Sarah sighed. I wasn't sure whether her sigh was related to the situation or my attitude. "I think we need to talk to her, set some boundaries or something." Her upper body shuddered as if a chill had hit her without warning. "We can't tell her how to live her life, but lately, her actions have affected our lives." She placed a hand on mine. "Am I being too hard on her? We're all adults. Do we even have the right to say who she—?"

"In the past six months, she's slept with Courtney and Peter—both of whom are in relationships. No, you aren't being too hard on her. She's self-destructing before our eyes. Can't she be normal and sign up for Tinder, sleep with strangers? It'd decrease the odds of bumping into them at family events... or at our house."

"How do you know about Tinder?"

"I could ask the same of you."

"Please. I recently gave birth to two babies."

"I sorta remember that. Lots of screaming, crying, and begging. And that was before the twins arrived."

She slapped my hand. "Next time, you're giving birth. See how much you like it."

"I think we have our hands full at the moment."

"Nicely done, getting out of that. Now... Maddie. Are we in agreement that we need to have a sit-down with her?"

"Don't see a way around it, unless you want to talk to her on your own." I knew my tone was too hopeful, almost pleading.

She shook her head.

We rushed through our meals, and I dashed off, arriving one minute before my lecture.

"Good morning." I made my way to the front. "Sorry I'm late. Life with infant twins keeps me on my toes."

"That explains the puke on your shoulder," joked one student.

I glanced at my right shoulder and then my left.

"Made you look."

I laughed. "Let's get to it." Several students groaned, playfully I think. At least here, within these walls, I didn't have to deal with any type of family crap—not for a blissful one hour and fifteen minutes.

"Lizzie, do you have a moment?" Dr. Marcel gestured for me to step inside his office.

I settled into a plush chair. "How are you?"

His facial muscles strained, but he responded, "Okay. You?"

I stiffened. "Hanging in the best I can."

"Twins have a way of making you think you're always drinking from the fire hose."

And family drama, I added mentally. "That they do."

He tapped a pencil on his desk and gazed out of the window that overlooked the trees I'd been staring at earlier during breakfast. "I won't be teaching next semester, so I'm recruiting professors to take over my classes. I want you to take one."

"Is everything okay?" I practically whispered.

"Had a bit of a health scare, and it's made me come to terms with the fact that Lydia and I aren't spring chickens anymore. I want to relax some. Enjoy life a bit more. Do you think you can manage three courses? You'd still be considered part-time, but in the fall, you'd be officially added to the department, if you want."

I sat up straighter. "I absolutely accept." I paused. "But I should talk it over with Sarah."

"Of course. I understand."

"Did you have a class in mind for me?"

He smiled wanly. "I have an idea, but we can talk about that later, after I speak with a couple of others." Students already registered for spring, so it wouldn't do to yank the classes off the schedule, not without causing major headaches.

Dr. Marcel's eyes shone with relief. He probably suspected, as I did, that Sarah wouldn't have any objection to me accepting the offer.

"When are you and Sarah going to bring the twins over? I know Lydia would love to see the rug rats."

His desk phone rang, and he apologized with a shrug before answering, "Dr. Marcel."

I excused myself with a wave of the hand.

During my PhD program, the Marcels had been like parents to me, inviting me over for most holidays. I gripped the leather handle of my briefcase and marched outside into a cloudy, gray day that became drastically grayer by the second. Only one clear patch of sky hung over Horsetooth Mountain. I stopped in my tracks, trying to remember the last day I'd gone for a hike. No time for that today. I had to start preparing for the two classes already on my schedule next semester, and pronto if I also hoped to be ready for another class.

I walked into our kitchen to find Sarah sitting on a barstool, waving stuffed animals in front of Ollie, whose face was cherry-red from screaming.

"Now that's a welcome," I said to Ollie, who hushed some. "Is Mommy ignoring you, little girl?"

"Olivia is determined never to be ignored." Sarah turned to me. "How was your day?"

"Interesting. Dr. Marcel offered to bring me on board full-time in the fall."

"That's wonderful. We should celebrate." Sarah wheeled around to the drawer where we stored the takeout menus. "Thai? Chinese?"

"There's something else," I said. "He wants me to teach three classes this spring."

Sarah's eyes boggled. "Can you handle that much?"

"I think so. Won't really know until I try. I was thinking we should hire someone to help out here—cooking, cleaning, and laundry." My entire body clenched, preparing for her response.

"Agreed."

"Really? I was expecting you to put up a bit of a fight."

"I'd be an idiot to say I don't need help around the house." She jabbed a thumb at the messy kitchen. "You don't want the person to live with us, do you?"

"Nope. Strictly a day job. Part-time, really. Janice reached out. Her cousin will be attending CSU in the fall. She may need a job, and since Miranda is cutting back on her hours, it makes sense. Dottie wants me to keep an eye on her."

"We can barely keep our best friend in line. How will we manage Bailey?"

I laughed, still feeling overwhelmed by everything, but I was with my family; that was all I needed right now. "What do you keep saying? Somehow everything will work out."

— CHAPTER SEVENTEEN —

SATURDAY MORNING, I JOLTED AWAKE AROUND 4:00 A.M. TO A DISCONCERTINGLY quiet house. Sarah was in a deep sleep, and she didn't stir when I got up.

In the nursery, both babies slept peacefully. My brain whirred, ruminating over everything from teaching, Dad, Helen, Mom, Peter, Maddie, and Allen. Going back to sleep wasn't going to happen.

I tiptoed down the stairs, avoiding the second to last step, which always groaned in protest like an old person getting out of a chair, and camped out in my office, doing research on my laptop. Might as well get a jump start on next semester.

Sarah padded in an hour later. "I thought I'd find you hidden in here." I minimized the Internet window, and she squinted at the screensaver photo of Fred and Ollie that Maddie had set up for me. "Working?"

"I was, but I started wandering."

"Literally or figuratively?"

I rubbed my eyes. "I'm so tired I don't know." I clicked on the wireless mouse to maximize the screen again.

"Ah, doing some sleuthing." She perched in my lap and clicked the About Us tab on Helen's florist website.

"Is that bad? Stalking Helen online?"

"Oh please! You wouldn't even know where to begin if you wanted to be a legitimate online stalker." Her hands flew over the keyboard, and Helen's Facebook account appeared. "If you're curious about what Allen looks like, start here." She moved to get up, but I wrapped my arms around her, tugging her back onto my lap.

"Where are you going?" I kissed the nape of her neck.

"Don't you want to snoop in private?" She appraised my face to gauge my mood.

"No. I obviously need you." I peppered her neck with kisses.

"Keep that up and I'll stay." She swiveled back to the laptop. "You ready?"

"I don't know, but…"

Sarah clicked on the photos tab. We leaned closer to the screen. There weren't too many photos, but I picked out her eldest son with ease. He had his mother's kind brown eyes and mischievous smile.

The next photo in the collection was the one I sought: a black-and-white photo of a young man who wasn't looking at the camera full-on. He was staring at something off to the side, lost in his own thoughts, but he had Dad's cleft chin and his nose.

"He looks so young," Sarah whispered as if afraid she'd break Allen's concentration.

"He's still in high school. I wonder if this is his senior yearbook photo. Hard to believe he's old enough to be an uncle."

"Do you think he knows?"

I shrugged. "I hadn't considered that Allen might not know about Peter, me, or the twins." I massaged my forehead. "This is even more messed up than I thought."

Sarah scrolled down. "No photos of your dad."

"I didn't think we'd find any. Not that Mom was all that clever with a computer, but better safe than sorry. Maybe once they're married Helen may feel comfortable posting photos of Dad—old habits, though." I chuckled. "That's one thing we have in common—I don't have any photos of me with Dad from my childhood either."

Sarah drilled her elbow into my stomach.

Freddie stirred on the monitor. "Come on. Let's get him before he wakes up trouble."

A louder cry issued from the speaker of Ollie's monitor.

"Too late. All hands on deck." Sarah leaped up and stabbed out a hand to help me out of my seat, brushing her lips on my cheek when I stood. "We'll get through everything, one day at a time."

On today's agenda was our chat with Maddie.

We dropped the twins off at Rose's. She had a gaggle of female friends over, all of them dying to spend time with Freddie and Ollie. I was curious whether they'd still feel the same in two hours time. Not one of them was younger than fifty. I guessed it'd been years since any of them had changed a diaper. There was safety in numbers, though.

At the door, Sarah hugged her mom. "Thanks."

"Good luck with Maddie. Such a shame. Love does funny things to people, I guess. She always had her ducks in a row, even after she left Peter." Rose shook her head.

Maddie had moved in with Rose for a brief spell after she'd called off her wedding to Peter.

"We can't wrap our heads around it either," I said as we made our good-byes.

Outside of Maddie's apartment, I hesitated on the doorstep. "Here goes nothing" I said and knocked.

Doug answered, shuffling one arm into a jacket. "Hey, you two. Mads is in the shower, and I'm running seriously late." He shrugged on the other sleeve.

We all quickly hugged hello and good-bye, and we shut the door behind him.

"I thought he moved out a couple of months ago," I whispered.

"He did."

I shook my head and whispered again, "How does she keep track of everyone?"

"Name tags."

Both Sarah and I circled around. Maddie, her hair still wet, entered the front room all smiles, with just a hint of guilt in her eyes. "What can I get you? Water? Tea? Coffee? Wine?"

It was only ten in the morning, but I let her offer of wine slip for now. *One crisis at a time.* "Water works."

Sarah nodded.

Maddie returned carrying a tray that supported a glass pitcher of ice water, lemon slices bobbing at the top. Sarah and I took a seat on her bluish-gray sofa. The walls in the room were a pale off-white; the apartment manager didn't allow crazy color schemes. A stunning oil painting had once hung on the opposite wall, but all that remained was the faded outline of the frame. Often, Maddie pillaged her own apartment for things her clients might like.

After pouring three glasses of water, Maddie settled into a plush chair, looking like a prisoner about to face a firing squad.

"How does this work?" she asked after a minute. "You rant and rave, and I defend myself, making you yell even more, until we all end up crying and hugging it out?" She grinned, not seeming distressed, or not completely. Her inability to look me in the eyes was proof positive she wasn't entirely at ease.

"Can we skip the histrionics and just get to the heart of the matter?" Sarah jiggled her left leg, like a child waiting in a doctor's office.

"Which is?" Maddie's tone came across somewhat defensive.

"It starts with the letter P." I sipped my water.

Maddie inhaled deeply. "I know. Peter and I have talked, and it's been put to rest."

"Meaning… you won't be seeing my brother anymore?"

She arched an eyebrow, as if to say, *What business is it of yours?* Then she softened. "Nope. It was a mistake. A serious mistake we both regret. And before you ask, I broke things off with Courtney. And no, Doug and I are not back together."

An awkward silence followed. I sensed Sarah trying to get my attention, but I avoided her eye. If she wanted me to know where to take the conversation next, I didn't.

"We're concerned about you, that's all." Sarah meant it.

Maddie glanced at Sarah and then at me. "I know. Me too."

"Do you want to talk about it?" I reached for Sarah's hand, needing support.

Maddie laughed. "You must be worried if Lizzie's asking me to open up, but no. I think I need some time on my own to figure things out. I'm leaving tomorrow to visit my parents in California."

That was a relief. I didn't have any family members outside of Colorado—at least I didn't think I did. The way things were going, I might have another hidden family.

"Will you be gone long?" Sarah sounded upset that Maddie didn't want to open up to us.

"A week or two. Haven't really decided yet."

Was there a twelve-step program for people who kept sleeping with their best friends' family members? How long would it take?

"What about you, Lizzie? Your head must be spinning with your dad situation."

"It is. And then there's Allen."

"Who's Allen?"

I was used to Maddie knowing every aspect of my life before I did, so the fact that she didn't know about Allen suddenly worried me that the rift in our friendship was larger than I'd thought. I filled her in, with Sarah adding the details I omitted to keep me completely honest.

When it was all out there, Maddie stared out the window at her apartment parking lot. "I'm a little jealous. Lately, I've felt so alone, and now you have two babies and a brother you didn't know about, even a future stepmom. You really are lucky."

I followed her eyes to the half-empty parking lot. "The twins miss their Aunt Maddie. Any chance you want to come over for dinner tonight?"

"I'd like that very much."

"Good, because if you said no, we'd have to drag you kicking and screaming. No matter what, you'll always be a part of our family," Sarah said, patting her thigh.

"Great. Can we hug it out now?" Maddie asked, eyes glistening.

Before I pulled the SUV away from the curb outside of Rose's home, Sarah asked, "You're going to do it, aren't you?"

I shook my head, smiling as I glanced at the twins buckled into their car seats in the back. "That depends on what you mean. I do a lot of things every day." I eased the car into the street and made a left onto a side street a couple of blocks from our home. If someone had told me years ago that I'd live within a seven-minute drive from my mother-in-law, I'd have laughed in their face. Now that I was the mother of twins, having Rose so near wasn't half bad. Parenthood really altered a person's perspective.

Sarah, grabbing the headrest, peered into the backseat at the wide-eyed twins. "Mommy thinks she's so funny."

I gazed into the rearview mirror. "Other mommy thinks she knows everything," I told them.

Sarah rolled her eyes at me dramatically. "You're going to meet Allen."

I licked my lips. "I think so."

"What convinced you?"

I pulled the car over to the curb but left the engine running. "It's been a long time coming, I think. I was denied a family for years. It sucks, feeling so alone all the time. When I saw the forlorn look in Maddie's eyes earlier, I realized we'd switched places somehow. When I met her, she had everything going for her. Now she's—"

"Lost." Sarah's voice transformed the word into something even sadder than those measly four letters allowed.

"I don't want to do that to my own children. You and"—I jerked my thumb over my shoulder—"them, you all deserve so much more. My family isn't perfect, not by a long shot, but now they want to be a part of us, even Peter."

Sarah laced her fingers through the fingers of my free hand. "My gut wasn't wrong all these years. You really are an amazing person."

"Meeting Allen makes me amazing?"

"No, wanting to be the best parent you can be does."

"You know what makes you amazing?"

She squeezed my fingers tighter, and her face softened. "What?"

"Me."

She thumped my shoulder with a fist. "You aren't too off the mark."

"Then why'd you hit me?" I sagged my shoulder, feigning a bone break.

"Because you're still a Petrie."

"So are they." I bobbed my head to the twins in the backseat, both now slumbering sweetly.

She stared back at them. "They're beautiful, aren't they?"

"Just like the woman who gave birth to them." I boosted her hand to my lips and kissed her fingertips. "Shall we have the entire family over for Christmas?"

Chapter Eighteen

Before Sarah rang the doorbell, she gave me a once-over and asked, "You okay?"

I nodded, not feeling confident at all.

She pressed the bell; no turning back now.

The massive wooden door swung open to reveal Helen. "Welcome." She piloted us in. "Here, let me help." Helen took the bulging baby bag from my left hand. In my right, I carried Ollie in her car seat.

"I remember lugging all this stuff around not too long ago," she said, smiling.

The entryway to her home was huge but not overly decorated. A figurine of a ballet dancer sat on a shelf over the staircase, and she led us off to the right, down a soft yellow hallway. Sarah's heels *click-clacked* on the newly polished wood floor as she carried a giggling Freddie.

"It's so nice out for November, so everyone is outside. Your father is manning the grill." Her smile was heartfelt, honest. Charles Allen Petrie wasn't the type of guy who typically manned a grill. Actually, any man who had a chauffeur to drive him to the grocery store probably wasn't the type of guy to expertly throw a few steaks on when he returned. "Hope you like your steaks chargrilled, emphasis on char," she added with a laugh.

Sarah and I laughed with her as Helen shepherded us through a kitchen that had more shine than Mr. Clean's bald head. Spotless as it was, it was still a kitchen for serious cooks: the wear and tear seen on the knobs of the oven and the hanging pots and pans was testimony to Helen being the true chef in the family.

Family. The thought struck me like a stone. My dad was a member of Helen's family. He had been for years, and I hadn't had a clue. Would that traitorous thought ever not feel so traitorous? How did Peter feel? He had hitched his professional life to my father's reputation, and he always made it appear as if "our family" was a top priority. I'd lost count of how many articles I'd seen in the papers featuring a photo of the semi-smiling father and son Petrie. Would those photos include other sons from now on?

"Lizzie and Sarah, so glad you could make it." Dad set his tongs on the grill's shelf and strode toward us. "Sarah, you look lovely." He gave her a peck on the cheek. Now that my father was the type to grill, he was also the type to give my wife a peck on the cheek, apparently. "May I?" He moved to Olivia in her car seat.

"Of course." I unclipped Ollie. "Say hi to your grandpa, Ollie."

Dad cuddled her like a pro. Had he ever held me that way when I was a baby?

Jesus, Lizzie. Get the fuck over it.

"Hello, Ollie." He stared into her cooing face.

Freddie fussed in his seat.

"I think he's saying, 'What about me?'" Helen held out her hands for Fred.

Sarah freed our son and glanced at me, misty-eyed, before handing him over. She nodded. "Say hi to Grandma, Fred."

Helen and my father stared into each other's eyes, both slightly teary as well. Fortunately, their attention didn't land on me. My feelings were all over the board: happy, relieved, and scared that everything was illusionary.

"Hey there, little Freddie." Helen wiggled his tiny hand. "Lucky for you, you don't have to eat any steak."

Dad puffed his chest out. "What do you mean? The steaks —" He reeled around, his face paling when he saw the smoke circling in the dark blue sky.

A man clad in jeans and an Eddie Bauer plaid button-up dashed to the grill and started pulling the filets to safety. Laughing, he said, "Everyone wanted well-done, right?"

"Is there another way?" Sarah fought a giggle.

"That's what Lea & Perrins is for, to give the meat flavor." Helen rubbed her chin against Freddie's fuzzy head.

"I bet shoe leather has more flavor than those," interrupted a kid who didn't yet have a hair on his chin. His scrawny neck poked out of a lightweight Gap sweater. He had a dimple in his left cheek and two in his right. I couldn't peel my eyes away from him.

"Hush, Allen. Your father tried. That's what matters. Now, I better go inside and prepare the rest of the meal." Helen handed Freddie back to me, snapping me out of my stare.

"I'll help you." Sarah followed her into the kitchen.

Helen stopped abruptly. "Goodness, where are my manners? Sarah and Lizzie, this is—"

"Hi, I'm Gabe," Helen's firstborn interrupted, sticking his hand out. I shook it. "And this here is Allen." Gabe tossed a brotherly arm over his shorter sibling's shoulder.

Allen nodded shyly, as did I.

"And these are Lizzie's twins. Ollie." Dad raised Olivia as a way of introduction. "And Freddie." He gestured to the baby in my arms.

"Aren't you a handsome fella?" Gabe played with one of Freddie's socked feet. "He has your eyes."

I started to agree when I realized Gabe was referring to my father's eyes, not mine. Allen, Freddie, and I all had Dad's blue eyes.

Sarah rubbed my back.

"And you, beautiful." Gabe stroked Ollie's cheek with a fingertip. "You have the cutest nose." He tweaked it gently, delighting Olivia.

It was clear Gabe was the businessman in the family. Unlike, Peter, though, he didn't have a smarmy way about him. I didn't believe one-tenth of the crap that spilled out of Peter's mouth. With Gabe, so far I'd believed at least half.

Sarah and Helen retreated inside, but seconds later, Sarah stuck her head out the door. "Charles, Helen wants to know if you can put two more steaks on the grill—Peter and Tie are on their way. Also, she asked for you not to massacre them this time." She sniggered, already feeling like part of Helen's family.

"Shall I do it, Pops?" Allen looked hopeful.

"Go ahead. Your mother clearly doesn't trust me. Besides, it's my turn to hold Freddie." Dad handed Ollie to Gabe and took Fred from my arms.

I studied Gabe, trying to determine whether he really wanted to hold Ollie, and was surprised to witness him cooing in her ear, completely at ease. Helen's sons were better people than most, I decided—not that I had too much experience. Too bad Helen hadn't raised Peter. Was it too late for my brother? For me, for that matter?

"Peter's about fifteen minutes out." Helen reappeared on the deck, with Sarah in tow. "What can I get you to drink, Lizzie?"

"Water is fine."

"Are you sure? We have cream soda."

"I haven't had cream soda in years."

"It was your favorite when you were a kid. That and root beer were your go-to drinks." Dad didn't look at me, and I wondered why.

"Finally, a beer Lizzie will drink." Sarah prodded my shoulder with hers.

"I take it you aren't much of a drinker," Gabe said.

"She hasn't had much to drink since we found out I was pregnant. Me, I pumped earlier so I could have a glass of wine tonight."

No one seemed ill at ease when Sarah mentioned pumping breast milk for the twins. It still amazed me that she was so free talking about breastfeeding.

"Red or white, Sarah?" Gabe clasped his hands together, eager to play cohost.

"Red, please."

Ollie let loose a howl.

"Feeling left out, baby girl?" Sarah took Ollie from Gabe's arms. "I need to get her bottle from inside."

"Let me show you two to the study. It's quiet and cozy." Helen gestured Sarah inside.

"Is she the fussy one?" Dad asked.

"That's an understatement. Fred takes after me."

"You and Allen have that in common. Allen never cried as a baby."

My half brother turned a shy shade of pink, and I shuffled my feet.

Helen returned with two cream sodas on the rocks, handing one to me and the other to Allen.

I laughed, slightly unnerved. "Another thing we have in common."

"And history." Helen swiped Allen's bangs from his eyes, much to his dismay. "Allen is considering studying European history."

"Really?" I asked. "Do you have a time period in mind?"

"The Russian Revolution." His eyes met mine briefly before flittering toward the aspens in the yard.

"Ah." I rolled back on my heels, squinting at the gold, red, and orange leaves on the oak tree in the corner. "I should introduce you to Michael Paulson, one of the scholars I met at a conference last year. We're both scheduled to speak at an event in Boulder this spring."

"You know Michael Paulson?" Allen's voice squeaked.

"Not intimately but we had dinner together last year. You a fan?"

Allen nodded vigorously. "One of his books got me hooked on the time period. Before I read that, I'd planned on studying the American Civil War, my second-favorite time period."

"For his high school graduation, we're traveling to Fredericksburg and Gettysburg." Helen smiled at her youngest son like a mother bestowing a priceless gift.

"And Washington DC," Allen added, the corners of his mouth coiling up ever so slightly, making him look even more like my enigmatic father.

Helen shivered and rubbed her hands together. "Shall we move inside?" The temperature had cooled several degrees since our arrival.

"Yes, we don't want the youngest Petries catching a cold, do we?" Dad snuggled Fred, who calmly accepted the attention. All this time, I'd thought my son was so much like me, but seeing him in Dad's arms made it clear that he took after his grandfather. I wondered whether Freddie's stoicism would be a help or a hindrance in the years to come. I was only beginning to grasp how different my father was around Helen, Gabe, and Allen.

The doorbell rang.

"I'll get it." Helen was off before anyone had a chance to blink. Soon enough, she returned with the final dinner guests.

"Ah, Peter. So glad you could make it." Dad stuck out his palm, and Peter shook it, businessman-like. "Allow me to make the introductions. This is Gabe, Helen's oldest, and this strapping young lad is Allen..." He let the rest of the statement fade away. No one had to be told Allen was Peter's half brother.

Peter shook Gabe's hand formally, the same way he had Dad's. When it was time to shake Allen's hand, he hesitated. The younger man blushed even redder.

Nice going, Peter, making Allen uncomfortable in his own home.

"I'm Tie-Fannie." Tie wrapped her arms around Gabe and Allen in her enthusiastic, bone-crushing fashion.

"That's an unusual way of pronouncing Tiffany." Gabe clearly wasn't the type to let someone's nonsense go unnoticed. I waited for him to call her a bullshitter or what was the hip term: jive turkey?

"Most call me Tie," she said, unabashedly.

"Tie it is. What's your poison?"

She eyed Sarah's wine but placed a hand on her belly. "Water."

"And, Pete, I know you like bourbon. I picked up a bottle of Blanton's especially for you." Gabe about-faced and left the room.

Peter blinked excessively. He still hadn't said a word. I had never heard anyone call him Pete before. One look at Peter's face confirmed he wasn't entirely sure how to take it either.

Helen ushered us into the dining room.

Sarah, carrying Ollie on her right hip, joined us.

"Gimme, gimme, gimme!" Tie squealed, thrusting her waiting arms toward Olivia.

Olivia, much to my chagrin, cooed at Tie's boisterous greeting. To add insult to my shock, once safely settled into Tie's arms, Ollie flashed her the widest grin.

"Don't worry. In a week, Ollie will outgrow her," Sarah whispered in my ear, and I had to stifle a laugh with my palm.

"Cap, would you mind helping me bring the food out?" Helen rubbed Dad's back.

Dad rounded about to Allen. "Time to get to know your nephew." Before Allen had a chance to protest, Freddie was placed in his arms.

Peter visibly bristled. Why was he so outraged? Fred was my son. Or was it the verbalization that Allen was a blood relation?

"Hello, Fred." Allen meandered to the far side of the room and stared out a window that overlooked the Castle Pines golf course. The entire wall consisted of yellowish, burnt-orange bricks with four large windows set among them. I wondered whether golf balls ever came crashing through.

I turned to Peter, who was still surveying the room. The house had an elegant, cabin-like feel. In the corner was an adobe-style fireplace. Rustic wooden beams jutted along the ceiling. An antique rug sat under a massive cherry table and chairs, with a modest chandelier above. The features blended well together, making the home feel lived in, the complete opposite of the home I'd grown up in.

Gabe returned with the drinks, including a refill of my cream soda.

"Soda, Elizabeth? Really?" Peter swished his bourbon and took a long sip, as if at a liquor tasting for billionaires.

"I'm driving." I didn't know why I defended my drink choice.

"I imagine having two little ones at home makes it hard to drink. How much sleep have you two had?" Gabe's eyes were kind.

Sarah laughed. "Sleep? I think I remember what that is."

"Here we go." Helen carried in a tray laden with food and placed it on the hutch to the side. Dad's tray was twice the size. "Please, everyone fix a plate and take a seat wherever suits you."

Peter set his drink down by the chair at the head of the table, much to my amusement. Gabe grinned and set his drink opposite Peter. Secretly, I hoped Peter would challenge him to arm wrestle. I suspected Gabe would handily whoop Peter's ass.

"I'll get the car seats for the twinkies," I said.

"Thanks, sweetheart. I'll fix you a plate."

By the time I returned and settled the twins in their seats, everyone was ready to eat. Dad and Helen sat next to each other, whispering like schoolkids with crushes. Allen sat next to Gabe and me, while Tie was as far away from Peter as she could get. Sarah met my eye, communicating that she'd noticed.

Dad stood and raised his glass. "Helen and I would like to thank all of you for coming. Tomorrow, this woman"—he gazed down at Helen—"is going to make me the happiest of men by becoming my wife, and it's an honor to have all of you share in the event."

Peter shifted in his seat.

Dad forged on, even though I was certain he picked up on it. "It's been a long road to this day, as all of you know." He met everyone's eyes, staying fixed on Peter's a moment longer than necessary. "But that's life. Nothing can be perfect, but having a partner with you through thick and thin makes it bearable."

Dad briefly turned his attention to Tie. I would have paid one hundred bucks to know what she was thinking. Was it Dad's way of warning her about her husband, or a way of telling Peter to squash whatever rebuttal was surely bubbling under the surface?

Sarah nudged my leg with hers under the table.

Dad sniffed, showing the most emotion I'd ever seen him display. "To Helen. Thank you."

We all toasted Helen and my father.

A quiet settled over the table as everyone tucked into their food.

"Peter, I hear you're a golf man. One of my buddies has bailed for our game next Saturday. Care to join us? Oscar Mendez and Reggie Whitcomb are the other two." Gabe's smile was inviting.

I wasn't normally the type to know the who's who of the world, but even a business neophyte such as myself recognized the names. The first was an Internet entrepreneur, along the lines of Mark Zuckerberg, and the second was the son of a successful hedge fund manager. Their photos were constantly in the news.

"Next Saturday, you say?" Peter rubbed his chin, but it was clear he was frothing at the mouth like a coyote about to pounce on a rabbit. "I'm pretty sure I can clear my calendar."

"That's Kit's birthday," Tie piped up.

Peter cleared his throat. "I'm sure Kit will understand if I'm a little late to his party."

"He'll probably take it as a gift—you not being there at all." Tie sipped her drink innocently, her face devoid of any emotion.

Gabe laughed good-naturedly. "Good. It's settled."

"How do you know Mendez and Whitcomb?" Sarah asked.

"We went to school together." Gabe cracked black pepper over his burnt steak and potatoes au gratin.

"Where was that?" Sarah dipped a slice of filet into peppercorn sauce, leaving it longer than normal, maybe in the hope of softening the meat.

"Harvard."

"Wow! The flower business must pay well." Tie's eyes bugged out.

My father stared down at his plate.

"I've been fortunate." Helen motioned for my father to pass her the silver salt and pepper shakers.

Peter looked to my father and then to Gabe, processing the information in the way only Peter could: how much had that taken away from his inheritance?

"I'm a Stanford man, myself." Peter tousled his gel-free hair. I tried remembering how many hairstyles I'd seen him wear over the past few months. Mine was always slicked back in a ponytail these days. "Elizabeth never left the state and settled for CSU."

"You make it sound like a bad thing," I interrupted. "I have a beautiful wife, two amazing children, and I work with the top historian in my field."

"And she doesn't have to go golfing to beg people to invest with her." Tie popped a glazed carrot into her mouth.

Peter stared at his wife. His expression barely hid his disdain. I imagined he was fantasizing about wrapping her autumn-colored scarf around her bird-like neck until it snapped.

"The life of a businessman is only glamorous in the society pages." Gabe poured more wine into his glass. "Anyone else need a refill?" He raised the bottle.

"Yes, please. Water," Tie purred as if Gabe had forgotten she was pregnant. "I do love a man who knows how to treat a woman."

Sarah sucked in her bottom lip, stifling a laugh. Helen and Dad were engaged in a private conversation, speaking softly to one another. Allen reacted by fidgeting in his seat.

"Oh, I'm sure you have scores of men falling at your feet. Isn't that right, Peter?" Gabe poured ice water into her glass, filling it nearly to the brim.

"Not sure about scores. The retarded boy down the street has taken a shine to her, though." Peter laughed maliciously.

Everyone else at the table stopped what they were doing to gawk at him in disgust. Normally, Peter wouldn't back down, but this time his shoulders sagged and he followed up with, "He's such a sweet boy. We donate money to his school. The best school for children like him."

"He's not mentally challenged. He's deaf." Tie rolled her eyes. "He mows everyone's yards in the neighborhood to raise money for his school."

"Is that why he never responds when I tell him to ensure the lines in the lawn are perfectly straight?" Peter's face was incredulous. "It does explain why he talks like he was raised by wolves or something." He waved a hand dismissively before addressing Allen. "Do you have a part-time job?"

Allen shook his head.

"That's not true. During school breaks, you help out at the shop in Denver." Helen rushed to Allen's defense. She turned to Peter. "We think his studies should come first. He wants to be a professor, like Lizzie." Helen smiled broadly.

"Another professional trivial pursuit player in the making," Peter said, winking. "Kidding, of course."

Nothing about his tone or posture indicated he was joking.

Again, everyone at the table fell silent.

I examined Allen, who blushed like he wanted to disappear under the table. "Tell me about your upcoming trip. It's been years since I've been to DC." I rested my forearms on the table. "I do have one tip. You have to visit the house where Lincoln died. Seeing the small bed where they laid the tall, mortally wounded man—it's depressing, yet gruesomely fascinating. It's near the theater where he was shot, of course."

Allen perked up in his seat and launched into a monologue about all the things he wanted to see.

When he mentioned the Holocaust museum, I interjected. "The section with all the shoes is quite emotional. I mean, it's just shoes, but the sheer number is overwhelming. Frankly, that aspect gets the point across the most. Each pair belonged to a human being who was meticulously murdered."

"I'm surprised the Germans didn't sell them. They could have made a killing, considering the scarcity brought on by the war." Peter poured a substantial dose of bourbon into his tumbler.

"Such a businessman, ignoring the humanity of Lizzie's statement and zeroing in on lost profit margin." Tie's voice bordered on humor, or was it just shock?

Peter tugged on the neck of his sweater. "I didn't round up and kill the poor bastards. I'm just saying I'm surprised the Germans didn't sell the shit."

"So you aren't Hitler, more like Switzerland, hoarding prized works of arts and gold." Tie quirked a brow.

"Exactly!" Peter's businessman smile amazed the hell out of me. How had he managed to take Tie's comment as a compliment?

Tie mentioning the role Switzerland had played shocked me even more than Peter's ability to brush off the dig. Sarah had been right all along: Tie was no fool. Maybe Sarah would be right. Maybe Peter would ask for a divorce sooner rather than later, even if they had a child on the way.

Sensing that the conversation needed steering to safer waters, I asked, "Have you found out whether you're having a boy or girl yet?"

Tie shook her head. "I want to be surprised. Did you two know?"

"We did. Our big shock was finding out about the twins."

Sarah laughed. "I think it took three full minutes before Lizzie's heart restarted."

"Maybe longer." I met Sarah's gaze and then glanced over my shoulder at the sleeping babies. "Can't imagine my life without them now."

"Children have that way about them." Helen smiled at her boys.

Peter folded his hands and rested his chin on them, a thoughtful look in his eyes. Was it possible that my brother was looking forward to meeting his child?

— Chapter Nineteen —

ALL THE SCENTS OF CHRISTMAS, REAL AND MANUFACTURED, SWIRLED AROUND my head as the three of us dashed around the house, putting the finishing touches up before all the branches of the family tree arrived.

"Did you light the candle in the bathroom upstairs?" Sarah marched into the kitchen, looking like Dwight D. Eisenhower on D-Day. One hand clutched a clipboard that spelled out her battle plan, an endless to-do list that had been making my life hell since the day after Thanksgiving.

Maddie eyed me, and I shrugged one shoulder.

Sarah grunted. "Why do I even bother asking for help?" She about-faced to take care of the monumental task Maddie and I had neglected.

"I've never seen her like this, not even on our wedding day." I dried my hands on a dish towel draped over my shoulder.

"Don't take it personally." Maddie cranked the temperature on the Crock-Pot from low to high. She was making her famous Swedish meatballs, a laborious task, but well worth it.

"It's kinda hard not to take it personally when she looks at me like I'm the worst thing that's happened to human history since Nero fiddling while Rome burned."

Maddie laughed. "The fifty-fourth history reference since five this morning. Sarah wants this day to be perfect for you. She knows how nervous you are." She squeezed my shoulder. "How nervous are you, by the way?"

I flung out my hand, showing her how much it shook. "Let's say I won't be a great team player if we break out the Operation board game."

"Like you've ever played that game before."

"True, but now we own two sets, and the twins aren't even walking yet." I laughed. The first couple of hours this morning had involved me, Sarah, Maddie, and Rose unwrapping gifts for Freddie and Ollie. For the first few minutes, both of them had wriggled and clapped with delight, but they'd soon lost the thrill and just tried to eat wrapping paper instead. Fred actually nodded off before we were halfway done. "What about you?"

Maddie slanted one eyebrow.

"Is this the first time you'll be seeing Peter since that night?"

She nodded.

"And Tie will be with him."

She made another up and down motion with her head.

"And Kit and Courtney are coming."

She sucked in a breath.

"I'm not judging, but should I know about any other *situations,* just so I don't step in it?" I stuck two palms in the air, but not fast enough. She thwacked me with a wet dishrag. "Ouch!"

"By the way, is your stepbrother good-looking?"

"Don't even think about it." I narrowed my eyes.

"What about Gabe? Is he off-limits?"

I got an eyeful of the ceiling. "Huh. Interesting thought. He is in the flower business, and you're an interior designer. Might be a match made in heaven."

"Because of our business connections? Sometimes you really do think like a Petrie." Her laughter was a mix of amusement and disgust.

"What are you two doing?" Sarah stood in the kitchen doorway with her clipboard and red pen raised.

Luckily, Freddie reached out a hand and played with his toes, giggling, and Sarah's stern face melted into happiness. Ollie joined in the game, laughing louder than Fred. The sibling rivalry had already started.

I wrapped my arms around Sarah's waist. "Today is going to be perfect. Thanks for everything you've done." I brushed my lips against hers.

Sarah beamed. "Nice try," she muttered. "Can you get the twins dressed in their Christmas outfits?" She clicked her pen and struck the chore off the list.

I sighed melodramatically. "My tasks are never done." Turning to the twinkies, I added, "Come on, kiddos. Time to make you look ridiculous."

Both Maddie and Sarah slapped my arm.

Our house had never been so loud, or so sweltering, given the roaring fireplaces in the living room and TV room.

"Lizzie, the place looks wonderful." Dr. Marcel held his arm crooked for his wife to clutch.

"I can't take all the credit. This is Sarah's doing, and our friend Maddie is an interior designer."

Mrs. Marcel's eyes panned the spacious living room. "It's more elaborate than a window display in New York City."

I smiled, swallowing a comment about the astronomical price of transforming our house into Santa's workshop. Not to mention that it was going to take a team of cleaners to vacuum up all the fake snow and glitter throughout the house.

Dr. Marcel leaned closer. "Are your father and his new wife here yet?"

"Not yet. They're stopping to see Helen's family first."

"You nervous?" Mrs. Marcel's smile matched the warmth of her husband's. She wore black slacks and a red and white sweater that swallowed her body.

"A little."

Mrs. Marcel hooted. "Translation: you'd rather give a lecture in your birthday suit."

I laughed with the Marcels. "Something like that."

Dr. Marcel squeezed my arm. "One day at a time. Things will get easier."

Maddie brushed past, and I reached for her arm. "Maddie, I'd like you to meet the Marcels."

Maddie smiled knowingly. "Oh, you're the two who raised this cretin during her PhD program."

Everyone laughed, and Maddie eased them into a conversation so I could make my escape. On the back deck, I stumbled into Kit and Courtney.

"Hello." Kit took a drag on a cigarette. "I can't believe this place." He waved a hand to all the lit-up Christmas ornaments in the backyard, including a replica of Snoopy's doghouse with twinkling lights and a Charlie Brown tree.

"Sarah loves the holidays." I leaned against the deck railing. "You two hiding?"

"Yes. You?"

"Absolutely." I wrenched the collar of my green Grinch Christmas sweater, a gift from Maddie. "It's like Hades in there."

Courtney offered me a cigarette.

"No thanks. So have you two set a date yet?" I grinned.

"Nope," they chorused, giggling like naughty schoolkids who'd just activated a fire alarm.

Sarah sidled up next to me. "I thought I'd find you out here."

"Busted!" Kit laughed, accidentally sloshing his eggnog onto the snow. "This shit is good." He and Courtney drained their glasses.

I said to Sarah, "Maybe we shouldn't let Maddie mix the rum into the eggnog next year."

"Are you serious?" Courtney motioned for Kit to refill her glass. "She's an artist. An eggnog aficionado. You can't stifle her freedom of expression."

Kit nodded enthusiastically. "I usually hate eggnog, but this is my third glass, soon to be fourth."

At least two people were smashed, and it wasn't even seven at night. Even Rose had one before the guests arrived.

Sarah tugged my arm and whispered, "They're here."

My heart leaped into my throat, and I nodded as if I just found out I had to run a marathon to the North Pole barefoot or no children would receive a gift.

More people had streamed into the living room in my absence. Peter and Tie huddled by the fourteen-foot Christmas tree. I hadn't thought Sarah would choose such a tall tree, but she'd informed me it would be a crime not to take advantage of the room's arched ceiling. Maddie had to buy an extra-large ladder to get the ornament on top.

I raised a hand to greet Peter, and he tipped his bourbon glass in my direction. It was our first communication since the wedding, which had been a surprisingly modest affair.

My father, Helen, Gabe, and Allen were engaged in conversation with the Marcels, Maddie, and Rose. Sarah threaded her arm through mine and rested her head on my shoulder. "It's okay. You got this."

"Dad, you made it." I approached with my hand out.

He grasped it and pulled me into a hug.

Helen embraced me next.

"I was just telling your father you were my best student in my thirty-five years, and the only former student I've hired to teach on my staff." Dr. Marcel's face showed he meant every word.

Maddie, with Freddie in his elf pajamas on her hip, said, "I paid him fifty bucks to say that."

"Fifty? I thought you said one fifty." Dr. Marcel jostled her arm. In his other arm, he held Ollie, dressed in PJs that matched her twin's.

Everyone laughed. I caught a glimpse of Peter's scowl out of the corner of my eye.

Dad gripped my shoulder. "I always knew this one was smart as a whip. It's always the quiet ones, right Allen?"

Allen turned three shades of scarlet.

"Cap, don't embarrass the boy. Be useful and get us some eggnog." Helen shooed her husband and sons away.

"Anything you say, dear."

It felt like I was in an alternate universe: one where my father was a doting husband and proud father, and one in which I wasn't the hidden child anymore. I glanced in Peter's direction again.

Tie, clutching her baby bump with both hands, was speaking earnestly to Kit and Courtney while Peter managed to have his back turned to everyone in the room. Maddie followed my gaze and shrugged.

"Shall we hit up the food?" Mrs. Marcel and her ever-loving husband, with Rose in tow, retreated to the kitchen where the buffet was set up.

Dad, Allen, and Gabe returned with eggnog.

Peter spun around, and I motioned for him to join us.

"I was thinking. Since Allen and Gabe live so close to a golf course, we should all play this spring," I said.

"You play golf?" Peter's eyes bulged. "Since when?"

"Uh, not really. But how hard can it be? You play." I elbowed Peter, and he actually grinned.

Sarah gave me a *good for you* nod. It had been her idea to propose a golf game with my siblings. To me, it felt weird adding an "s" to that word.

"Careful, Peter." Maddie sidled up and met his shocked face. "I've played putt-putt with Lizzie, and she has a remarkable short game. Only takes her ten shots to sink the ball."

"So, when you say remarkable, do you mean jaw-dropping or *I can't believe what I'm seeing*?" Gabe said, seeming somewhat shy around Maddie.

Maddie was nodding and laughing too hard to reply.

"Hey now! I did get a hole in one."

Sarah circled her arm around my waist. "That's right. The ball bounced right off a lighthouse, smacked into a pirate ship, boinged into a windmill, and then swirled around the hole twice before going in. Too bad it was the hole *after* the one we were playing."

"Can't win them all." I nuzzled my cheek against her head. "Although I did with you," I whispered in her ear.

Peter sidled up on my other side. "I think I can teach you a thing or two about golf, if you're willing to put in the time."

"Of course! As long as I don't have to wear your silly golf pants and shirt, I'm willing to bet that in six months I'll clean your clock."

"Shall we say ten dollars?" Peter put his hand out, and I shook it, laughing.

The rest of the guests gravitated toward the laughter.

I raised my glass. "I'd like to make a toast."

"You can't help going into lecture mode, can you?" Maddie laughed.

I restrained my desire to give her the middle finger. "Unlike my lectures, I'll make this short and sweet."

Maddie started to say something else, but Sarah's withering look zipped her lips shut.

"To family and friends, thank you for sharing our twins' first Christmas with us. This year has been insanely crazy in a wonderful way. Not only did we welcome our children into the world, but we also embraced new family members"—I waved to Helen, her boys, and Kit and Courtney—"whom I hope to get to know better in the new year. We're keen to meet Fred and Ollie's cousin."

Tie cradled her belly, and Peter smiled slightly.

"And now that we have your names and numbers, expect to hear from us. We're in desperate need of babysitters."

The twins cooed, momentarily drawing all attention away from me. Sarah leaned against me. "I love you."

"I love you too," I whispered right back.

I waited a few seconds for the laughter to subside and then lifted my glass above my head. "Merry Christmas, and may everyone's wishes come true."

AUTHOR'S NOTE

Thank you for reading *A Family Woman*. If you enjoyed the novel, please consider leaving a review on Goodreads or Amazon. No matter how long or short, I would very much appreciate your feedback.

You can follow me, T. B. Markinson, on Twitter at @IHeartLesfic or email me at tbm@tbmarkinson.com. I would love to know your thoughts.

ABOUT THE AUTHOR

TB Markinson is an American living in England. When she isn't writing, she's traveling the world, watching sports on the telly, visiting pubs, or reading. Not necessarily in that order.

Her novels have hit Amazon bestseller lists for lesbian fiction and lesbian romance. For a full listing of TB's novels, please visit her Amazon page.

Feel free to visit TB's website at www.lesbianromancesbytbm.com to say hello. She also runs I Heart Lesfic, a place for authors and fans of lesfic to come together to celebrate and chat about lesbian fiction. On her 50 Year Project blog, TB chronicles her challenge to visit 192 countries, read 1,001 books, and to watch the AFI's top 100 movies.

Printed in Great Britain
by Amazon